Avon Books are available at special quantity discounts for bulk purchases for sales promotions, premiums, fund raising or educational use. Special books, or book excerpts, can also be created to fit specific needs.

For details write or telephone the office of the Director of Special Markets, Avon Books, Dept. FP, 1790 Broadway, New York, New York 10019, 212-399-1357.

THE ORDER OF THE DAY

An Unidentified Flying Opus

Márcio Souza

Translated by Thomas Colchie

 A BARD BOOK / PUBLISHED BY AVON BOOKS

Published in Brazil by Editora Marco Zero Ltda.

AVON BOOKS
A division of
The Hearst Corporation
1790 Broadway
New York, New York 10019

Copyright © 1983 by Márcio Souza
English translation copyright © 1986 by Thomas Colchie
Published by arrangement with the author
Library of Congress Catalog Card Number: 85-91532
ISBN: 0-380-89765-2

First Bard Printing: July 1986

BARD TRADEMARK REG. U.S. PAT. OFF. AND IN OTHER COUNTRIES,
MARCA REGISTRADA, HECHO EN U.S.A.

Printed in the U.S.A.

OPM   10   9   8   7   6   5   4   3   2   1

UNIDENTIFIED FLYING OPUS
IN WHICH HIGH-RANKING MILITARY OFFICERS
UNDERGO A CRISIS
TO THE DELIGHT OF THOSE WHO WILL NEVER
BE AWARDED ANY PURPLE HEART

"We have no competency to interpret orders of the day."
—A high government official,
May 9th, 1983.

Author's Note

ORDER OF THE DAY, the dictionary tells us, signifies a predetermined sequence of tasks or business to be accomplished in a given day. In general, this sequence entails a roster of more or less routine matters to be discussed and decided upon by an empowered assembly.

At certain progressive gatherings where questions of principle are more important than the facts themselves, the making-up of orders of the day has a tendency to become more relevant than the actual analysis and resolution of the specific subjects under consideration. It was only a short while ago that I ceased to participate in such reunions.

But ORDER OF THE DAY also signifies a manly speech composed by military chieftains and read aloud, in an unequivocally masculine tone of voice, at all military installations on certain occasions deemed to be civic or during solemnities involving a change of command. I'm still trying to free myself from a preoccupation with pronouncements of this type.

The title of the present novel, however, must be understood simply as a symptomatic reference to the second sense of the term.

Brazilian literature is rich in multiple forms of expression. Some of these forms, though of great historical and political import, have tended to be overlooked—an oversight that has occasionally proved fatal. For shame, such a lack of civic vigilance on the part of *belles lettres!*

Actually, until 1964, letters were highly esteemed among us. We had Pero Vaz de Caminha's letter, from 1501. We had Getúlio Vargas's, from 1954. The first was more or less an inventory of the New World; the second, decidedly a last will and testament. Then after '64 things began to change. It was a time of manifestos: the Manifesto of the Joint Chiefs of Staff; the Manifesto of the Manufacturing Class; the Intellectuals' Manifesto, and so on.

How poignant were such manifestos!
How indignant, at times . . .
I signed a few.

After the manifestos came the Institutional Acts. A numbered succession of them from our military keepers. In five acts, like all the old tragedies. Balanced and concise, with enviable syntactic precision. The country was, of course, in no mood for playing with words. . . .

I didn't sign any of them.

A fair number of people want to forget that they did.

They say that such Institutional Acts hark back to the purest Luso-Brazilian cultural tradition—all the way back to João das Regras or John-of-the-Rules, a fifteenth-century technocrat from the House of Avis, in Portugal.

Now we seem to be living in the emotive age of orders of the day. Of all styles, definitely the most serpentine. At times, such creations seem the work of experts in explosives or camouflage, of strategists in the insane. A well constructed order of the day takes on the laxative savor of a judgment from the Oracle of Delphi. And like all oracles, they have created legions of interpreters—all, of course, authoritative.

Being a perfect idiot in the face of such oracles, I am in the habit of reading them with the same attention span I devote to skimming my monthly horoscope. But somehow it always turns out to be right!

Every order of the day seems to aspire to the sublime. And manifest an elevated poetic tenor. Just the way certain carnivorous plants secrete nectar, I imagine. Still, they are clearly virile, with no affectations and a vigorous cadence: not unlike the mopping of the mess hall in a barracks. And the vocabulary never jeopardizes the requisite stridency of diction. Can you imagine some brigadier general fumbling his syllables before an astonished gathering of journalists and troops on parade? I know one story about a stuttering sergeant that goes something like this:

> He stomped and shouted in his boots
> And always fucked the raw recruits
> But not his wife . . . I wonder why-yi-yi!
> Sergeant Stutter, the D-D-D I-yi-yi!

Sorry, readers, but poetry from the barracks is like that. . . .

The sublimity of orders of the day lends itself to the issuing of political threats or warnings. In the manner of the local anesthetic used by dentists to pull out teeth. The elevated poetic tenor highlights the inherent contrast between the limitless love the military holds for democratic institutions and the violence they generally shower upon those same institutions in order to defend them from the danger of Communist subversion. Like the hot breath of the lion on the back of the neck of its prey. And orders of the day are an eminently oral form of composition, depending upon inflection, gesture, etc. On paper, they become incomprehensible. Well, to me the whole military is incomprehensible.

The remote inventor of orders of the day in Brazil was, by the merest of chances, not actually a soldier. He was a Carioca poet named Olavo Bilac. Entitled our Prince of Poets, he even wrote advertisement-sonnets for remedies to fight venereal diseases—in perfect Parnassian form. Venereal diseases are endemic to life in the barracks. Parnassian diseases are more typical of the Academy of Letters.

It was Olavo Bilac also who invented compulsory military service in Brazil, although he himself had never performed military service. Olavo Bilac happened to be cross-eyed, and all the lads old enough to be eligible for military service used to have a good laugh whenever old Bilac walked by. May the Lord have pity on the Prince of Poets' soul!

This novel is dedicated to all the altruistic interpreters of orders of the day, but especially to those of them who work for the daily papers. They have performed an enormous service to us all.

I have a journalist friend who is crazy about his job of interpreting orders of the day. Recently he confided to me a very important fact about orders of the day.

"You know something," he told me, "an order of the day is no good for lyrics to a samba."

I agreed: the rhythm of a samba is quite different from an Independence Day parade. As we Brazilians are tired of realizing...

But I also dedicate this novel, and rightly so, to all the enlisted men who are serving in the Armed Forces at this very moment. They are the only ones who are constantly obliged to expose themselves— out of professional duty—to the reading of orders of the day.

Personally, I would prefer never to be mixed up with enlisted men for the rest of my life. That particular brand of sublimity doesn't appeal to me. I detest that species of elevated poetical tenor. And as for military shades of green, I'd rather stick to the shade of the Amazon forest. It's difficult enough to distinguish olive-green in the Amazon forest. The real problem is that the Amazon forest will most likely be extinguished long before the olive-green of the barracks. All the better, I suppose, for orders of the day.

I have never been a soldier. Not that I take any pride in the fact. But I have made an occasional effort to attempt to comprehend the mysteries and rituals of life in the barracks. A question of survival, if you get my meaning.

By the way, my most invaluable source of information on life in the barracks has turned out to be certain more boisterous orders of the day. A few of them have left me rather perplexed. . . . Obviously life in the barracks would leave me equally perplexed. I am so viscerally opposed to certain types of camaraderie that I could never interest myself, for example, in joining the Boy Scouts. Oswald de Andrade, a novelist of the twenties who was never a soldier either, once compared the Scouts to Martians.

I happen to think this whole business of army uniforms rather extraterrestrial. They have something in common with those dangerous invaders in the old Hollywood science fiction flicks from during the Cold War.

And they walk among us. . . .

Run for your lives!

I've always suspected the *Blob* to have been olive-green in color. Besides, aren't members of any crew from a flying saucer generally called little green men?

By the time I reached the age to perform my military service, certain philosophical attitudes had already matured in me that hardly rejoiced at the prospect of my becoming a soldier. It proved to be one of the most anguished moments of my life. During that period I found few adjectives sufficiently strong to adequately insult the memory of the poet Olavo Bilac. Cross-eyed! Bloated! He seemed like an alien from the planet Uranus. Wasn't he the one who claimed to "hear" stars? Nevertheless, I was obliged to report to my local draft board.

I was ordered to present myself at the old 27th Battalion Headquarters, which has since become the Military Command of Amazonia and occupies one-sixteenth of the entire city of Manaus. There I underwent a humiliating medical exam: Take off your clothes! Fall in line! The army doctor looking on with a pensive air. The smell of disinfectant . . . I was sent off—nearly in a panic—for other tests, since the laws covering military service gave me the right, as a student in my last year of science at the Colegio Dom Bosco, to serve my country in the ROTC. That, as you no doubt imagine, stands for Reserve Officers' Training Corps. Besides becoming a soldier, I was to be dressed out as a lieutenant. At the time I was reading *The Metamorphosis* by Franz Kafka—no humbug of a metaphor for my own situation.

It was the first year they were to have any ROTC program in Manaus and they had twenty slots to fill. There we were, some forty student candidates being paraded in front of the captain. He promptly shipped us off to some new installation, in the São Jorge district, where we were to undergo an additional medical examination and a battery of physical aptitude tests: shimmying up a rope, sprinting a hundred meters, pumping a few dozen push-ups in between, and so on. Even a paraplegic would have fared better than I did on those tests. Still, I bluffed my way through like a professional poker player and slipped by with honors. They also presented me with a mimeographed sheet depicting the style of uniform to be worn by the future lieutenant. I was to purchase it—at my own expense—from a military tailor's shop. They gave me another date to re-present myself.

A week later, six A.M., I was standing on parade all over again in front of the same captain. He curtly interviewed each one of us and made the final selection, dismissing those in excess of his quota. When my turn came, I answered the captain's questions with childish abruptness. When he asked if I wanted to join the army, what came into my head was No! And I said so. Then immediately there came the next question of why I didn't want to serve my country. A thought came into my head, and nearly would have escaped my lips if the captain had not flashed me a look to the effect of "Don't be a fool, son," and then written on my chart that I preferred to continue with my studies. The thought that had come into my head was to proclaim myself against the military establishment. This was in 1965—the coup had taken place the year before. It was my first intimate experience with the military. There were to be others, much more harrowing. . . . It was also my first taste of alien psychology. I continue to prefer science fiction movies.

Perhaps that explains the climate of close encounters and flying saucers that pervades this novel. Nothing more reminiscent of *Star Trek* than a four-star general reading an order of the day. Nothing more *Lost in Space* than a Brazilian society brought to its knees by the anti-Communist fervor of the armed forces. Nothing so similar to *Invasion of the Body Snatchers* as the vigilant paranoia of the National Security Laws.

A question of politics . . .

The language of science fiction . . .

There once was a stuttering sergeant, and so on and so forth.

Then in 1968, I paid a visit to ITJW—that's Intensive Training in Jungle Warfare. The course was administered by the Military Command of Amazonia and provided training to an elite force in anti-guerrilla combat. In '68, this business of guerrilla warfare was taken very seriously. Vietnam was running full-steam ahead. Che Guevara was in Bolivia. The Caparaó resistance, in the mountains of Rio de Janeiro, had gone badly. The fierce and protracted guerrilla action in Araguaia, to the north, was about to begin.

As soon as I arrived at the headquarters of ITJW, I felt as if I were on the set of that old film *The Thing from Another World*. At the time I was not an avid reader of science fiction. I was too busy perusing my General Giap, that otherworldly strategist who had won an extraterrestrial battle on an asteroid called Dien Bien Phu.

My visit coincided with that of a group of army colonels from Superior Officers' Training School. They seemed to adore swinging from one liana vine to another across the Amazon jungle. Then after three treacherous kilometers of narrow trails filled with Vietcong traps, we got to sit in an auditorium where we had to listen to some major. What he told us had nothing to do with any order of the day. Among other statements typical of the galactic logic of the barracks was the following: that the Americans were losing the war to the yellow race because they were chicken and smoked pot. Brazilians, on the other hand, would never lose a war like that. I sat there trying to imagine General Westmoreland having a drag in Song My. . . . Araguaia would soon erupt to demonstrate the difficulties of a well-managed guerrilla action, even in Brazil. But what really got to me was the major's brand of rhetoric. He sounded like some sort of alien villain from a grade-B sci-fi, ready to take over the planet Earth. They were already the masters of most of South America. And as with all extraterrestrials, I noted the degree to which the military lived isolated from the real world, protected by that species of energy field known as hierarchical order, or rank. The major was a profoundly isolated human being. A frightened extraterrestrial. Like E.T. Only more vindictive. . . .

* * *

It was years later that a new type of guerrilla started in Amazonia. Glowing lights began to be sighted along the frontier—very selective lights, mind you. First, in the state of Maranhão—this was in 1977—where they appeared only to landless peasants who had occupied the area of the future Carajás mining project. Blinking lights which appeared in the wee hours before dawn, they blinded their victims and drained their blood. The locals started calling the phenomenon the *Chupa-chupa*, a reference to the creature's addiction to guzzling hemoglobin.

In 1978, it appeared in Vigia and in Mosqueiro, in the neighboring state of Pará. And in order to have the privilege of a close encounter, all that was required was any sort of proof of membership among the disinherited of the Earth. By the following year, it had already spread to Amazonas State, with sightings in Parintins and later in Maués. At the moment of this writing, it has become bold enough to occasionally startle even farmhands from Iranduba, a municipality just outside of Manaus. And the capital itself has not been immune to nocturnal visits: wandering lights have been robbing the sleep of slum dwellers from Coroado and Compensa to Gloria and São José. A woman who had never lost sleep over earning only half the minimum wage has now refused to bed down in her squatter's hovel in Compensa; not with that *Chupa-chupa* hovering bluishly in her kitchen.

A family of peasants who used to slumber like angels, even though their debts continued to pile up with the banks, now spend each night camping in the open air. It seems that one of them spotted the *Chupa-chupa* just above the church in Iranduba and suffered an electric shock.

A team of five officers was promptly dispatched to Iranduba.

Nothing came of it.

One of the peasants, however, had managed to get off a shell with his shotgun, nicking a piece of rubberlike material from the *Chupa-chupa*. The piece vanished into thin air, from the hand of a colonel.

On Sunday, January 23, 1983, soldiers at the zoological park of the JOCCA—Jungle Operations Company for Commando Actions, run by ITJW—were treated to an unaccustomed throng. The guard was reinforced and armed with machine guns.

The visitors were not tourists interested in viewing the collection of animals captured from all over the Amazon jungle. These were victims of the *Chupa-chupa*. A rumor had been circulating to the effect that the creature was imprisoned there in the park. And that it had something to do with the Americans. Or the Japanese, who knows?

Some of the visitors went as far as to offer money to the guards, just to have a glimpse of the *Chupa-chupa*. Others were hoping for the opportunity to settle accounts with their bare hands. You see, they hadn't slept for quite some time and tended to be a bit edgy.

The military authorities denied everything. And the zoological park was closed to the public, as of that same Sunday, January 23, 1983.

Which is why the events and characters described in this novel are clearly fictitious. Since it narrates a tale of extraterrestrials, any resemblance to persons living or dead, to institutions in this or any other galaxy, or to events taking place in other dimensions, would have to be purely coincidental.

Tell the world . . . Tell everybody . . . Look up in the sky!

THE DAY THE EARTH STOOD STILL

MONDAY, AUGUST 15

Since early morning the radio had carried the story: an unidentified flying object was creating panic among inhabitants of the small town of Valéria. Local residents were abandoning their community and fleeing for assistance to the distant county seat.

Vera's first reaction was to get up out of bed and rush down to the harbor. For the last six months she had worked feverishly in Parintins. She would wake up full of enthusiasm, only to waste half the day lecturing the president of the Rural Workers Union. Vera had come to the county seat hoping to convince farmers to experiment with new planting methods along the river plain. At a loss to make any sense of what she was saying, the farmers merely laughed. Had she been an officer from the state bank, they might have attempted to seek additional financing. Or were she, instead, one of those insufferable college students that seasonally drift into the area, they could have sent her packing—with the utmost civility, of course—back to the state capital. But the fact of Vera's being employed by the Ministry of Agriculture left them no other choice than to tolerate her with abiding good humor.

Basically "clean," though always looking to grub another joint somewhere, Vera Martins would show up first thing each morning at the union office. Her white skin had already been deeply bronzed by the months of sun, and her shoulders and arms were splashed with freckles. Still, her hands were so delicate that the head of the union thought they must be made of tissue paper. Oh, the attractive young agronomist from São Paulo definitely interested him, a fact he continued to demonstrate by grinning like a dunce while she flipped her way through index cards; while for her, the toll of each morning's effort at self-control was like feeding one's nerves to a blender.

"The plain might produce as much as three profitable harvests a

3

year," she would explain while the president of the union, with maddening complaisance, stuck to filing his nails and leering broadly. "It worked in Egypt. . . ."

Vera felt like putting a match to her index cards, convinced by now of the futility of her profession. She was fed up with this union rep and his idiot's delight at *anything but* agricultural innovation. And he himself, to his partial credit, was beginning to suspect that he might soon be rid of this pretty agronomist from the Ministry of Agriculture.

Parintins was undoubtedly the most perfect hole anyone could imagine to destroy one's illusions. And Vera had actually dug her own way into that fiery pit. Sprawled on the right bank of the Amazon, Parintins seemed to have slipped into a protracted coma.

Afflicted with a typical romantic conservationist fever, Vera Martins had completed her university studies in São Paulo, two years before, only to discover later in Parintins what she never could have dreamed: heat enough to bake one's cerebellum, lethargy enough to eradicate thought, and isolation sufficient to drive the most devout Tibetan monk into a straitjacket. Like many students of her generation—educated in universities dominated by fear and deception—she exhibited a casualness bordering on apathy and let her life be ruled by consummate disdain for ordinary common sense. Her first sleepless night in a pool of sweat, however, was enough to provoke fissures in her illusions, and the dogged grin on the face of the union rep had thoroughly drained her of hope. The Amazon—fascinating, immense and permanently threatened—was not exactly an ecological campground, which would have been more appropriate to the level of her frustration and her bouts of despair. In those stifling early morning hours of the Lower Amazon, Vera Martins had begun to discover what it really meant to be ruled by an implacable disdain for common sense, as exemplified by that perverse ecological determinism that was enough to drive man and nature into the void of indifference. She was all of twenty-five years of age, and considered herself extremely plucky for having managed, in less than a month, to get a job with the Ministry of Agriculture. Now she passed each day in a continual state of anxiety because she was terrified of metamorphosing into a witless technocrat.

It was clear, however, that people did not look upon her so indifferently as that. The union rep would smile benignly at her agricultural models while peeping now and again, with a genuinely conservative sense of etiquette, at the curve of her knees. The old mayor of the town would offer her countless helpings of powdered guaraná, strong and bitter-tasting, as if the better to keep her quiet. The Capuchin bishop took exception to the elliptical bikinis she would wear to bathe in the channel, and the mestizos paused to ogle at her as she pedaled by on her bicycle. And finally, there was the young disc jockey from the local radio station; timid but infatuated, he insisted on dedicating to her those mawkish melodies that were like nothing she had ever heard in her life.

She made no friends, however, and in six months had only once been treated like a human being: when she spent two days in a hospital ward after having suddenly come down with an infection. It was there in that polyclinic, while lamenting her overbearing, seemingly tactless personality, that she first heard talk of unidentified objects—*"Chupa-chupa,"* as the popular imagination had already dubbed them, because of their marked appetite for sucking blood—visiting havoc on the remote community of Valéria.

Vera then felt true hatred for the first time in her life, although the object of her hatred was too vast to engender a response. Her hatred was of the decrepit luxuriance of nature in the Amazon, capable of reducing a human specimen to a grinning idiot.

When Vera arrived at the harbor it was nearly ten o'clock. The sun was so hot that her shoulders felt as if they had been horse-whipped. Soldiers of the Military Police, barefoot and out of their gear, were helping women and children off a tiny wooden boat over-loaded with passengers.

The small community of Valéria was situated way out in the far-thermost reaches of the county, where the locals produced a coarse, toasted manioc meal for export to Manaus. Vera had never gone to Valéria, just as she had refrained from setting foot in any other community after experiencing the crude hospitality of Parintins. There was real panic in the faces of those passengers, something she could also surmise by the mute urgency of their movements as they swiftly disembarked.

"I had a feeling you might show up, miss," the mayor observed dryly, cradling a screaming infant in his arms.

"I heard the story on the radio," Vera told him. "I gather it's not the first time something like this has happened out in Valéria, is that true?"

The mayor was trying unsuccessfully to calm the child.

"Well, it's nothing very special. These people are just a bit scared, that's all."

"It looks to me like the whole community is here," Vera commented, seeing how many people were climbing onto the docks.

Still, the port was not so busy as it had been earlier in the day. Before sunrise there were often hundreds of such boats and canoes in the harbor, loaded with animals, fruits, fish, flour and a variety of other wares. You could find almost anything there in those early morning hours before dawn. Occasionally, Vera would actually visit the docks at such an hour, to have some banana pudding or other fare, particularly when she was "blasted" from marijuana or had given in to some other diversion like drinking beer and dancing on into the night with her young disc jockey. But the sun at present seemed to have permanently stalled above the murky yellow waters of the river; and few people were venturing to stroll along the wharf, which extended like a T from the steep bank of the waterfront. No one in town seemed to take an interest in the peculiar drama of these residents from Valéria, as if the sudden appearance of crowds of people fleeing the *Chupa-chupa* was the most ordinary thing in the world.

"They say the pastor out there has disappeared, that he was carried off by the *Chupa-chupa;* is it true?" Vera hazarded.

The mayor shook his head vehemently *no,* while still attempting futilely to distract the baby in his arms.

"That's just another silly rumor, miss. They do love a tall tale, these river folk . . . but it's best not to take them too seriously."

Earlier, while Vera was having coffee at the hotel, the kitchen girl had told her that the Adventist pastor—new to Valéria, but well respected—was apparently attacked by one of those objects and seemed to have vanished without a trace. An eighteen-year-old boy who had tried to rescue him from the thing had suffered a kind of electric shock and was rushed to the hospital with hyper-anemia. According to what they were saying here in the city, the pastor and the local priest were the only ones not afraid of the *Chupa-chupa.* So the disappearance of the pastor seemed like a warning.

"The priest didn't come?" Vera asked, noting the absence of the young father of Germanic complexion from Rio Grande do Sul.

"Are you returning to Manaus, tomorrow, miss?" the mayor ventured, changing the subject. The last thing he wanted at the moment was any more talk of that priest.

For nearly a month now the mayor had been quizzing her daily, with an eagerness he could barely suppress, as to when she was finally going to return to Manaus.

"Yes, tomorrow, after lunch."

"So, you'll be taking the plane?"

She nodded. "Who knows? I might even run into that flying saucer."

The mayor, immune to her humor, finally delivered the child into the arms of one of the women.

"You don't intend to order an investigation?" she persisted.

"Good Lord, no. What in the world for? Before you know it they'll all be back in Valéria, slapping their knees with laughter over the big scare they got out of this one."

"You know your people well. . . ."

The mayor took her comment as a compliment. Now serving his second term in office, he felt too old for any other job; and besides, he enjoyed governing his people, with an earnest negligence that endeared him to all. To be sure, the city of Parintins was a small and peaceful place, even reasonably rich by Amazonian standards, with rarely a headache for its lucky mayor.

The boat was already empty, as the residents of Valéria huddled together inside the warehouse among baskets, crates and bundles of clothes. None of them showed any sign of animation; they were simply there, simply waiting, and Vera Martins could not help being amazed at how tacitly these river people surrendered to life's imperatives.

"Have any of you people places to stay?" the mayor asked.

A powerful-looking farmer stepped forward, respectfully removing his hat. "We'll manage," he replied humbly, apparently in charge of these refugees. "All of us have relatives here."

"Anything at all, then, just let me know," the mayor insisted.

"Much obliged."

Silently the motley group of river men began to shuffle about the warehouse, patiently gathering their belongings. They would soon disappear into the homes of relatives and neighbors, and there relate their adventures. Forgetfulness would set in later.

Vera turned her attention to the women, all of them surrounded by their children. An impenetrable stoicism could be read deep inside each and every stare, in every gesture executed with a slow deliberation. What could have driven out such tranquil people? Why had they abandoned their homes, their fields? Whatever it was, it must have been truly terrifying, not simply frightening. Vera's imagination worked feverishly, but failed to stanch her curiosity. The small amount of time she had lived with such people was already enough to make her realize that, deep in the Amazon, people did not scare that easily.

"You shouldn't worry your head, miss," the mayor told her, seeing that she was still intrigued.

Unconcerned himself, he headed off under the shade of his umbrella in the direction of his private, air-conditioned office. The mayor's casual attitude was as mystifying as the refugees' panic. It was obvious to Vera how much she had still to understand; all her faculties seemed to have atrophied from prolonged exposure to the vast indecipherability of the Amazon. Yet it was clear that more than fifty people had abandoned their homes, while a mayor was acting as if nothing had happened. He might have at least sent a couple of policemen to investigate matters on the spot. Of course, any governmental authority would be skeptical of reports involving UFOs, especially from the likes of river dwellers. Yet the mayor seemed to exaggerate even his own skepticism. A pity that the newspapers of Manaus were so provincial; here was a perfect subject for a genuine piece of investigative journalism.

The harbor shimmered above the majestic current of the river, as gigantic islands of earth and grass floated lazily downriver, heading for the ocean. In search of a bit of shade, Vera tiptoed through the pigshit that so often fouled the streets of Parintins. People were gathered in the shade, here and there, under the marquees and canopies of the commercial buildings, where they passed day after day sipping beer and playing dominoes.

The following afternoon she would take the flight to Manaus, and all these events would become as distant as they were unreal. Her bags had already been packed for a good month now. Had she ever really unpacked them? In Manaus, she would be required to write up a detailed memorandum to be sent on to Brasília. The idea of a memorandum irritated her so that she even contemplated drafting one shallow enough for the bureaucratic minds of the Ministry of Agriculture. In the face of such a task, however, the mayor's behavior no longer appeared to be all that unreasonable: how to explain to the state authorities that a group of superstitious river hicks were sighting luminous objects in the skies above the Amazon? and *not* sound ridiculous? As ridiculous as to claim to other bureaucrats in Brasília that the project for harvesting from the river plain had faintest hope of being implemented. Her life's work was certainly turning into a positive bore, an extended yawn—an infuriating development for someone who had planned to save the entire Amazon Basin, single-handed, from the claws of destruction.

Later That Morning, at a Radio Station in Parintins

Independence Radio Network, the most popular station in the Lower Amazon, was the pride of Parintins. The studio comprised two small rooms filled with the very latest in sound equipment and vinyl upholstered furniture. The air conditioners ran night and day to prevent heat and humidity from knocking out equipment or otherwise interrupting programming of that awful music Vera felt must be some sort of local concoction from the darkest Amazon.

Slouching back in the DJ's seat, she was slowly drifting off to sleep. The musty smell and deliciously cool air reminded her that technology could sometimes be a blessing. Outside the window, the humidity was steadily evaporating, making the landscape swim beneath the violent rays of sun that just a while ago had been pounding her scalp and searing her flesh. The studio was like a refuge where she might revive her faculties, because out in that heat she always felt in a vertiginous state of Zen meditation: her head empty and unreal; a useless, but nonetheless painful, bodily appendage.

"Vera, look, I managed to find at least one of them for you."

The young DJ had just walked into the studio with a boy dressed in shorts and a flashy pair of imported sneakers. Vera shook off her lethargy and bounced out of the chair to greet him.

"You're incredible, Jorge," she warbled, pecking him on the cheek.

Looking quite proud of himself in his new role of investigative reporter, Jorge pulled up a stool for her.

"Sit down."

"I don't want to get in your way," she said, half sitting and half leaning against the stool behind her.

"I had a heck of a time finding this one," he said, pointing to the boy with his thumb. "The whole gang of them seems to have gone into hiding."

Vera kept staring at the boy. The drowsiness had left her and she could barely contain her excitement. The boy was obviously still nervous and stared timidly at the floor. His face was serious, mature, though she read a hint of trachoma in the crystal-clear brown eyes.

"You actually saw a flying saucer?" she could not refrain from asking.

The boy looked up at her, puzzled.

"The *Chupa-chupa*, you saw it?"

"Wait," Jorge interrupted, "first let me turn on the tape."

The experience the boy related was, in fact, unique. From out of the jungle, gliding at incredible speed just above the crown of tallest trees, a white light—fantastically bright—had swooped down and headed directly for him. The boy had no idea what it was; he had never seen anything like it and had begun to run. Fear is far too limited an emotion to contain the sum he felt, since suddenly the sky—in the logic of the river dweller—had presented the same onus of mystery that until then was the exclusive province of the great river.

Vera and Jorge sat mesmerized as the boy related his tale.

Meanwhile, at the Presidential Palace in Brasília

The President of Brazil felt uncomfortable in his armchair. Ever since he had taken his seat that morning, for the daily meeting with his cabinet ministers, something had been troubling him. And it was not simply the gravity of events that the ministerial head of the National Service for Information—acronym: SNI—so bluntly referred to, with that monotone voice of contained aggression, that particularly disturbed him. After all, it was precisely the function of the SNI to gather intelligence; and the present state of national affairs seemed to be rapidly approaching the twilight zone, as one political commentator had put it on television the previous night with an aptness the President found compelling if only for its metaphorical clarity. The President himself was not much given to such elegant, almost bookish turns of phrase; but he envied those who could so easily draw their refined circumlocutions out of the proverbial hat, much as he might lead his favorite mount to jump effortlessly over some unanticipated obstacle in the field.

Over the last two days, the city of São Paulo had been transformed into a megalopolitan version of the northeastern villages periodically overrun by starving refugees bent on sacking stores and shops for food. In this case a peaceful protest of the unemployed had escaped the control of its organizers, turning loose a rebellious mob that eventually looted a substantial part of the city's commercial district, including the old shops around the Praça da Sé, in what was once the center of the city.

The state governor, according to the SNI's reports, was for the moment in control of the situation. But the minister continued to press for the additional presence of federal forces, given that in his view the governor—elected by a party of the opposition—showed himself to be vacillating, even conciliatory toward what the SNI would classify as agitators, and appeared to be placing the blame on some mysterious form of right-wing subversion, thereby concealing the obvious participation of notorious Communist elements.

"But the governor is handling the situation adequately for the moment, isn't he?" The customary expression on the President's face, of perennial displeasure at the duties of office, was even more pronounced than usual. "The looting and vandalism have been halted as of yesterday afternoon. Your own reports have confirmed the fact, if I understood you correctly."

The Minister for Military Affairs and the Minister for Civil Affairs both agreed with the President. Relations between either one of them and the minister in charge of the nation's network of intelligence were icy at best.

"The Minister of Labor is staying on in São Paulo," the head of Civil Affairs informed the President. "And for the moment that's the only branch of the federal government that rightfully can be involved in the matter."

The explosive general in charge of the SNI stared contemptuously at the old jurist. He could not abide the presence of a civilian in the midst of this decidedly military gathering. Ever since that man had taken over the Office of Civil Affairs, the traditional morning session with the President had lost its flavor. It was no longer that fraternity of comrades in arms assembled there to discuss matters frankly, using the blunt language that only the intimacy of the barracks can confer upon a man. This civilian meddler had reduced everything to a tedious exchange of etiquette that made any soldier want to puke.

"I agree that the spread of disturbances was a direct consequence of a lack of initiative on the governor's part," the Minister for Civil Affairs continued without so much as a glance at the irritated general from the SNI. Instead, his watery eyes remained fixed upon the President, who seemed unable to find a comfortable position in the brown leather armchair. "But what else was to be expected? The personality of the governor of São Paulo has never been a mystery to anyone. He's not a man accustomed to making instant decisions, but he is going to have to learn that it's a necessity if he expects to stay in office."

"I still can't understand how such a thing got started in the first place," said the President, shifting positions in his chair and grimacing with pain. "I think this story of losing control of some rally by the unemployed may be fine for the newspapers, but I don't buy it: a well-managed herd of horses doesn't just bolt from a little thunder and lightning."

Everyone laughed except the general from the SNI. He loathed the false effusion of such timid titters, above all from the Minister for Civil Affairs. And this was hardly the time for effusiveness, however timidly it was being managed.

The meeting dragged on for another two hours and nothing concrete was decided. The President would receive intelligence updates periodically from the SNI, and the press secretary would announce to journalists that the administration was continuing to "monitor the situation with grave attention."

Finally, when the two ministers for Civil and Military Affairs had left the room, the director of the SNI was left alone with the President, who continued twisting about in his chair without a moment's respite.

"Are you feeling all right, Mr. President?"

"Of course I am," the President snarled. "Why do you ask?"

The general remained silent for several minutes, simply leafing through some official documents he carried with him in a plastic portfolio. His silence irritated the President because it seemed maliciously insinuating.

"So, what's on your mind?" the President asked gruffly, still moving around uncomfortably in his seat.

"Are you sure you're all right?" insisted the general.

"What in hell do you mean by that?"

Snapping closed his portfolio of documents, the head of the SNI turned his full attention to the bilious head of state.

"You're the one who's been shifting around the whole time in that chair. You'd think you were sitting on a nail."

"The problem is one that lies outside even your jurisdiction."

"Good enough, Mr. President," the general temporized, "but if I were you I'd consult my physician."

"Physician? What in hell would I have a doctor look at a chair for?"

"Not the chair . . . you! That chair is perfectly fine."

"Well, there must be a loose spring in the upholstery or something."

"That chair doesn't have any springs. I examined that chair personally when this room was redecorated for you. If there's a problem, it must be with you."

"With me?"

"Mr. President, you suffer from hemorrhoids, don't you?"

The President flew out of his seat.

"Am I going to have to put up with your insults as well?"

"I'm only trying to help, sir. It's hardly normal for a person to spend his every moment attempting to find the right position in a chair."

"I happen to be a cavalry officer, General," the President remonstrated.

"For that very reason," insisted the general, himself an artillery man.

Discreetly, the President proceeded to examine the area of his body under suspicion, then took a few tentative steps across the cabinet room. His discomfort apparently had ceased from the instant he leapt out of his chair. He was about to inspect the chair more closely but was sidetracked by his intelligence minister.

"In any case, we have a bit of a problem to discuss," the general began.

"What do you mean?"

"Concerning the next head of the Joint Chiefs of Staff."

"Fischer? What's the matter with him?"

"It's not exactly with him, Mr. President, although for my own part I consider him a horse's ass. It's the General Staff though, Mr. President. There are already signs of growing displeasure among the various units. The army base in Rio talks about nothing else these days."

"I don't understand. Fischer's been an outstanding officer."

"But he's from the Air Force."

"So what? Even officers from Artillery fill important posts nowadays."

The general's expression grew more and more peeved.

"You have no sense of humor, General," the President chided.

"The General Staff believes," the director of the SNI continued, ignoring the President's remark, "that this is not the proper moment to be appointing Brigadier General Fischer to head the Joint Chiefs of Staff for the Armed Forces."

"Normal rotation, that's all. We've already had two admirals during my stay in office."

"The General Staff seems to harbor the opinion that you haven't managed the thing properly."

"What! So I haven't managed the thing properly, have I? Haven't secured the reins of the country firmly in hand, I suppose? Well, it may interest them to know that in a process of liberalization such as the one we're attempting, the experienced horseman has to know just when to snap the reins and let the horse break out of a trot."

"That may be so, but the Staff seems to feel that you haven't even put the horse's bridle on securely; that at any moment the horse could very well throw its rider."

The President smiled condescendingly; he was on his own philosophical turf now. If there was one thing in the world he was thoroughly versed in, it was the equestrian arts. It was, if nothing else, his profound knowledge of horses that enabled him to confront the hardships, surprises, headache and tedium of public life. Even the ups and downs of his private life were governed by that specialized knowledge. There were times when his own wife would grow positively incensed with his manner of behavior at home, which to her frequently rivaled the vulgarity of a dedicated veterinarian.

"That staff doesn't know what the hell they're talking about," he opined.

A questioning wrinkle slithered across the brow of the ministerial head of the SNI.

"The important thing, General," the President continued more serenely, "is not whether the bridle is properly strapped on the animal. It's not even a matter of whether you have the reins firmly in hand. Those are merely mechanical tasks for the man in the saddle. Any rider can manage them decently enough."

"But the President is no ordinary rider."

"Obviously, my friend. And if a horseman knows his trade, he will, of course, watch that the bridle is carefully adjusted on the animal; and he will also manage the reins with precise movements in order not to confuse the poor animal. But there is still one thing about which a rider can do nothing; yet if he's worth his salt, he's prepared for the thing to occur no matter what the circumstances."

The head of the SNI was growing paler and paler, his hands in a cold sweat clenching his portfolio of classified documents.

"Do you know the one thing a horseman has to keep in mind, no matter how skillfully he handles his mount?"

"No, Mr. President," the general hissed, unable to contain his impatience.

"That the horse can decide at any moment to take a shit wherever he damn well pleases."

The President smiled at the head of the SNI in triumph. His greatest pleasure was to pontificate matters equestrian to his cabinet advisers.

"It is the knowledge of that fact that permits the horseman to be both flexible and politic. You can deprive a horse of a considerable portion of his freedom of choice; take hold of his reins, force him to trot to the left or the right; get him to leap over obstacles, ford rivers, and a lot more; but the moment any mount has the desire to, no rider in the world is going to prevent him from shitting on the spot. I don't care if it's the marble floor of the palace or the bed of roses around our National Monument. That is the margin of liberty, the escape valve, of every horse. And the same principle applies to the people of this country."

The general from the SNI got up to leave. Before exiting through the doorway of the cabinet room, however, he took one more opportunity to admonish: "I think there are times when even a mule should *not* be allowed to *shit!*"

Furious, the President let his body fall back into the seat of the armchair, insulted by the lack of either political or equestrian sensibilities on the part of his minister from the SNI. He knew perfectly well who was at the bottom of those objections to the appointment of Brigadier General Bernardo Fischer. The director of the SNI—true, he was on intimate terms with the President for many years; both of them graduates of the class of 1959, from Superior Officers' Training School—had lately for some reason begun to develop a peculiar jealousy toward anybody who enjoyed access to the presidential cabinet. On the heels of his pronounced antipathy toward the Minister for Civil Affairs, he was now attempting to make a case against the selection of an officer from the Air Force as head of the Joint Chiefs of Staff. Behind it all, the President knew, was the question of his own succession. Once at the helm of the Joint Chiefs, Fischer would undeniably have jockeyed himself into favorable position for the nomination; he was an obstinate, ambitious man who surmounted poor health with an unquenchable appetite for work. And it was exactly for this reason that Fischer had won the President's approval.

The upholstering on the armchair continued to plague him with discomfort. Upon dropping back into the chair, with such a violent temper, he had nearly had his thoughts eclipsed by the severity of pain that immediately enveloped his posterior. The circumstance was befogging his judgment. He did not have such a clear idea in any case as to why he had decided to name Brigadier General Fischer to the post—he had acted almost out of pure impulse, as if simply to complicate the path of the countless other candidates to his own succession. That Fischer had earned a reputation as an element of the extreme right was not a matter to preoccupy the President at the moment.

He got up from the armchair once more and commenced to examine the upholstery of the seat. After a bit of probing, he could feel that a particularly hard object was lodged more or less in the center of the seat. Indeed, it formed a slight protuberance at precisely the strategic spot to deprive any mortal of his sporting good humor.

He gripped one edge of the seat cover and gave it a hard wrench. A few upholstery nails gave way and the foam plastic wadding bulged out from under the leatherette lining. The President proceeded to pry one hand into the stuffing and took hold of what was definitely a metallic object. He withdrew his hand instinctively and beat a hasty retreat to the doorway. It could be a bomb; someone trying to kill him. He shouted for his aide-de-camp. Soon the cabinet room was swarming with security agents.

"I can't understand it," snarled the general from the SNI, who had returned with the other ministers.

"Hemorrhoids, eh?" the President countered with sarcasm.

The object was a fairly sophisticated listening device. It had somehow gone undetected by the team of security men who made a daily sweep of the presidential offices.

"They must have recorded some rather strange sounds." The President smiled in an attempt to minimize the damage. "As I see it, it must be the operation of a foreign power."

"Do we give this to the newspapers?" the press secretary inquired nervously, scrutinizing the portraits that hung on the walls while running a hand under tables and chairs.

"Keep the press out of this," barked the director of the SNI. "I want a complete blackout on this investigation."

"Oh, don't be ridiculous," the President intervened. "Of course the press has to be informed—that way your office will need to come up with a decent explanation for all this."

One of the SNI agents was already on his way out of the cabinet room with the minuscule artifact in hand, when the Minister for Military Affairs brusquely halted his departure.

"Young man, that piece of equipment stays with me."

The agent turned doubtfully to the director of the SNI, awaiting instructions.

"The President's security is entrusted to my office," the general in charge of Military Affairs insisted.

Noting the outlines of an ironical smile beginning to form on the lips of the Minister for Civil Affairs, the general from SNI acquiesced with a gesture of disdain.

"Suit yourself . . ."

The young agent tossed the apparatus into the air, and the Minister for Military Affairs had to rush to catch it before it fell to the floor.

"Didn't I tell you, General," the President observed to the irate minister from the SNI, "the horse will shit wherever it damn well pleases."

A half hour later, the presidential retinue was on its way to the Chief Executive's ranch, Granja do Torto. Suddenly, with no advance warning to security guards, the presidential limousine pulled over to the edge of the curb by a lonely bus stop; and to the complete surprise of his immediate advisers, the President got out of the limousine, took out a telephone credit card and began to dial a number in a public booth.

Someone obviously answered, because the President began to give a brief summary of what had just transpired back in his cabinet room.

"Well, I can no longer just stand idly by, Mr. President," said the voice on the other end of the line.

"Now don't go jumping the gun on me," the President warned.

"You think I'm too old for this sort of thing, don't you?"

"It's not exactly that—"

"It is exactly that; but the way I see it, either we take urgent steps or we're liable to be swallowed up by events."

"But don't you think that—"

"Look, it's obvious they're trying to topple you, Mr. President. And they happen to be the agents of extremely powerful forces."

"You shouldn't get involved in this," the President reflected uneasily.

"It's obvious that I'm already involved. I intend to enter the fray and give them a run for their money, or my name isn't Pessoa."

"General Pessoa!" the President repeated anxiously, but the line had already been disconnected.

SATURDAY, AUGUST 20

The small cassette recorder began to emit a disagreeably high-pitched tone, and Paulo Veronezzi shut it off. What he had just finished hearing would not have aroused more than a mild curiosity in him, were it not for his companion lying on the bed with the sheet pulled up to her chin. Paulo let out a whistle and popped the cassette out of the recorder. Vera had been watching his every reaction.

"You were there when the kid was recorded?"

His question, intended to display interest, rang as falsely to her as his whistling. Still, Vera nodded, her flowing hair splaying over the pillow behind her as she summoned the expression of an amazed witness to her eyes.

A trace of irritation began to fester inside of Paulo Veronezzi, which merely increased his own embarrassment. He was gradually realizing the extent to which he regarded her with an attitude of superiority, with a presumptuousness that bordered on the sadistic and a detachment that only served to exacerbate her excitement with respect to purported events in the Amazon interior.

"The boy must be about thirteen," Vera added, apparently oblivious of her friend's preoccupations. "But he's already quite mature. You know how fast kids grow up around here."

Paulo was still weighing the cassette tape in his hand, when the only thought on his mind at the moment was how to get out of all this. He was hardly in Manaus to hunt down flying saucers. His job, thank God, had not the least flavor of adventure.

"It's the only thing of consequence to happen to me in six months of life in the Amazon," Vera continued. "Yet no one in Parintins seemed to pay the slightest attention, as if it were all perfectly normal."

"It's a pretty screwy part of the world, all right."

Paulo was leaning back on the windowsill, where the open curtains allowed the rays of sunset to penetrate the room, dissipating the shadows with a yellowish hue. Vera could not see his face against the vermilion twilight.

"The boy seemed to be in total shock, I wish you'd seen him."

"Well, you can hardly blame him. Imagine coming face-to-face with a weird contraption like that in the middle of the jungle . . . I'd light out of there fast."

"You would? I'd be rather curious; besides, I've always wanted to see a flying saucer. You'd be amazed at how many people have. There was a time when I used to follow that sort of thing, reading everything I could lay my hands on. I kept imagining how it would be to live in a future world, where all our terrible problems would have already been solved: hunger, war, aging, all the heavy issues we have to live with. It would be mind-boggling—intergalactic travel from one star to another. Don't you think?"

"I don't know. I guess I never much bothered about that sort of thing."

"But these things exist, they're for real, lots of people have witnessed them."

"Right, and you have a lot of wacko people around here too."

"But this isn't something crazy. There are millions of stars out there, and there must be millions of planets as well, where intelligent life is possible. It makes no sense to believe that just one fucking planet in the universe was conceived for intelligence and has remained unique in its technological development. That's obviously trash."

"Trash from a science fiction novel . . ."

Vera sat up in bed abruptly, letting the sheet drop to her thighs and revealing her sun-bronzed, small-breasted torso punctuated by its pink nipples.

"But the boy did see something, some sort of creature that answered his signals. Something intelligent, and responsive to other intelligent beings."

After five days in Manaus, she had nearly forgotten the incident: completely absorbed with the task of composing her report, she had let the cassette tape lie hidden at the bottom of her knapsack under layers of books and dirty clothes. And now the final result of it all was merely to be exposed to the complacent attention of Paulo Veronezzi.

"Anyway, you don't have to act so superior with me."

"Come on, it's not that at all."

"You're so transparent, Paulo."

"Well, you're the one who's letting yourself get carried away with all this business. I run into you on the street, and all of a sudden you start hitting me with flying saucers, farmers in a panic. How do you think I'm going to behave?"

She had met Paulo on the street quite by accident that afternoon. They had ended up at the hotel where he was staying. Vera had felt a desperate need to unburden herself to someone, somebody intimate enough to understand the same language she herself spoke. But it turned out that Paulo Veronezzi had no intention of fulfilling that role.

"You just don't want to get involved . . . isn't that it?"

"That's not it, Vera," Paulo protested with an odious yellow smile. "It's just that I already have a job to do here, it's as simple as that."

"You're not one to open yourself up to anybody, I know. That must be why you're always surrounding yourself with airhead groupies, to keep yourself looking above it all."

"Take it easy, Vera, will you? This isn't getting us anywhere."

She did not wish to irritate him more than he already was. She preferred to excuse the shortcomings of his machismo because he was rather tall, quite athletic-looking, with that square chin of an Italian and the Latin look of panic whenever a woman dared to stare straight into those big dark eyes.

Vera was trying that very moment to do just that, but could read no panic there because his head and shoulders were only a black silhouette against the violet sky; and all was reduced to that tone of displeasure in the voice, of irritation: a nervous male simply making ends meet with a mediocre job.

"This must be what they call maturity, right?" Vera asked, giving voice to her thoughts.

"What?" Paulo had no idea what she was talking about and continued to draw his blank in silence.

"You used to work for the *Jornal da Tarde* when I first knew you, remember?" she said finally.

"So?"

"I just mean you were already in your profession while studying for your degree."

"I've always had to work."

"You even got a prize for journalism, didn't you: that series of articles on political prisoners. Politics usually doesn't turn me on, but I read every installment."

"And I lost my job because of them."

"How did you manage?"

"Took a job in advertising; you know, editing copy, that sort of thing. We haven't seen each other in a long time. Somebody told me just recently that you'd gotten yourself a job out here. I couldn't imagine why."

"So now you're back with the paper again?"

"No, for the last year or so I've been with *Isto É*, not the worst magazine."

They fell silent again, the hum of the air conditioner subtly insinuating itself between them. Finally Paulo threw up his hands:

"You can't expect me to change my entire schedule just to cover some half-baked close encounters of the third kind with a dozen or so scared Indians . . ."

"They're not Indians," Vera chided sarcastically.

"I know," Paulo smiled, "but they're almost the same. . . ."

The tape cassette still lay there in his hand. The hotel room was comfortably cool, while outside the window the lights of the harbor rocked and flickered above the waterline. On a cart sat the remnants of the meal they had ordered, and on one of the armchairs, Vera's clothes.

The following day Paulo Veronezzi was going to have to climb into a Jeep at dawn and travel for four hours on a dirt road to the site of the hydroelectric works at Balbina. The magazine was putting together a cover story on the hydroelectrical power projects in the Amazon basin. The decision to focus on the one at Balbina was partly because the project was being financed with money from French interests but also partly because one result would be the flooding of an area inhabited by still wild, Waimiri-Atroari Indians. Fundamentally, however, it was a topic chosen to generate income from the advertising space to be sold to the countless firms involved in hydroelectrical construction, not to mention from the generous support of the Ministry for Mines and Energy.

"Meaning you're not about to help me?"

"My boss would bust my ass if I ever attempted to interest him in the subject of flying saucers."

"But it would make a terrific story. The *Chupa-chupa* has already frightened the wits out of over two hundred people. It's scaring off everybody in sight—these people are leaving everything they have: homes, property . . ."

"And now you want me to get bounced from another job!"

"No, I don't. How much time will it take you to visit the hydroelectric works and put together a story?"

"Oh, I don't know—I don't really even have to go there, I suppose. It would probably be enough to send the photographer out there. I've got all the information I want in that stack of papers over there."

The small table he pointed to at one end of the room was covered with papers, magazines and press releases sufficient to bury the telephone. Paulo Veronezzi was not of a very organized nature but overcame this particular failing by dint of a prodigious mnemonic ear which seemed to have the capacity to record everything spoken in a radius of three meters about his person.

"That meal is beginning to make the room smell fried."

Vera Martins switched on the table lamp and pivoted out of bed, throwing her nude, tanned figure into stark contrast with the walls of bright blue wallpaper. She dialed the front desk and asked them to come collect the tray. Meanwhile, Paulo Veronezzi was quietly gaping at the perfection of her body, was a bit numbed by it, aching to caress the soft curves of its thighs.

"Maybe you couldn't convince anybody out there, but you certainly made good use of the sun."

Vera hung up the phone and walked over to the window beside him; she pondered the intensity of the heat that lay just on the other side of the pane. She could not rid her mind of the mask of panic engraved on that boy's face. He had certainly experienced something extraordinary, and she knew she had to discover what it was. The problem still remained that nobody else seemed to care. People shunned the very mention of the subject, and now even Paulo seemed reluctant to investigate the incident in Valéria.

"Everybody wants to stay locked up in their routine little worlds," Vera began to complain aloud while rubbing her arms to ward off a chill. "No one is prepared to jeopardize anything. This whole affair is full of imponderables and defies comprehension. The expression on that boy's face said just that: that something had challenged his reason, something he could never hope to assimilate and simply go back to being what he was . . . an ordinary human being who had awakened rather early to go out into the fields, with no great questions or problems on his mind other than that of his own long-term survival."

"Forget it, Vera," Paulo insisted.

"It's such a shitty mess," she muttered furiously.

Paulo tossed the cassette tape onto the bed. The whole story was finally getting to him, as if it were not enough to have to do the swinish work he was paid for. He retrieved his shirt and started pulling it over his head. It stank of sweat that was still moist, but the room's cold temperature had begun to make him uncomfortable and all he needed now was to catch a chill.

"I had the idea it might interest you, that's all. I'm sorry."

"I understand, but I've got too much to do already, Vera."

"You're right, you have your assignment. Besides it's more important than my crazy notions . . . you'd better get on with it."

"Damn it, Vera, it's nothing all that important!"

She gave him a look of sympathy.

"Oh, it's a stupid-ass job like all of them. I head out tomorrow morning down some road full of dust to sweat my ass off while I interview some blowhard of an engineer."

When they had run into each other on the street earlier in the center of Manaus, while browsing through shops filled with imported wares, Vera had said nothing about flying saucers. She had looked like just another of the many tourists who crowded into the commercial heart of the city in search of the latest electronic gadget or some cheap Indian cottons. Still, she was always a bit spacey. Back at the university she had gotten all involved in oriental philosophy, reeking of incense and mouthing off mystical bullshit. And he had gotten fed up with the smell of incense and the smell of bullshit. Walking along the burning streets together that morning, she had behaved as a grown-up woman who had finally gotten some sense into her head. She confessed to him how difficult those lost months had been, even more the lack of any comprehension on the part of inhabitants from that ridiculous little town on the lower Amazon. Paulo was even faintly interested by her opinions concerning the horrors of living outside any large urban center, in refreshing contrast to the fashionable utopianists lately preaching a return to nature. He too was a strictly urban type who held no great affection for the dangers and discomforts such backward places generally exacted. In his travels as a reporter he felt mounting impatience toward his occasional contacts with the more primitive sectors of the country.

"I don't know how you managed to spend six months in the jungle," Paulo admitted, acknowledging after all that she did have a personality of sorts, or at least a strength of will that outclassed his own complacency. "I'd rather break a leg than have to spend six months like that so far away from São Paulo."

Vera Martins smiled, dropping her dress over her head and quickly brushing her hair. Her nearsightedness no longer gave her that squinting stare he enjoyed so much, for she had put her contact lenses back in.

"You leaving already?" he asked her.

"Don't you have to get up early tomorrow?"

"They'll be coming by to pick me up at around six."

Vera retrieved her purse and headed for the door. Paulo hastened to open the door for her but suddenly remembered that he was naked below the waist. So he stepped behind the door while Vera said goodbye.

"You'll phone me when you get back?"

He promised he would and blew her a kiss.

"Even if I don't run into any of your flying saucers."

Vera turned on him furiously.

"Oh, fuck you! I don't care whether you take me seriously or not—"

"I'm sorry, Vera, I didn't mean that."

She charged back into the room crying and throwing herself on the bed.

Paulo Veronezzi was taken aback by her reaction. He thought it typically feminine but rather badly timed. He was dying to get some sleep; his temples were pounding and his legs aching from all the walking he had done that entire day from one office to another in search of further information.

"I think I must be losing my mind," she said, sobbing uncontrollably, her head buried in the pillows. "All those weeks out there in that sweltering dump of a town have finally gotten to my nerves. Everybody laughing at my proposals like a pack of idiots. That city is so fucked up they don't even have a newsstand. The women order their photonovels from friends visiting Manaus the way other people order drugs. Nothing to do out there—even the programs arrive a day late."

"But don't they have some branch of the state university there?" Paulo asked, attempting to rekindle a conversation.

Vera rolled over on her back and stared at the ceiling. Her tears were smudging her makeup and a slender trail of black eyeliner was mapping each cheek.

"The loneliness was horrible," she admitted with rancor, a cold sob eclipsing her voice. "You have no idea what alienation is about until you've been to Parintins. The students know absolutely nothing, and when I say nothing I mean just that. They've never even heard of the Jari Project, can you imagine? And that's right in their own backyard. And the literature program—most of them have never read Jorge Amado; they don't even know who he is! It's worse than the heat, that kind of alienation—it rots a person bit by bit, turning anybody into a dolt. . . .

Paulo Veronezzi shut the door of his room and sat on the bed, observing Vera's anguished breathing and listening to her low sobs. She was clearly strained by the months of isolation, and her running into him this way had quite likely had the effect of a too-rapid ascent from the depths of emotional deprivation. That much he understood. But all he was looking for at the moment was a little companionship and nothing more—a girl with whom to spend some time alone after a long day of running back and forth in a terribly hot and unfamiliar city. A girl and a good air conditioner.

"Just forget about it, Paulo . . ."

He had lost track of what she was saying.

"About what?"

"Everything, everything I've told you . . ."

"Don't worry," he hastened to agree. "This stuff about flying saucers is all nonsense, for people who have nothing better to do."

"I suppose you're right, Paulo," she replied mournfully.

"Good enough," he concluded, animated by the possibility of an end to her crying. "I once had to interview this guy who called himself a 'ufologist,' completely off his rocker. An admiral or something like that . . . claimed he'd already talked with the flight crews of four flying saucers. You should have heard him. . . ."

Vera smiled timidly, gazing up at him with tenderness. She felt grateful in any case that at least he wasn't grinning at her like an idiot. And he had lost that expression of somebody who really didn't want to look at her.

Paulo took the cassette tape from the bed and stashed it into his suitcase. He still felt he wanted to listen to the tape more closely. The clear ring of the boy's voice, the high quality of the recording, had all transmitted a very strange emotion.

Meanwhile, Not Far from There

The prostitute, in her high-heeled shoes, was about to fall into the creek. A wooden plank measuring not more than a palm's width joined a floating hovel to the muddy bank. Manaus was full of such constructions along the countless fetid bayous that crisscrossed the city. They were generally palafittes or shacks floated upon rafts made out of tree trunks, where one could go have a beer, listen to the blare of a modern jukebox, play a miniature version of billiards or purchase, at the cost of a few pennies, any twelve-year-old prostitute who tickled one's fancy. The Bayou São Raimundo, an old and dilapidated district of Manaus, was filled with such dives and buzzing with hicks from the interior, with soldiers, and with overpainted, underdressed little girls.

The plank of wood did not offer the prostitute much support; in addition to which she was obviously drunk. Things were reeling in her head so thoroughly that she barely could make out the shack itself, lit up by a single red circular neon light. Another slide caused her to fall astraddle the plank as her legs sank into the putrid waters. She was so helplessly drunk that a stream of warm urine began to pour from between her legs, and the effort to call for help was altogether too much for her. The rough edges of the plank meanwhile had ripped her stockings and scraped her thighs; her shoes had dropped off her feet and were already floating downstream in the direction of the Rio Negro. Her whole frame bucked up and down with the swayings of the plank, and her two hands flailed the waters as if she were learning to swim. The flailing was desperate and unavailing, until she struck something bobbing just below the plank. As her eyes grew accustomed to the darkness, she was able to perceive with much effort that she was holding on to a kind of wet, shaggy ball—apparently made of rubber—which seemed to be the head of a mannequin. Overtaken by sheer reflex, her fingers clutched at the hair of it while she managed slowly to lift her legs and kneel on the plank. It was then she realized that what she was holding was a human head.

The shock was such that it instantly dissipated all of her insobriety. Those gathered inside the bar now heard a queer sort of howling and rushed out to see what was going on. The prostitute sat balancing herself on the quivering board while holding, lanternlike before her, a monstrous apparition that looked upon the world with an expression of horror.

Hours later, the riverbank was swarming with police. Patrol wagons had already rounded up the more inebriated habitués of that particular flophouse, inasmuch as the remaining customers—more in control of their reflexes—had managed to slither away into the opaque labyrinth of shacks and palafittes slung over the riverbank in defiance of every law including gravity. The prostitute, meanwhile, sat sobbing and trembling, still in shock, in the backseat of a metallic blue C-14 Chevrolet station wagon with false plates. Its driver was Captain Cruz, a muscular army officer dressed, typically enough, in civilian clothes.

Standing near the station wagon and wearing a sport shirt, slacks and a pair of eyeglasses with noticeably thick lenses, General Pessoa was peering down at the operation as his nervous hands fingered the leather strap hung around his neck and bearing a useless pair of binoculars. Teams of divers were probing the debris-infested waters, while at the deeper end of the bayou a patrol boat, with men from the fire department, was raking the bottom with a fine-mesh fishing net.

The operation promised to drag on into the morning, and General Pessoa strained to keep his eyes trained upon the darkness of the night and his ears attentive to the orders and shouts issuing from the men involved in the search. He felt certain that nothing would escape their vigilance: they were well trained and had spent their professional lives sifting through the bayous of Manaus in search of victims from either drownings or the countless topplings of shanties off the banks. Still, the general was not very optimistic about the outcome of his mission, though this was not the moment for doubt—the game was afoot and he would play it to the finish. As an officer assigned to the reserves, the most he could hope for from the Military Command of Amazonia was a degree of cooperation; the rest was up to him.

At the age of sixty, General Pessoa was recognized internationally in the field of paranormal research. Soon after graduating from Advanced Officers' Training School, he had attended a special reserve-officers meeting promoted by officers from the U.S. Air Force in Rio de Janeiro, where he watched in astonishment a documentary film shot on the night in which hundreds of UFOs flew over Washington, D.C. From that moment on he had steeped himself in the subject and begun to study a number of Brazilian incidents; at the time, under army auspices. The author of five extensive volumes on these mysterious visitors, to some of his colleagues he was little more than a harmless old fool; while to others, an eccentric who lived entirely for his army career but also nurtured a slightly unusual hobby. Still, his entry into the closed community of intelligence had nothing to do with his penchant for hunting down extraterrestrials. General Pessoa happened also to be the most qualified specialist in counterintelligence of his generation, with a brilliant passage through school at Fort Bragg, in 1967—a year, by the way, rich in sightings all across the northern United States. General Pessoa was one of the founders of the National Service for Information—the SNI—and the architect for the modernization of the Second Section of the Armed Forces Secret Service. Until 1977, he had worked in the Special Council on Information and Security, in the Ministry of Health; a post from which he then retired to civilian life, organizing CENAP: the National Center for Paranormal Research.

Now and then, searchlights cut through the darkness, and the hum of the motor launch, in low gear, grew louder with the occasional shifts in the wind's direction. The first signs of dawn would soon appear; the general was growing impatient, nervous that daybreak would bring the curious along with members of the press eager to pose too many questions.

The two-way radio in the station wagon began to emit an intermittent signal, and the general walked back to the vehicle. He reached in for the microphone and thumbed a button. Nothing happened.

"Damn gadget," he muttered to himself, annoyed.

Coming to his aid, Captain Cruz reached over and opened the channel for communication. As he passed the mike back to the general, a hoarse, metallic-sounding but perfectly audible voice was heard to say:

"Evening, General. Communications Center here, Department of Security. Over."

"Yes, General Pessoa here," he answered tiredly while looking in at the prostitute softly sobbing in the backseat of the wagon.

"General, the search there has been called off. We've already informed the lieutenant in command. . . ."

"But why call off the operation?"

"The body's been found, sir. If you wish to, you can check personally with the morgue; it's already on ice there."

The general nodded his head as he turned to the impassive face of Captain Cruz sitting at the wheel. The radio crackled and the metallic voice sounded urgent, or possibly annoyed. "Repeat, the body's been found. Operation suspended."

"Where did they find it?" the general finally responded.

Now there was a silence on the other end, punctuated by static, and then the voice replied still more raspily: "Why don't you check at the morgue, sir. Over and out."

The general handed the microphone back to the captain and wiped the sweat from his forehead with a hand, brushing off the moisture on his pants. The captain, exhausted by the lack of sleep, yawned and gripped the dashboard of the station wagon, stretching his arms.

"I want you to take a walk down to the edge of that bank there and find the lieutenant, Captain," the general ordered. "Tell him to get up here, tell him I want to have a word with him."

Cruz got out of the station wagon and started down the muddy slope, sliding in his boots now and then while precariously balancing a huge, athletic body. Soon the lieutenant showed up at the wagon and bent over the opened window to be able to address the general more easily.

"Well, Lieutenant, it looks like you're about to pack it up with your unit, eh?"

"That's right, sir. The body's apparently been recovered."

"Just the same, thanks for your help."

The lieutenant was wiping his nose with a rumpled handkerchief, and he grunted something inaudible by way of appreciation.

"Oh, one other thing, Lieutenant. I'd like you to drop the one in the backseat off at juvenile detention."

"You won't be needing her any further, sir?" the lieutenant inquired with a disdainful glance at the prostitute.

"No, I'm done with her."

The military police were all returning to the waiting vans, and off in the distance, the patrol boat was already headed for the Rio Negro. The lieutenant took the prostitute out by the arm and led her over to a gray patrol wagon that was half stuck in the mud.

It was still before daybreak when General Pessoa and Captain Cruz arrived at the police morgue. A guard opened the gates, and Cruz parked the station wagon close to the main entrance. The building itself was nearly all dark, though a few lights were flickering in the pathology lab. So this was the land of shadows, the general mused to himself, where he would now have to confront what remained of the man whose head the prostitute had lifted out of the bayou.

The drawers where the corpses were deposited lay mostly empty. The morgue did not generally house its cadavers for very long. The majority of them, when not claimed by the families, were sent on to the Anatomy Department at the university's Faculty of Medicine, immediately after autopsy and identification.

"His death was preceded by torturous agony," the young medical examiner on duty informed them in a low voice. "This much of the body was found washed up at a boat yard in the Aleixo district."

The examiner pulled out a drawer and lifted a sheet, depositing at the same time a spherical plastic sack where the head of the victim should have been. The general and Captain Cruz both stepped back with horror, unaccustomed to such a grisly sight. The examiner covered the body once more with the sheet and carefully rolled the drawer shut. The two military officers hastened to flee that depressingly frigid atmosphere, their nostrils burning with the unpleasant odor of formaldehyde.

"The body shows unmistakable signs of the torment the victim endured prior to death," the examiner continued in a self-consciously dramatic tone of voice. "All the nails were ripped off the fingers, probably with pliers. All the ribs were broken and the lungs perforated by bone splinters. He was found with a broomstick inserted up his anus, which ruptured the duodenum. The wrists bear the edema left by handcuffs and the soles of the feet have been burned by acids."

The examiner interrupted his speech to stare at the two officers in an accusatory way, then concluded: "I've been working here for two years and have never seen anything to match such barbarity."

General Pessoa looked at the medical examiner with an expression of pained embarrassment. He could never escape that same feeling every time a civilian made similarly veiled references linking the armed forces to cases of torture. Yet, almost immediately the embarrassment was displaced by another sensation: a sort of compensatory assuredness that he himself did not belong to that degenerate class of butchers-in-uniform who continually filled him with such shame. At least he was of a different stripe.

They entered the examiner's small office, only to suffer a second surprise. Seated at the young examiner's desk, with his head buried in the careful perusing of a stack of typewritten pages, was Colonel Nunes, the SNI's man in Manaus. Still, it was a familiar enough face to the general and his captain.

"I'll leave you gentlemen alone," the medical examiner suggested, eyeing the officers with obvious disgust. "No one will interrupt you here. Good morning, gentlemen."

Colonel Nunes looked up to fire a parting glance at the young examiner.

"Shithead civilians," he muttered aloud as the fellow closed the door behind him.

Captain Cruz crossed his arms and leaned against a metal file cabinet, while the general made himself comfortable in an armchair piled with papers, to the left of the desk where the colonel from the SNI had been sitting.

"You still think this has something to do with flying saucers, General?" Colonel Nunes asked, continuing to leaf through the typewritten pages after spreading some photographs across the desk. "The stiff had quite a file, you know."

The general, however, paid no attention to the provocative tone of his fellow officer, remaining totally calm and receptive-looking. Years of training had instilled in him an absolute self-control.

"If he was a Seventh-Day Adventist pastor, then I'm Jorge Amado," the colonel added dryly, still perusing the photographs.

"You have something you'd like to tell me, Colonel?" Pessoa asked him calmly.

"The actual name of the owner of that head was Mario Gardner— Mike to his friends. He was working for the CIA long before any of us had ever joined the Community."

General Pessoa sighed deeply, shaking his head as if in disapproval of all that had occurred.

"Sons of bitches!" exploded the colonel from the SNI. "These gringo bastards still think this is their own backyard. I'd like to know why the hell they didn't inform us they were plunking this lemon in our laps."

"Their explanation might tickle you, Colonel."

"What do you mean by that remark?"

"Just that Mario Gardner is their top expert on UFO phenomena."

"*Was* their top expert, General—he certainly isn't now."

"True enough, Colonel. At least on a physical plane he's no longer with us," Pessoa acknowledged.

"We were aware of the American's arrival." It was the taciturn captain's turn to speak.

"You *knew?* And you told us nothing?"

"Second Branch preferred to keep a lid on the facts for the time being," Cruz explained coolly.

Nunes reddened in a fury.

"Well, now that he's dead, he's not about to tell us himself."

"Perhaps he may tell us more now," General Pessoa reflected.

"Only if he shows up at a séance, General."

Captain Cruz stepped over to the desk and picked up a few of the photographs. His speech was slow and his voice heavy, without much inflection or emotion.

"We just wanted to find out what it was exactly the Americans were hoping to accomplish by sending their man into the jungle, precisely where some land disputes had been boiling over for the past ten years. The only thing that bothers me is that we sat back and did nothing."

Colonel Nunes's expression was akin to that of a deceived husband.

"We let the fellow come and go as he pleased," Cruz continued. "He'd arrived on a regular Varig flight, from Miami, and was welcomed by a group of genuine missionaries who apparently knew nothing of his intelligence activities. We confirmed as much with the missionaries themselves."

He went on to summarize the report: The American had landed at Eduardo Gomes Airport about three months ago. He carried a minimum of baggage and wore an old pair of sandals and a discreetly patterned long-sleeve print shirt. He acted like a different person, looking about timidly and shaking hands with the missionaries with the utmost filial piety. The passport presented to Customs and Immigration gave the name of Arthur Gary and listed his profession as registered nurse—an innocent little lie."

"The role of pastor wouldn't have stuck very well," the colonel observed with growing irritation. "He probably would have got his facts fouled up among all the true believers."

"He was a first-rate professional," General Pessoa corrected.

"Mike actually was a Seventh-Day Adventist," Cruz informed them.

The colonel from the SNI, meanwhile, was searching for something on one of the typewritten pages of dark blue paper designed to prevent photoduplication.

"But wasn't this guy a Cuban? I thought Cubans were Catholic."

"His parents were Cuban," Cruz explained, "but he emigrated to Miami in '58. By 1965 he was already involved in several shady operations. He seems to have converted some time in the sixties—imitation, you know how it is. He wanted to be American at all costs."

The colonel shook his head in disbelief, but went on listening to Cruz's narration.

"He was born in Matanzas. He got his American citizenship in '62: a reward for the fervor he'd demonstrated while engaged in a series of provocations directed against the Black Panthers movement. In 1964, he actually assassinated a leader of the movement in Orlando, Florida. In '66 he was already at work in Saigon, a specialist in interrogation. The man was very good, all right; dispatched some twenty important Communists to the arms of the Creator. He spoke several languages, including Italian and French, but since his Spanish was native he was constantly being sent on missions to Latin America."

"He even went to Chile, didn't he?" the general commented.

"Yes, and wreaked considerable havoc on the left while he was at it. But suddenly he changed. It was 1978, and he was traveling on some mission in the Atacama Desert when, with no explanation, he shows up alone on the outskirts of a small town called Sierra Gorda— his escort of five Chilean soldiers had disappeared somehow, and he's completely ragged and in a kind of trance. Well, they took him to a hospital in Calama, and there he tells them he had been kidnapped by extraterrestrials, back there in the middle of the desert. The soldiers and the Jeep they were all traveling in never were found, in spite of an intense search. Of course, not too many people believed Mike's story, and he was quickly returned to the United States. The following year, though, a magazine published in California called *Flying Saucers News* actually printed what more or less amounts to a deposition by Mike. In it, he claimed that they were driving along the highway that cuts through the Atacama Desert when they noticed a strange light following them at a considerable distance. At first he had paid no attention, thinking it must be a plane or perhaps a meteorological balloon. But the Chilean soldiers, the majority of whom were peasants, started to get a bit nervous, especially since the thing had begun to shorten the distance between itself and them. Mike ordered the driver to pull over and then tried to observe the light with a pair of binoculars. But the thing was still too far off; so he ordered them to proceed. It was at that point that the Jeep stalled out, while the UFO commenced to describe a different pattern of movement in the sky, finally approaching to some twenty meters distance from where they were. The soldiers cocked their machine guns but never managed to get off a shot. The UFO emitted a sort of luminous beam, paralyzing his men. Two crew members then descended from the craft: they were small, of the stature of children, and wore outfits not unlike the wet suits of skin divers. The two creatures took Mike by the hand and drew him floating back with them into the craft. Of what followed he had no recollection, only that he came to his senses again in the vicinity of the town where he eventually received emergency medical treatment."

"I met Mike last year, in Palo Alto," Pessoa remarked casually. "I was attending the annual MUFON convention—Mutual UFO Network. People there told me that he had repeatedly undergone regressive hypnosis at the hands of the CIA, and made some surprising revelations."

"And then lost his head here in the jungle," Nunes interjected.

"The Americans were onto something, Colonel, and it's no good resorting to sarcasm, even if it is one of the mind's basic reactions when confronted by something that challenges its powers of reason."

"But then why take the liberty of not informing us?"

"Colonel, would your people have believed them? What would have been the reaction of the community if the Americans came up with a story that they were about to put an agent into the field to investigate close encounters of the third kind in the Amazon jungle?"

The colonel returned to stuffing his papers back into their manila folder. His expression was one of total incredulity, but he made an effort to appear to be open-minded with the poor general who had obviously gone soft in the head.

"I can appreciate how you must feel, Colonel."

"It's simply my belief that this man was up to something else. Something far more concrete . . ."

"Like what, for example, Colonel?"

"Like drugs, for example."

"You mean you think he was—"

"Exactly, General, I think he was on the trail of a connection, but he paid with his life for such foolhardiness. If he had just enlisted our help . . ."

General Pessoa now gave vent to his own bit of irony:

"So you can close your case, Colonel."

"That's precisely what I intend to do. I've already phoned the American embassy. The governor, here, has agreed not to create a scandal and the entire matter is going to be dropped. At least it's served as a lesson to the gringos. The next time they'll think twice before pulling a stunt like that."

"Well, for me the case is still open," Pessoa stated flatly. "The death of that poor devil says a lot of things."

"You don't accept the hypothesis, then, of drugs, sir?"

"Not at all, Cruz. That man was killed because he knew too much about those lights everybody's calling the *Chupa-chupa*."

The captain lowered his head slightly and looked away from his commanding officer, not wanting to display the smile he could not prevent from coming to his lips.

"I know it seems ridiculous to you, Captain. But unfortunately that's the way it happens to be: the human animal refuses to accept the fact that there are more powerful forces at work beyond our control. We're too proud a creature for that."

"Sorry, sir."

"That's all right, Captain Cruz, I'm used to it. An old man like me should be home dressed in pajamas, taking care of his grandchildren or raising chickens. But if you'd been through half the experiences I've had, you'd offer me every reason to insist. There are moments, let me tell you, when I begin to think that it's just too heavy a burden for one man to bear."

The colonel from the SNI stood up, clasping the folder to his chest, and went to let himself out the door. The immaculately clean, empty corridor was already bathed in the light of day. The three officers stretched their tired limbs and walked slowly to the exit.

"I'm going to ship the stiff back to the gringos in a zinc casket, as a present," the colonel bragged.

No one laughed, however, not even him. The tension and exhaustion had left them all defeated.

"Who do you think killed the American, sir?"

The old general stood still for a moment and took Cruz by the shoulder. He held him with a firm, paternal hand while he spoke without the slightest embarrassment: "There are many types of visitors, Captain. Some of whom are not so peaceful. Yet they've already won a following here. The acolytes of such visitors are prepared for any task."

They reached the parking lot and said good-bye to the officer from the SNI. He's a lucky man, the general thought to himself; with all the certainties on his side, he has no need to trouble himself about anything.

"Don't you think it surprising," he said, turning to the captain, "that the CIA should keep a supposed crazy man in active service?"

"It's an interesting question, sir. But according to our information, the guy was pushing papers at some bureaucratic desk back at Andrews Air Force Base. The only thing we haven't figured out is how he wound up here."

A Few Months Before, at Andrews Air Force Base, in the United States

The bitter winter had frozen the valley bathed by the Potomac, and Mike Gardner was watching the screen of a computer terminal far from the centers of political decision-making at the hub of the nation. He was in a subterranean vault deep in the bowels of the two hundred hectares of land occupied by Andrews Air Force Base between the Potomac and the Chesapeake. Mike Gardner was working for a special section of the Department of Consular Operations at the CIA.

He was eating fried tortillas flooded with ketchup, while peering attentively at the data which printed itself across the screen—the fruit of patient harvesting that Mike had been carrying out since 1977. It was data collected in South America, a region of few surprises but which the CIA kept under constant surveillance, if only to be cautious, ever since the Falkland Islands War. But his own interest was hardly military, and his work had very little to do with the political crises and other such tribulations besetting this troubled world of ours. His special section was charged with documenting all sightings of UFOs over that particular subcontinent. And to tell the truth, things were getting pretty hot down there lately.

Mike did not know whether it was the winter or the solitude, but he had the strangest feeling that something was about to happen. This same peculiar sensation would come over him every morning of late, as soon as he would leave his billeting and climb aboard the base's internal bus to arrive at his underground chamber. The growing number of sightings in South America was perhaps one of the reasons for this state of excitement; yet, what really made him uncomfortable was the tingling he had begun to feel in his hands and feet—the identical symptoms he had experienced that moment when the two aliens had taken hold of him out there in the Atacama Desert.

On this particular morning, while he was downing his tortillas, the lights of his chamber began to grow dim and finally the computer went dead. Mike suddenly felt a jolting shock at the base of his spine and realized he was somehow paralyzed where he sat, with the food making its descent only through the peristaltic movements of his gullet. Then the electricity seemed to have been restored, for the computer began to print on the screen a series of unintelligible characters that nevertheless were perfectly comprehensible to him. The phenomenon lasted a few short seconds and then ceased, leaving him lethargic and with a splitting headache. He made a futile attempt to recall the message from the computer's memory banks, but gradually understood that no record remained. The aliens had once again contacted him. Such a thing posed no problem for them, regardless of the extraordinary security in effect at Andrews Air Force Base. Much was still obscure to Mike Gardner, but if he really wished to know the answers, he would have to go after them deep in the Amazon jungle.

With the arrival of spring, Mike Gardner boarded a plane in Miami and headed for his tragic end. He died without learning the answer to so many questions.

SUNDAY, AUGUST 21

The lights along the Esplanade of the Ministries were twinkling cold and distant while, inside his suite at the Hotel Nacional, in Brasília, Pavel Aksentyevich was admiring an expensive silk tie. He had purchased the tie earlier that afternoon, for a very steep price, at one of those sophisticated shops in the Conjunto Nacional. It was to be a present to his brother-in-law—Secretary to the Political Bureau for the Western Sector of the Party, in Moscow—who was trying to pull strings so that Pavel and his family might leave the tiny apartment where they were living for a larger one, with two bedrooms, in a modern complex along the Entuziastov Highway.

Pavel worked in public relations promoting the Moscow Circus, but was also a high functionary in a special section of the Twelfth Department at KGB. The basis of his mission was to act as a courier for coded communications while also looking into the activities of various international organizations investigating paranormal phenomena—a particularly strong interest of the Soviet government. Trained in physics at the University of Moscow, he was first drawn to the subject when he witnessed demonstrations by the great female magician Ilena—healer and clairvoyant—of her powers of telekinesis. Pavel himself possessed certain considerably developed powers, and now here he was in that extraordinary city of Brasília, where there would periodically gather as many as twenty thousand mediums in a single locale in order to enter into contact with luminous beings from other galaxies. Well, to be honest, he had to admit that Brazil was hardly a country to fit into logical analysis.

Pavel had flown to the capital from Lima, where he had been received with icy, mistrustful cordiality by a woman from the embassy there. He himself felt no particular warmth for any of Latin America—it was a territory that proved particularly hard on the Russians. Even in Brazil, that land of endemic informality, he had sensed a degree of antipathy that deprived him of finding any pleasure in his travels. This was his first time in Brasília, and already he preferred Rio de Janeiro, a city he felt to be incomparable, almost hypnotic in its beauty. Brasília was another matter: there was something verging on the maniacal in the ordered configuration of buildings which appeared to be levitating above their enormous lawns. Brasília seemed vacant, disquieting, with its automobiles spiraling like meteors along interminable traffic lanes. It was a city that thwarted traditional formulas for human contact, driving its inhabitants either into total isolation or in search of other planes of existence. Here, capitalism had succeeded in constructing a city that was pure metaphysics, despite the fact of its having been designed by an orthodox Communist.

Sometime around one o'clock in the morning, two men arrived outside the door to Pavel Aksentyevich's suite. One of the two knocked quietly and the door opened.

"So late, comrades?" Pavel questioned sleepily, making way for his visitors and turning on the overhead light.

"We weren't told to come at any special hour, comrade," replied the one who entered last and was wearing a leather Windbreaker.

"Which one of you's Henrique?" Pavel asked them.

The skinnier of the two, with an oval face and a dark pencil mustache, smiled.

"He couldn't come," he answered finally in perfect Russian, staring straight into Pavel's eyes.

He did not appear to be Russian, although he produced a Moscow accent with fluent mastery. It was the Latin features and slender athletic physique that gave him away. He must have been nearing forty.

"I'm afraid I don't understand," Pavel replied, a nervous tautness overtaking his facial muscles.

"Relax, comrade."

The other intruder did not appear to be Russian, either, but was tall and powerful, with tousled hair and the flattened nose of a boxer.

"Who are you?" Pavel asked, backing away against a dresser and staring woefully at the two strangers.

"We're your friends, as long as you behave properly," the boxer answered gruffly in Portuguese.

Pavel did not understand him, and began to reach for the inside breast pocket of his jacket. He had a reasonable command of Spanish, but could only fathom Portuguese when it was articulated very slowly.

"I wouldn't do that," the thin one warned him in Russian. "We would hate to have to prevent you. The Master wants you in one piece."

"I don't carry a weapon," Pavel attempted to reassure him, "but who do you think I am?"

The boxer, meanwhile, had drawn out an INA .32 revolver and

pointed it straight at Pavel's head. He was staring at the Russian like
someone drugged, while making his way over to the bed and cautiously removing the passport from Pavel's jacket. He examined it
carefully, keeping one eye on its owner, and then handed it to his
companion.

"It's him all right," he remarked.

The other simply slipped the passport into his own hip pocket.

"I was afraid we had the wrong one," the other continued. "You
know how it is when you're out of practice."

"You can't do this to me," Pavlov protested in desperation.

"Take it easy, friend."

"You're going to produce a crisis between my government and
yours."

"I doubt that," said the shorter one.

As a Russian, he had already heard enough stories of the vicious-
ness of the forces of repression in Brazil. They were not so frequent
as those about Argentina, Chile or Central America, but still a lot of
people had lost their lives there or at least disappeared without a trace.

"There's got to be some mistake . . . I'm employed in the Moscow
Circus, do you realize that?"

"What's he saying?" the boxer asked his companion.

"The same old shit," the other replied with a wave of the hand.

"Let's get him out of here, this place is beginning to smell bad."

Pavel Aksentyevich could not believe that this was happening to
him. People working in the Twelfth Department seldom wound up in
tight spots of this magnitude—the most that normally occurred was
to have a visa denied or be expelled discreetly through diplomatic
channels. But these fellows were behaving as if he were an agent
from S-Department and trained in sabotage, infiltration and God knows
what other lethal arts.

"Let's take a walk, Baba-Yaga!"

The thin one had called him that, and Pavel trembled: Baba-Yaga,
the legendary witch—then they knew exactly what he did.

"Ptyíthwi!" Pavel shouted with rage. The thin one eyed him com-
plicitously.

"What's that mumbo jumbo about?" the boxer demanded of his
partner.

The thin one, meanwhile, was rummaging through Pavel's luggage
and did not bother to explain things to the boxer. He came across a
bottle of vodka, still unopened, and read the label.

"This is the real stuff," he observed, taking the bottle out and then
closing the suitcase. "We haven't forgotten anything, have we?"

He grabbed the suitcase after having checked the rest of the room. Pavel always traveled lightly, since it was never prudent to show up at customs with a lot of baggage. And he was completely clean: he had not even contacted his referentura at the embassy. From an intelligence point of view, he was wholly useless, in whosoever hands he might be.

"Now then, comrade, you're going to be very well behaved about heading downstairs with us. And there will be no playing hero of the working class, correct?" The shorter one's Russian could have fooled Andropov himself.

Pavel Aksentyevich stepped out into the corridor, as waves of panic ebbed and flowed within him—ominous as the vast plateau that extended darkly in every direction outside. His feet behaved like twin fifty-kilo weights that had to be dragged painfully along. They stepped into the elevator together, and he felt the barrel of the INA revolver nosing into his ribs, but out of view to anyone else who might chance to get on at another floor.

"You like my Russian?" the thin one inquired.

"Letter-perfect," Pavel replied in a disagreeably quavering voice. The thin one smiled with satisfaction.

"I'm a bird: a *ptyíthwi,* as you say."

"So I noticed," Pavel confirmed without wanting to say more. His voice was an embarrassment to him—hoarse and tremulous as a trumpet out of tune.

"I studied five years at Patrice Lumumba, comrade, and then took a powder."

"Oh, really?"

"They were about to send me packing because I was screwing around with the wife of one of the managers of the GUM Stores."

He was lying, obviously. No one was expelled from the Soviet Union just for sleeping with store managers' wives. The government would have had to spend all its time signing expulsion orders. Not to mention that the Jews and dissidents would be queueing up at the bedroom doors of every store manager in town.

"She couldn't resist a little Latin blood," the shorter one insisted, and gave out with a laugh as the elevator softly landed in the lobby. The doors opened and the three walked out and headed casually toward the parking lot. The shops in the gallery were already dark, and the last show of any movie had exited long ago. That's how it was on Sundays, when nearly everybody went to bed early in that city of bureaucrats.

But, just as they were getting into the car, a youth with long hair and tight-fitting jeans stepped out of the darkness. He began frantically snapping the shutter of his Nikon automatic, which flashed repeatedly. Reacting instinctively, the two thugs posted themselves menacingly in front of the Volkswagen they had just opened and proceeded to wave obscenities at the young man whose camera was still flashing. Then they scrambled into their Bug, and drove slowly off, crossing the Rodoviaria to take the Eixo Monumental, where they gradually picked up more speed.

"How do you like the nerve of that guy!" the boxer commented in a fury, now driving the car as if he were at Le Mans.

Pavel swayed from side to side in the backseat, his hands cuffed, putting his weight against the suitcase to try to keep his balance.

"You were just photographed by the CIA, comrade."

If it was true, Pavel thought to himself, then this country really was turning out to be a land of lunatics.

He turned to look behind them, and could see they were not being followed. At least no automobile seemed to take an interest in pursuing such a bizarre kidnapping.

Pavel Aksentyevich closed his eyes, the better to think: he must put all that was happening to him into some kind of logical sequence. Perhaps that would calm him down a little and even lend him some courage. One thing he had already concluded: these men were not government agents. If they had been, they would never have allowed themselves to be photographed like that. And they were poorly armed, just a .32-caliber. And reckless, to boot. Even as terrorists they were operating very carelessly. He had had a hunch from the very outset that they might be no more than common criminals. He had read too many accounts with respect to the high incidence of crimes in Third World countries to think otherwise. Yet, the pattern of their actions did not really jibe with ordinary criminality. Actually, they seemed like a pair of fanatics. Maybe that was why they continually eyed him with such a curious intensity, and with such arrogance. And that thin one who spoke the fine Russian displayed such quick reflexes and tense muscles that he seemed to be positively burning with fever. Clearly that fellow could not be fitted into any facile category.

They had not bothered to blindfold Pavel; perhaps they were not even worried whether the Russian saw where he was being taken. In any case, he kept his eyes peeled in order to observe everything. They were already out of the Plano Piloto, and now continued—at a good 100 kph, he observed—along an excellent asphalt highway with neither lights nor traffic.

After more than an hour of driving, the car finally began to slow down. Just ahead, at a soft curve in the road, Pavel Aksentyevich could make out a sort of gigantic ellipse fantastically illuminated within the surrounding darkness. He could do nothing, he knew, and he began to regret the amount of money wasted on that elegant tie. Quite likely, his brother-in-law would never hear from him again.

A Few Hours Earlier, Some Thirty Kilometers from Brasília

A black Mercedes pulled up at the entrance to an enormous marble stairway that descended along a slope to form a Greek-style amphitheater. At the far end, crowning a species of pedestal in the form of a temple with a single door, was a stone statue some twenty meters tall: the figure of Sylyon, galactic visitant in his flowing white tunic; his right hand pressing the staff of power to his bosom; the Runic swastika raised to the heavens in his left. Sylyon, inhabitant of the star Canopus and a being from the very highest astral plane, gazed eastward with his oblique stare devoid of pupils.

The amphitheater itself was some one hundred meters in diameter, with the representation of a golden pyramid at its center, from which there issued six radii terminating at the base of six blocks of cement in the guise of thrones.

Two guards, each with a sawed-off shotgun, jumped out of the Mercedes and stationed themselves immediately at the front and rear of the vehicle. Then a skinny tallish fellow, obviously advanced in years, climbed out and proceeded with surprising alacrity down the long stairway to the only entrance to the temple.

The door opened, and the elderly figure continued his descent, down a long ramp lit indirectly by neon lamps. Each step he took, with his vigorous gait and erect carriage, echoed from the floor of polished concrete. The sloped corridor displayed no furniture or decoration, and led to a vestibule with three identical steel doors, all of them shut. The old fellow took a magnetized plastic card from his pocket and inserted it into the electronic identification box. The middle door slid open with a muffled hiss and he stepped inside.

The ambiance was one of extreme tranquility, and a feeling of the utmost serenity pervaded the salon. The elderly gentleman had just entered the most intimate private sector of the Valley of the Seven Moons: the most potent core of spiritual irradiation on the entire continent. A powerful system of central air conditioning held the temperature to a constant 17° Centigrade in a room filled with an array of videos and LEDs which were blinking in the shadows. A third-generation mainframe computer, storing in its memory nearly all the mystical wealth of humanity along with the revelations of the great Sylyon, pulsed with life in the sanctuary of its anti-atomic shelter beneath the vast Planalto Central.

Two rather young technocrats with crew cuts stood up from their chairs and hastened to salute the new arrival.

"At ease, my sons," the old man grunted in reply.

One of the two then addressed himself with great formality to the old fellow.

"We've recovered the material, all in perfect order, Master."

"Excellent," the old man rejoiced. "When can we have a look?"

"At once, Master."

The youth offered the Master a high stool and then took his own place in front of a keyboard with a TV monitor. He typed in some orders, and almost immediately the monitor commenced to display a series of images in motion. They were the images of lights coursing through a night sky and picked up by extremely sensitive polyspectral scanners.

The old fellow laughed convulsively as the images metamorphosed across the screen to display the lines and contours of these luminous objects in all their aerodynamic complexity.

The phenomena which had been recorded with an ordinary domestic brand of videocassette tape, of the Betamax variety, amounted to several appearances of unidentified flying objects in the skies above Amazonia. One of the sequences was particularly stunning: the object hovered in the air and then suddenly descended upon a clearing in order to shoot a beam of light at a family of terrified peasants. It might easily have passed for some footage produced by a very sophisticated special-effects studio, had it not been found lying among the belongings of a dead Adventist missionary in Manaus.

"Interesting footage," the young man ventured to remark.

"And the gentleman from the CIA?"

"Dead, Master."

"Dead! But he was supposed to have been brought here alive. How could this have happened?"

"An accident, Master. Our men went a bit overboard."

"They disobeyed my command."

"And they'll be punished, I can assure you."

The old man got up and paced around the room filled with flashing lights and the faint hum of the computer.

"There's no possibility that this film might be a fraud?"

"We are still checking out the possibility, sir. In ten days we should have the results of our tests."

"So long?"

"To make absolutely certain, Master. But if it should turn out to be authentic, then it will qualify as the most precious document in our entire archive."

"You're right to be cautious. The CIA could very well have planted some fake footage on him just to mislead us. They must think us very primitive if they did, or very naive."

"His body has been discovered, Master."

The old fellow shook his head in a gesture of annoyance, the murmur of his respiration rising above the low hum of electronic equipment.

"Master, you should know that General Pessoa has gone to Manaus to investigate."

"The traitor!" he cried. "Is he working alone?"

"He moves about in the company of a certain captain from Second Section. Still, it appears no one takes him very seriously."

The old fellow cackled on, while the two technicians remained silent. They had already anticipated this sort of reaction. The Master was a fiery old character who surmounted the grave illness consuming his body only by cultivating an inflexible discipline for work.

"Have you found out the identity of the CIA agent?"

"We have, Master."

The technician struck a different combination of keys, which caused the monitor to cease displaying the UFO. A few lines of static followed, and then an image was restored, this time of a man—front and profile—who was clearly entering middle age.

"Mario Gardner, Master. Central Intelligence Agent since the early sixties. He came through here once before, on his way to Chile. Spent two years hiding in the Consular Office, in Rio. Lately, he'd been working as a specialist in close encounters. His cover in Parintins was that of an Adventist missionary."

"The Americans are tireless in their service."

"The CIA has apparently been tracking sightings in Amazonia since 1977. They sent their best authority into the field to investigate. And obviously they did not inform our government. Being very discreet . . ."

"It's a subject no one likes to be frank about."

"The CIA must be disturbed by the possible repercussions of this case. A great many Brazilian papers already were placing the blame on the Americans: claiming that the lights were some form of psychological warfare meant to drive peasants from lands potentially rich in minerals or suitable for raising cattle."

"The selective pattern of the sightings really is rather intriguing."

"A source at the American Embassy has advised us that Gardner was actually working on his own."

"Is that a possibility?"

"Perhaps. But clearly the CIA would not wish to be seen as involved in such matters. Plus, there's the problem of infiltrating an agent without the American government's knowledge."

"And our own Community?"

"Not a word. They swallowed the American agent with absolute silence."

"As always . . . What *beautiful* patriots."

"Our real problem, Master, is the intrusion of General Pessoa."

"Well, he can do very little. He's working all alone—and on the wrong side."

"Still, one must be cautious enough not to underestimate the general. Pessoa has powerful allies on the astral plane."

"But Sylyon is much farther along the evolutionary path."

"Look at this, Master."

The technician once again began to type at the keyboard. The video of the monitor turned gray, then gave birth to a green field and the inscription FACTOR QUAZGAA.

JUST A MOMENT, the computer replied.

The old fellow watched with amazement as the computer speedily assembled all factors involved in the question put to it.

ASSESSMENT FOLLOWS, the computer explained.

The three men waited anxiously until the video began to spell out, letter by letter, digit by digit, its coded reply:

        PRONOUNCED IMPONDERABILITY
        QUAZGAA DEVELOPING
        PROBABILITY SUCCESS REDUCED 300
        INTERMITTENT SUSPENSION SYLYON
        SOLUTION URGENT
        TOLERABLE PERFORMANCE MISSION TO DATE
        AXIS MODIFYING
        DIMENSION ZERO
        END OF ASSESSMENT

The old man slammed his fist down on the console.

"Forgive me," he apologized to his shocked technicians. "I couldn't control myself."

"The situation is critical, indeed, Master. Quazgaa may have already made contact with General Pessoa. He always likes to work with someone."

"Quazgaa is only an emissary. He cannot challenge Sylyon."

"But Quazgaa's lords are powerful and have challenged Sylyon for centuries."

The old fellow paced the room's penumbra, his mind somewhere beyond the thousand blinking lights. His thoughts soared, and he rued his mistake bitterly. He should never have allowed the CIA spy to be eliminated. His greatest error, however, was to have sent a small group of young men with absolutely no training to accomplish so delicate a mission. The risk was too high, and the youngest among them were still at that turbulent, impulsive age when professionalism and impeccability counted for very little.

"What do you think should be done, Master?"

"Bring me General Pessoa. I want to see whether this Quazgaa is as powerful as we think."

"Do you really feel that's the thing to do, sir?"

"Bring him to me, I say, and the sooner the better!"

A red light began to blink insistently, and one of the technicians picked up a phone.

"Marvelous," the fellow exclaimed, holding his ear to the receiver.

"What is it?" the old man demanded.

The technician replaced the receiver, staring contentedly first at the image on the video and then at his Master, who stood tensely beside him.

"The Russian is in our hands, Master."

"Fantastic," the old fellow applauded, almost skipping with delight. "I thought he would be more difficult to come up with. I hope they haven't committed any further idiocies."

"He's being brought down here this very moment."

"Have him taken to the Meditation Room. I wish to speak to him personally."

"He was like a sitting duck, Master. He arrived by himself and checked right into the Hotel Nacional."

"A very capitalist duck," the old man observed ironically.

"But he's our man, all right: Pavel Aksentyevich, parapsychologist, authority on poltergeists and UFOs, physicist, agent for the KGB. He has true telekinetic powers and is versed in a variety of oriental arts of self-defense. But he didn't resist being apprehended."

"By the way, are you performing any service for the public sector today?"

The technician consulted his agenda.

"This morning we're computing our services to the National Bank for Household Finance. According to our contract with them, it's due on Tuesday. And this afternoon we begin processing data for the construction company that will pour the concrete for Phase Three of the Itaipu project."

"Excellent, my boys. These services bring in substantial revenues for the Community of the Valley of the Seven Moons. And this is a month of sizable expenditures: we begin our annual period of donating food to the poor, and you know what happens around here whenever we distribute food."

The technicians both smiled, but the old man continued to purse his lips in an expression of pain. The Master was actually quite sick; his heart was failing and his skeletal frame functioned only because of being propelled by a will of iron, the mark of the old man's unflinching character. According to military doctors, at least, the venerable Grand Master of the Valley of the Seven Moons, Brigadier General Bernardo Fischer, future ministerial head of the Joint Chiefs of Staff of the Armed Forces of Brazil, was a lost cause—a matter of months, at best. Or rather, this is what they had predicted two years ago. Yet here he was, sucking in the powers of his astral connections, inflexible, suffering acute pain, nearly incapable of ingesting any earthly foods, but still firm in his resolve with respect to a higher mission of transforming the world.

"One other thing, Master."

The old man paused, waiting for the horrible sensation of burning he felt in his thorax to finally pass.

"Here is the text of the order of the day you are to read at the inauguration ceremony as the new Chief Minister. It was transmitted by Sylyon through our computer."

He took the pages in hand and began to peruse them.

"It's very good, Master," the technician remarked. "It should provoke quite a furor."

The old fellow bid them "Good day, my sons," and headed for the door to the deserted ramp of the Temple of Sylyon.

The technicians paused from their work to follow his exodus with fervent admiration. They were the faithful, well-trained men whom he had practically lifted out of the gutter where society had buried them. He had personally molded these idealists after having rescued them from alcoholism, drugs, desperation. They were youths who had descended to the lowest levels of Karma, boys who had come out of the bowels of political oppression, ex-torturers finally abandoned to their own devices and condemned by their hypocritical superiors. The old man's steps echoed loudly and then less so, as he made his way upward, until only the timid hum of magnetic tapes spinning through the computer filled the air. Thereupon, his young acolytes returned to their tasks.

MONDAY, AUGUST 22

Paulo Veronezzi was submerged to his chin in the tub of his hotel room. A murky water enveloped his body, but the fact did not seem to disturb him. Next to the tub, on the floor, a half-empty bottle of whiskey bore witness to the effort he was making to have a tolerable last night in Manaus.

Suddenly Vera Martins entered the bathroom with a newspaper folded under her arm. With her hair combed back, a bit of makeup on her face and the white dress she wore, she looked rather different from her habitual image of permanent representative of the counter-culture.

"Well, you certainly must have been having a wonderful time of it," she exploded sarcastically, while noting the muddy water in the tub and the worn-out expression on Paulo's face. "What in the world made you stay in Balbina all of Sunday?"

"Oh, I was just jerking off," he replied in a fury. "Of course, the damn Jeep happened to blow all four tires and we lost our only means of transportation. Not to mention no one gave a fuck about the predicament of two journalists. God, have I had enough of eating dirt in this place."

Vera unplugged the bathtub to drain the yellowish water and run a clean tub. She began massaging Paulo's shoulders as the tub began to refill. He seemed to fall asleep momentarily with his head lolling back against the enamel rim.

"Have you read the paper yet?" she asked him finally.

"Do I look like I've had an occasion to read the paper, Vera?" he muttered with a sigh, unable to conceal his irritation. They had hardly arranged to meet like this; he had simply agreed to call when he got back—but here she was, when all he could think about was getting out of Manaus as quickly as possible.

"They found the body of some American."

"Fascinating . . ."

"A prostitute discovered his head bobbing in some inlet over at São Raimundo. The rest of him was found washed up in a boat yard in Aleixo. It was apparently a gruesome death."

"Must have been a mugging—after his dollars."

"No, it seems there was no mugging. The police have the idea it was a drug-war retaliation."

"Well, Manaus is part of the Bolivian connection. They ship it by the ton through here on its way to Miami. I suppose it makes sense."

"Only there's something a bit strange. Look at this: they have his picture on the front page."

Paulo finally opened his eyes again to have a look. It was a blurry photograph, probably from a passport—serious-looking, with no particular expression. His name was Arthur Gary.

"A rather honest-looking face for a drug trafficker."

"I know this man, Paulo."

"Don't tell me he was your supplier?"

"I never touch the stuff, Paulo. A little grass now and then, that's about my speed. I know the fellow because he was living back there in Valéria. I'd run across him lots of times whenever he came to Parintins. This is the Adventist pastor."

Paulo Veronezzi climbed out of the tub and began to dry himself.

"But it doesn't make any sense," he observed. "A Seventh Day Adventist involved in the drug trade?"

It was exactly what Vera herself could not understand: a preacher from one of the most conservative religions imaginable.

"I have the strangest feeling this all has to do with those UFOs," she said, finally abandoning her discretion.

Paulo exploded with laughter.

"Are you trying to tell me that the guy was murdered by extraterrestials? Attacked by little green men?"

"I'm not kidding, Paulo. Something very sinister is happening here, I can feel it."

"And this is what you came here to tell me?"

"That's right, it is—because you're the only real journalist around. You don't expect me to run to some newspaper reporter from Manaus, do you? You know as well as I do what their papers are like. . . ."

"Please, spare me—"

"Exactly! But somebody has to do something."

"Why me, Vera? Why do I have to do something?"

She could not answer. She kept staring at the photograph on the front page of the paper: barely recognizable, but him nonetheless. He had died in some horrible fashion, suffering unspeakable torments of a kind that some ordinary drug slaying could never explain. Yet Vera could not really describe what it was that rang sinister to her except that something did not add up: something peculiar which struck the finely tuned chords of her intuition. From the instant that she had read the paper, she could no longer think of anything else. She had recognized the victim immediately: it was the man who always came into Parintins to buy whatever he needed wearing the same sandals and ridiculous straw hat for protection against the sun. The Catholic priest from the community of Valéria had described him as an old-style fundamentalist, fanatically opposed to Ecumenicalism.

She had actually called Paulo's hotel several times on Sunday, but he had stayed out of town that entire day and only returned late this afternoon. She had already been hanging around his hotel from early that morning, feverishly awaiting his arrival. She had barely even touched her coffee, overcome with a feeling of nausea every time she turned back to the paper.

"I've heard the army is investigating the matter now."

Paulo took the paper and read the story. Its text was a shambles, ridiculously edited—a mixture of police blotter-ese and the syntax of a mental retard. Yet the confusion of data and incoherency of fact were not intentional. It was simply that whoever did the article had obviously never heard of logic.

"Christ, this text is crazy," he muttered incredulously. "And they have the nerve to call a rag like this *A Crítica*."

"There's a rumor going around that the fellow was really from the CIA."

"I wouldn't put it past the CIA to go chasing after flying saucers."

He walked over to the phone and called long distance.

At that hour the editorial room of the magazine would be a veritable morgue. *Isto É* had a variety of closings throughout the week, beginning on Tuesdays when the culture pages and the main spreads on the arts were decided. The editors of all the sections generally took Monday to review the previous week and plan strategies for the next issue. If he was lucky, he still might find his boss there making the rounds of the various editorial desks, a cold cigarette butt still on his lips, getting ready for the *via-crucis* of all the bars in Pinheiros, far from newspaper gossip and political rumor-mongering.

The phone rang once at the other end and was immediately picked up.

"I want to speak to Beto. This is Paulo . . ." Someone said something at the other end and Paulo laughed humorlessly: "Oh, fuck you! Get Beto to the phone, I'm calling from Manaus."

He waited a few seconds and then his boss got on the line.

"I've got it all sewn up, Beto," he confirmed, after hearing his boss out. The bastard hadn't even bothered to ask him why he was calling. He probably thought Paulo was already back in São Paulo, calling him from some dive.

"I'm still in Manaus . . . right, I ought to be leaving tomorrow, just after lunch. I'll be arriving around eight . . . Christ, what do you expect out here in the jungle . . . this is Amazonas, you remember? Listen, Beto, I want to know if you've heard anything about this American guy who wound up dead here? Nothing, right? . . . Of course you haven't. Word just appeared in the police reports of some rag that comes out here on Mondays . . . Pay attention, Beto, I'm telling you it's serious."

But the editor was clearly in no mood to listen to stories about some murdered American.

"What if I tell you the guy was passing himself off as a Protestant minister while up to his neck in CIA? . . . How do I know? Everyone knows out here. I just wanted to check if I can hang around a little longer," he concluded reluctantly. "I want to look into it, that's all. I can send the hydroelectric material on with the photographer."

He still listened awhile longer and then hung up. His expression was not the slightest bit encouraging. "Son of a bitch!"

"What did he say?" Vera had held her breath through practically the entire conversation. "Well, how did it go, Paulo?"

"He said I can stay, but on my own account. Says the magazine's on too tight a budget to pay my expenses."

"You can move in with me," Vera offered eagerly. "My place is huge, almost an apartment: it belongs to the ministry."

Paulo Veronezzi looked at her with rage: she really was determined to get him mixed up in this story.

The phone rang. It was his boss, calling him back. He wanted Paulo in São Paulo before the end of the week. That would give him only until Thursday, but Paulo was relieved. At least there would be a definite cap on his availability; he would not have to worry about an endless entanglement in the whole affair.

"That's good enough," he told him, "I couldn't put up with this place any longer than that."

Vera Martins could hardly contain her delight, and sat back in an easy chair to prop her legs up on the footboard of Paulo's bed.

"How great that you're going to stay."

She had very lovely legs deeply tanned by the sun.

"But you just keep in mind I have to be back in São Paulo by Thursday, come hell or high water." He did not take his eyes off that pair of legs slowly surfacing from beneath the hem of her white linen dress.

"Well, at least that's something," she said happily, aware of where his eyes were focused.

"Sure, but what about my expenses? How are we supposed to get to that Indian village or whatever it is?"

"You mean Parintins?"

"Right, how are we going to get there?"

"It's an hour and a half by plane. They have flights there every day, Paulo."

"But how are we going to pay for our tickets?"

"We won't. I'll get them from the ministry." She was lying, of course. She had already planned everything: she would pay for their tickets out of her own pocket and he would never even suspect. "We can leave first thing tomorrow, as soon as we get out to the airport."

Paulo stood scratching his head absentmindedly, while lighting up a cigarette.

"Do you have a typewriter over at your place?"

"I've a portable, a good one. I use it whenever I travel."

"Well, I'll need it. I have to wrap up my story and send it off with the photographer."

"Then let's go to my place, right now. You can bring your things there right away."

"This room's already paid for until tomorrow at noon."

"You prefer me to bring the typewriter here? I could be back in a half hour."

If he got started on the thing right away, he could wrap up the rest of that hydroelectrical nonsense in a good two hours and still have time to go out for a few drinks. And he began to think the company of Vera Martins might be quite pleasant after all.

"No, let's move into your place and be done with it," he concluded, emptying the drawers of the dresser into his suitcase.

Meanwhile, in Brasília

The NCPR—National Center for Paranormal Research—was particularly quiet that late afternoon. Only one member of the staff was on duty: the young Raul Pessoa, a student of medicine at the University of Brasília and the youngest son of the Center's founder. Seen from the outside, surrounded by green lawns and the stout trunks of stubby fig trees, the building might have been taken for the modest, cheery residence of some middle-class family from the Asa Sul. The Center had been housed there for the past five years, with the customary discretion of such organizations and the tacit compliance of its neighbors. These were generally middle-echelon civil servants, most of them without children, who spent the greater part of their time either at the office or away for the weekend.

The staff of the Center was not a very large one: five well-chosen, very dedicated individuals who were attracted to a field that continually afforded them new surprises. The house itself had three bedrooms. Raul was seated in the living room, which was used as the reception area, reading another science fiction novel, a favorite pastime of his. The NCPR maintained a meticulously catalogued archive, wherein were registered some of the most extraordinary cases ever recorded in the field of UFOs. The archive occupied one of the bedrooms, the other two serving as reading room and conference hall for the weekly gatherings of the Center's research staff. From time to time the place was also visited by journalists in need of a story; at such times, whoever was on duty was charged to receive the press cordially and provide whatever assistance might be required.

The other researchers also lived right there in Brasília. The most experienced among them was Major Nelson, an old compatriot of General Pessoa who had retired from the military and was now working for Petrobrás. The major had experienced two close encounters of the third kind and researched nearly a hundred sightings in central Brazil alone. Nelson also cultivated ties with the same alien who had established contact with General Pessoa: the emissary Quazgaa, crew member of an interplanetary patrol ship and master of a variety of miraculous gifts, who had cured one of the major's daughters of a terminal illness. The girl's name was Ariadne; she was twenty-five and also did research for the Center. At seventeen, however, after having wandered about the interior of the state of Minas Gerais with a gang of hippies and a knapsack, she had returned home stricken with Chagas disease. The illness spread rapidly and she was soon hospitalized, her condition grave, at the Military Hospital in Brasília. The doctors had already given up any hope, since her heart was by that time thoroughly deformed. Then, on a weekend in Goiás Velho, where he was investigating a sighting, Major Nelson was surprised by a UFO that stalled out the motor of his car, forcing him to pull up in front of a being who unexpectedly materialized in the middle of the highway. The being—tall, with long hair and dark complexion—did not seem to be using any special equipment to permit him to breathe in the terrestrial atmosphere. Wearing an outfit completely fitted to its body, the being introduced itself as Quazgaa, saying that it was aware of the tragedy afflicting the major. Nelson, deeply moved, confessed what had happened to his daughter. Quazgaa then promised to help, declaring that at five P.M. on the following day he would visit the hospital where Ariadne was being cared for. The major returned to Brasília behaving as if he had found the pot of gold at the end of the rainbow and confiding everything to General Pessoa. The next day, at the appointed hour, the two friends stood waiting in the room of a dying Ariadne, when the alien calmly entered wearing ordinary terrestrial clothes, as if he were no more than one of the doctors who looked in on the unfortunate patient now and then. Quazgaa then took a tiny incandescent sphere out of a pocket and somehow caused it to levitate above the bed of the young girl. Afterwards, he exited without so much as a word and vanished into the labyrinth of hospital corridors. The convalescence and eventual recovery by Ariadne is still commented upon by the medical staff at the Military Hospital and must be one of the rare recorded cases of a total cure of Chagas disease. Complete recovery took some fifteen days—a period during which Ariadne, undergoing every sort of cardiological examination imaginable, gave no evidence of ever having suffered a lesion. She herself, to this day, had no memory of her benefactor—the miracle took place in 1974—but had since witnessed several close encounters of the first kind and was at present employed at the Center's library. The two remaining researchers were on the young side as well: Jorge, a graduate of Annapolis in engineering, twenty-nine and cataloguer of the Center's archives; and Maurício, a lawyer, twenty-seven, an employee of Banco do Brasil and author of a manual on extraterrestrials describing seventy-eight specific types of visitors—a mini-best-seller among aficionados and already translated into Spanish.

Raul Pessoa, whose greatest pleasure came from taking his seventy horsepower motorcycle out to race down the Eixo Monumental, felt slightly troubled at the thought of his father's sudden return to the field. The old man was no longer of an age to be doing such things. The general was still a powerful man, of course, but he was getting on in years and ought to show some discretion. This trip to Manaus and the renewal of contacts with old friends in the intelligence community did not make his son any happier, either. Raul had yet to forget the years of humiliation spent at school, ostracized by his classmates simply because his father was in the military. If his fellow students had actually known what his father's position was inside the service, they would no doubt have crucified him. Some moments had been especially difficult to endure in silence, as when for example the coeds began refusing to go out with him in order to avoid being stigmatized by their classmates too. So it was with considerable relief that he had received the news of his father's transfer to the reserves and, eventually, of his decision to retire from the Ministry of Health in order to devote his time to research for the Center.

Raul's calm, introverted nature had helped to shield him to a degree from that whole unsavory period, and now he seemed to have found a true calling in his work for the NCPR. His degree in medicine would eventually provide him with a solid enough profession; in another year he would begin his internship at the Military Hospital, and beyond that he had no clear sense of the direction his career would take. Perhaps he would set up practice with the medical group of some private company and thus have more time to spare in order to move ahead with his research of the last two years, which concerned the proliferation of centers devoted to the occult throughout the Federal Capital.

In this regard Brasília was certainly an incredible city. Over a two-year period he had already discovered some four hundred sites where a variety of Afro-Brazilian rites were practiced—from Quimbanda to Candomblé, not to mention the diversity of cults of a more esoteric order, some of them extremely well organized with all the modern innovations of electronic religion. More fascinating still was the degree to which these cults cut across social strata: you could find every imaginable sort of member, from construction workers to ministers of state, minor technocrats to major generals—a complete microcosm of the entire social order existed in each and every center, whether spiritist tent or mystic temple. In a city which otherwise epitomized the most restricted sort of social interaction between the classes, it was not uncommon to discover abandoned dispatches scattered on Mondays or Fridays all over the Plano Piloto. Or to hear stories to make one's hair stand on end concerning political bigwigs indulging in Black Magic as a means of keeping the reins of power.

The idea for such an investigation had come to him during a visit to the Venusian Theosophic Church, headed by an intimate of his father, the famous clairvoyant Mother Tereza, politically one of the most powerful women in the nation during the darkest period of the military regime. While on this visit, he had come upon the director of the Federal Savings and Loan Association, there in the flesh, overcome by a mystical trance, sacrificing a black chicken with his bare teeth.

"All the upper crust attend my church," Mother Tereza had explained to Raul, witnessing his perplexity. "We have come to expect no less from them. They are, after all, simply men and women who have the fear of God in them and wish to perfect their Karma. Look at our Minister for Foreign Relations; isn't he conducting an enlightened foreign policy? What courage the man has, don't you think? He actually comes here to the church to seek the advice of our Guiding Hand."

Mother Tereza's "Guiding Hand" was an enlightened spirit, a scientist-pneuma who had already visited our solar system in previous ages. His name was Flávio, a somewhat ordinary name for so extraordinary an influence.

"Flávio has always condemned brutality," Mother Tereza continued. "He hopes to teach mankind a return to simplicity. A number of military heads, including some four-star generals, have been severely admonished by him regarding the practice of torture in the barracks. He has urged them to banish that lowly behavior which only serves to reduce the Karma of both the torturer and the tortured."

The subject of torture would surface again with reference to still another sect—less influential than that of Mother Tereza's but with broad representation among senators and federal deputies. It was the Tent of Transcendental Love, founded by an ex-homesteader who had migrated from Piauí, a man with a cavernous voice and a brow furrowed by wrinkles. He was called "Lord" Rogério—not a claim to nobility but merely the nickname he had picked up because of his miraculous powers.

According to Lord Rogério, then, there were negative entities from a parallel universe that had infiltrated the military by entering the bodies of a number of officers from the armed forces. They were a species of malefic beings who dedicated themselves to the annihilation of humanity out of envy for the human possibility of free choice.

They initially took possession of a general who was more or less General Costa e Silva's right-hand man during the term of his presidency, hence one of the most influential men in the regime. This possessed general—with the help of men from the Military Police of the state of São Paulo and a fakir with chiromantic powers—organized a kind of terrorist falange. The group practiced a variety of assaults and assassinations which were laid on the doorsteps of known Communists and subversives. They went as far as to dynamite an auto parked in front of the Department of Political and Social Order—the DOPS. Then one day the DOPS managed to apprehend the two lieutenants involved, along with their fakir. The officers confessed everything immediately, no problem; but the fakir wouldn't open his mouth. He suffered for his silence, but was convinced he was about to be saved by flying saucers. Well, they hung him upside down on the "parrot's perch" and tortured him with electric shocks, but he felt nothing because he had entered into a trance. Annoyed by his indifference, the torturers lit a fire under the fakir's trussed body hanging in its trance on the "parrot's perch." The fellow was nearly roasted alive. Yet, mysteriously, he disappeared from the cell in which he was imprisoned, there in the DOPS, and was never seen again. Some prisoners claimed that they had heard strange noises on the night of his disappearance. The warder, however, hadn't noticed anything unusual. Only a guard who happened to be on duty on the roof of the building at the time still swears that he witnessed the fakir's departure through sheer levitation, surmounting walls and rooftop alike, finally to be swallowed up in a flying saucer hovering above the building in space. The guard insists that he even drew his revolver, but can't explain what subsequently transpired: he was found asleep, the next morning, by the warden and given a month in the same cell.

These cases and others no less extraordinary were all meticulously catalogued in the NCPR's archives. Raul had even pondered writing a book on the subject, a book that would finally reveal to the public one of the more secret aspects of real political power in the nation's capital. Millions of cruzeiros annually were channeled directly or indirectly to this end: through donations, collections and legislative appropriations—the work of the faithful, whether poverty-stricken followers or influential leaders.

The telephone rang and Raul Pessoa put down the book he had barely glanced through. At first he did not even recognize the voice, the connection was so bad. Soon enough, however, his face lost a bit of its worried expression to the nervous intensity now sparkling in his eyes.

"Dad, is that you?" He was gripping the receiver with such force that his fingers began to turn white. "I can hardly believe it's you calling from way out there in the middle of the jungle."

The connection worsened, and his father's voice was reduced to an electronic gargle devoid of signification.

"I can't hear what you're saying," he insisted, knowing his father must be cursing the phone by now. The old man detested any sort of apparatus, even if he *had* entered into contact with some of the most unbelievable kinds.

On the other end of the line, General Pessoa was shouting into the receiver, cupping his hand to the mouthpiece in order to amplify his voice. An electrical crackle suddenly returned the line to normal.

"Son, can you hear me now?"

"Much better, Dad. How are things? Taking good care of yourself?"

"I'm just fine, my boy, but listen: Go find Nelson, today, right away, and tell him our pal Mike Gardner is dead."

"Don't I know that name?"

"It's the fellow I met in Palo Alto, remember?"

"Wasn't he from the CIA, Dad?"

"I'm still not sure, son. In any case, he was down here on his own initiative when something went haywire. I don't really know, of course. Maybe he was following orders from above. Whatever the case, it's a pity he didn't look us up first."

Raul switched on the tape recorder. He preferred to simply play it later for the major than to try to explain his father's message secondhand. He did not have the general's memory for things.

"Dad, we've all been worried about you out there by yourself."

"I'm not by myself. I've got plenty of friends here helping me out, wherever they can be of assistance. Don't worry—one more day and I wrap it up here and head for home."

Raul realized only too clearly that his father was attempting to reassure him—those so-called friends he had in the intelligence community merely humored him but then laughed at him behind his back as some kind of nut.

"I'm going to need Nelson's help. Let me explain, son: there's a real possibility that Mike Gardner was killed by the acolytes of Sylyon. The sightings here follow the typical pattern of Sylyon's negativism. He treats us all like guinea pigs with no wills of our own; that much we already know. The lights here have been dubbed *Chupa-chupa* by the locals: they are clearly aggressive lights, vampire lights. They attack human beings, suck out their blood, spreading terror. Nothing in the way of a peaceful mission, you can be sure. And the whole thing has been masterfully planned, infiltrating the very halls of government. People very high up and very ambitious, who think themselves above the law or the nation's will. What's worse, they imagine themselves superior in everything."

"What do you want Nelson to do, Pop?"

"Hold on a minute, son, I have to supply him with the necessary coordinates."

"Sorry, old man."

"What Nelson must do is get out the Jeep and drive to a point of contact with Quazgaa. We have to have some sort of contact or we're goners."

"When will you get back?"

"I think I've got a lead that will take me to the acolytes. They must be stopped as swiftly as possible. I'll have to lend a hand, here, to my friends until they nail some of them. But it shouldn't take long—another day or so and I'll wrap the whole thing up."

"Anything else?"

"Nelson will know the rest. You just give him whatever help he needs, will you, son?"

"If he likes, I can drive the Jeep for him . . . what do you think?"

"It may take a bit of time; that won't affect your schoolwork, will it?"

"No problem—I can still miss a few more classes, I'm on top of my work."

"Good enough, I'll hang up now. Be careful, son."

"You too, Dad."

The line went dead and Raul noticed it was already dark outside. He took a last look around the house, checking to see that doors and windows were locked securely. With the rash of burglaries in the neighborhood, it was no time to make things easier for them—the NCPR was hardly rich, but everything there would be sorely missed if carried off by some misguided thief. He turned out the light in the reception room and locked the door behind him, descending the steps to his motorcycle and stowing his books and leather case in the rear saddlebags. The traffic was mild, with the majority of neighbors already ensconced at home before a dinner plate or a TV set. He guessed he would find Nelson at the same old bar over in W3, where he generally sat downing drinks until about nine o'clock before going home to his widower's apartment.

As he was about to start up the engine, he noticed a woman hurriedly approaching him. The shadow of the trees prevented him from being able to make out her face, but he hardly gave the matter much thought. She was obviously a beautiful woman wearing very tight jeans and a white cotton shirt with something printed across the chest.

Each effort to start the motor curiously ended in failure. Finally, the engine died completely. He was jumping futilely down on the starter pedal for the seventh or eighth time when the woman came up to him and placed her hand gently on his shoulder.

He looked up at her, fascinated.

"I'm Quazgaa," the woman told him in sibilant tones.

When Raul finally came back to his senses, he was racing at high speed along the Eixo Monumental and feeling the delicious pressure of the woman's arms around his waist. The wind whipped against his face and Raul Pessoa felt indescribable pleasure.

At About the Same Time, Some Thirty Kilometers from Brasília

Pavel Aksentyevich had wakened to a room floored in black marble with walls covered in moss-green silk. The easy chairs and padded carpets were restfully seductive in that tranquil ambiance of soft lighting and bland temperature. What first attracted Pavel's curiosity, however, was the console of electronic buttons in one of the four corners of the room, with its twenty-two-inch TV monitor beneath a rack of four fire extinguishers of the type used in automobiles. He had never seen anything similar save perhaps when browsing through North American magazines. Yet, from an almost exaggerated sense of caution, he had refrained from touching the console. They had still not served him anything to eat and he was thirsty and hungry. Since the room had no clock and his captors had removed his wristwatch, he could only guess the time by the measure of complaints of his enfeebled organism—depleted by anxiety and exhausted from its high consumption of histamines.

Fed up with pacing back and forth to no purpose, Pavel had settled down upon one of the sofas and attempted to sleep again. But sleep would not come and the uncomfortable vigil finally left him mentally drained, as if he had pushed himself over the edge into another reality.

He woke up, suddenly frightened, his legs asleep and his stomach craving. Staring at him with an expression of tender regard was a tall, skinny, elderly man.

Pavel Aksentyevich trembled as if he were already on another planet.

"Calm yourself, brother," said the old man, placing a hand on the Russian's icy forehead. "I'm not going to do you any harm."

"Could you talk a bit more slowly, please. I'm not very accustomed to Portuguese."

"Of course, my brother. Try to calm down," the other answered, speaking in measured tones, almost didactically.

The Russian leaned back on the sofa, feeling the blood flowing through his veins with an uncomfortable tingling. His heart was still pounding, and his thirst had left his lips dry and chapped.

"I need water," Pavel pleaded.

The old man walked over to the console and pushed a button.

"Bring him his meal," he ordered. "I apologize, brother Pavel, I did not intend to cause you such discomfort."

"How do you know my name?" the Russian muttered confusedly.

The other gave no answer. Then someone knocked on the door and the other allowed him to enter with a service cart from which Pavel already detected the appetizing odors of food.

The cart was wheeled over to the sofa and the Russian sat up. The waiter began to serve him deftly while Pavel flung himself at the meal. He drank gluttonously under the watchful eye of the old man who remained standing. Only when the meal had entirely vanished from its platters did Pavel Aksentyevich pay any attention to the other's facial expression. The old fellow seemed to suffer a continuous onslaught of pains in his chest, making his lips contract tightly and lending an ashen paleness to his flesh.

"Are you ill?" the Russian asked out of simple curiosity.

"I'm not myself," the old man replied vaguely.

Pavel stood up and fixed his full attention upon the other: he fell into a kind of deep sleep, eyes closed and both hands pressing against his thighs. A plate left its place on the cart and smoothly levitated across the room, finally landing on the floor without a sound.

"Extraordinary," murmured the old man.

"Silence!" Pavel's entire body was trembling. "You're a very sick man," he concluded. "I can see by your aura that your vital radiance is nearly extinguished. There is some other force that still sustains you, though I've yet to determine what it is."

"Enough!" the old man shouted, taking refuge near the rack of fire extinguishers.

The Russian immediately returned to his normal self.

"There's no point in trying to impress me with circus tricks," the other warned.

The old man raised his left hand and pointed a finger at the Russian's shoulder. At once that portion of his body was racked with needlelike pain. Pavel bent over but was instantly thrown back by a second force. He fell to the marble floor, squirming in agony.

"Please!" he begged hoarsely.

The other lowered his hand and the pain ceased.

"I'll have no more games, brother Pavel."

A silver tray flew off the cart and slammed into the old man's chest, knocking him to the floor.

"Now we're on the same level, sir," the Russian retorted.

The other remained on his back as if he had fainted. Pavel got to his feet while beginning to smell a sweetish odor of burning flesh. From the old man, still panting inertly on the floor, there slowly issued a wisp of yellowish smoke.

"And it will do you no good to try and do me further harm," the Russian warned him cautiously, "I'm well protected now."

He proceeded to help the old man over to the sofa where he had him sit down.

"I'm Brigadier General Bernardo Fischer," the old man said to introduce himself. "Hurry, the fire extinguisher . . ."

Pavel Aksentyevich extended his hand and shook the more delicate one of his captor without understanding directly what the old man was asking for.

"I am, as apparently you know, Pavel Aksentyevich, director of public relations for the Moscow Circus."

The brigadier general let out a scream and wrenched his hand away. He flung himself toward the rack and took down a fire extinguisher, then sprayed his own legs which were already enveloped in a dense smoke.

"Why am I here, General?"

"Because you wished to be here, brother."

A good answer, Pavel thought, but one which did not serve to alleviate any of his doubts.

"Actually, I ought to be seeing city officials concerning the forthcoming trip by the Moscow Circus to your capital. That's my job, you know, to make necessary arrangements prior to the Circus's arrival."

"I'm not particularly fond of circuses," the old man remarked, still holding the empty extinguisher.

"Neither am I," the Russian confessed, staring at the other's trousers mired in chemical foam.

"Circuses appeal to the most primitive instincts in man," the brigadier general went on to elaborate. "And what is worse, they offer catharsis to those very instincts. In the ring of a circus, human effort is put on the same pathetic level as that of a trained beast. Pitiful. The dexterity of a potentially fatal leap, the millimeter's feat of walking on a tightrope wire—all is reduced to the antics of a pachyderm dancing the rumba or a seal tooting a trumpet."

"You haven't brought me here to philosophize about circuses—"

"In the same way that you have hardly come here to facilitate the performance of one . . ."

The Russian was growing impatient.

"Don't be in such a hurry," the brigadier warned. "No conversation is entirely worthless."

"I would prefer to discuss more concrete matters. For example: the real motive for my being kidnapped."

"Are you a Communist?"

"What?"

"You heard me, brother Pavel."

"No, as a matter of fact I don't belong to the Party."

"What do you think of Communism?"

"Nothing special."

"Then why do you work for KGB if you're not a Communist?"

"I'm a patriot, sir."

"Patriot! Rather empty little word, don't you think?"

The Russian stood up and began pacing about.

"Do sit down, here," the brigadier general ordered, pointing to a place beside him on the sofa.

The Russian obeyed since there was hardly an alternative—he had already exhausted all the possible steps to be spanned in the room.

"Within a few more days, all atomic weapons will have been eliminated from this world."

"How will that be possible? Nowadays you military men are equipped to destroy the world several times over. It's you and your kind who have changed the entire globe into a circus, if you want to know my opinion."

"I'm going to tell you exactly how it happened that I was reborn to the true science," the brigadier continued calmly, though a throb of pain in his chest periodically blanched his face of its color. "This was years ago when I was still brimming with health, a young officer who naively believed in the political process. One day there was a sailors' mutiny. The rebels took over the headquarters of the Automobile Club of Brazil, in Rio, and demanded a series of absurdities that went counter to the very discipline and hierarchy that gives definition to the armed forces. I was ordered to go there and negotiate with them. From my point of view, they should have stormed the place and thrown the mutineers into prison. The penalty for mutiny is death—at least in all the great navies of the world. The damn thing was, the President of the Republic only wished to ingratiate himself with certain sectors and at the same time to demoralize our class. As an officer of the Air Force, I simply donned my uniform and complied with the President's orders. The mutineers refused to even listen to what I had to say. I was forced to run through an improvised gauntlet and to suffer the humiliation of having my bottom felt by more than two hundred species of human trash. I walked out of that place with pride completely shattered. I went home. I lived in a house in Tijuca with my mother at the time. It was an old mansion that belonged to my family, with a garden and lawn. My mother was at the door waiting for me. I walked into the yard and went toward her but never managed to reach her. I vanished, right before the eyes of my own mother! I evaporated into thin air and was expelled from our universe to another . . . There was no trace of me for two years, until I reappeared without explanation, in 1968, to discover I was in charge of PARA-SAR, a specially trained commando unit of the Paratroop Service for Assault and Rescue Operations in the Brazilian Air Force. The spot where I had vanished had been permanently stained—the soil had acquired a particularly dark coloration, as if it had suffered the impact of tremendously high temperatures—and my mother had distinctly heard my voice pleading for help."

"You were expelled to another dimension?" Pavel asked with growing interest.

"I have tapes of the deposition I made under regressive hypnosis. When we have a moment I'll play them for you."

"I'd very much like to hear them."

"My only regret is not to have seen my mother alive again. The poor soul passed on just a few months after the incident."

"I'm terribly sorry."

"We have a congenital illness in our family: my ancestors habitually have expired by spontaneous combustion. Mother was lost while having a walk in the garden. Her roasted bones were found intact, inside her clothes, by our gardener. The nearby plants were not even singed by her. An inquest was held, and even to this day some of the organs of security insist that she must have suffered a terrorist assault."

The brigadier got up from the sofa and went over to the electric console. The waiter soon returned and wheeled away the serving cart.

"And you, brother Pavel," the other turned to say: "What *are* you doing in Brasília?"

"I guarantee you one thing: I have no intention of passing on to any other dimension—I feel quite at home in the present one."

"But I know what brings my brother here," Fischer went on, further activating the electronic controls. The video came on and commenced to display the sequence of images recorded on the videocassette recovered from the body of the American agent.

"You were after this, weren't you?" the brigadier insisted.

Pavel was marveling at the show of lights played out against the black backdrop of the Amazonian firmament.

"We still don't know if it's authentic," the other cautioned, "but there's no real question that the time is coming."

The video went out, but the Russian continued to focus his attention on the milky blank screen. Those images had seemed perfect, much superior to anything found in the archives of the Institute for Parapsychology, back in Moscow.

"Sylyon has need of you, Pavel, my brother."

"Sylyon?"

"The Starry-One. He needs someone with telekinetic powers such as you yourself possess, to carry forward his plans for the transformation of the world. We have yet to find an initiate with such powers. You have been led to us, brother, by the hands of Sylyon."

Pavel Aksentyevich reflected on his two kidnappers and guessed that Sylyon's hands were more like two iron fists.

Meanwhile, Somewhere Along the Eixo Monumental

The motorcycle sped along the macadamized pavement at more than 120 kilometers per hour. The wind was buffeting Raul Pessoa's hair as he relished the motor pulsing between his legs and Quazgaa's fingers caressing his body. The hands were truly knowledgeable and possessed an extraordinary sense of touch.

She rested her head on his shoulder while pressing her body closer and closer to Raul's back. Her body transmitted a heat of lassitude that commingled with the sheer joy of speed.

This was surely not the normal pattern of behavior when it came to extraterrestrials.

The motorcycle raced past the apartment buildings around Itamarati, along the Asa Norte, and headed toward the lake highway. The night was still moonlit, and the sky clear, almost cloudless, as was typical of the skies of Brasília.

She began to unbutton his shirt and massage the muscles of his chest. Raul Pessoa felt an unending thrill of contentment. His trembling increased as Quazgaa lowered one of her hands and started delicately stroking his fly. The sensation was delicious, but the boy was beginning to lose control of the bike. He kept slowing down, urging her to continue. But the motorcycle did not respond to his lowering the throttle, and rather continued at the same vertiginous speed until gradually he realized that the machine was out of his control. His body froze and an irrational fear overtook him. Quazgaa realized as much and ceased to caress him, sliding back a bit from the contact that, until then, she had maintained with Raul's body.

They continued at high speed along the highway, north of the lake. The road was empty, and suddenly Raul no longer felt the presence of the woman on the rear seat. He wanted to glance back, but his muscles would not obey him. He began to grow tired, a somnolence tingling throughout his whole body; and the motorcycle flew like a meteor across the asphalt. If he did not immediately bring the bike under control, he was certain to suffer a devastating, perhaps fatal accident.

It was then that he noticed the woman was levitating just above his head. She had circled in the air, and floated just in front, staring back at him. Suddenly the motor died and through sheer inertia rolled on along the highway—out of control and headed for a tree trunk twisted by the drought. The impact tossed Raul into a clump of high grass.

Stunned, he still managed to get to his feet and begin walking around in circles searching for the woman. But he did not succeed in finding her: she had vanished without a trace. He went over to examine the bike. The impact had bent the front wheel and partially crushed the gas tank. Clearly he would be left without any means of transportation for quite some time, since he would only have enough money to pay for repairs at the end of the month. What he had to do now was get out of his present predicament, pull the motorbike along the road to some busier locale and attempt to hitch a ride.

Raul slowly lifted the bike from the ground and tried to push it, but the task proved too difficult—he did not have the strength to drag his beloved machine for more than half a meter. He sat back on the ground and felt a temptation to burst into tears. Gradually his body returned to its normal rhythm and he began to have a look around, to familiarize himself with his surroundings. He would have to sleep the night there and search for help in the morning. If her intention had been to delay him, the woman had succeeded—totally, he thought with irritation.

It was then that he heard a strange noise and his senses grew alert. The sound came from the highway, and Raul took out a heavy lug wrench from the back of his bike, for protection. A stranger appeared, dressed in a bedraggled cape and a beret, bearing a knapsack over his shoulder. He paused to size up Raul with his lug wrench poised to defend himself.

"I'm only a tramp," the man reassured him. "Don't be afraid. I saw the whole thing and thought you might be seriously injured."

"I'm okay, but I think the motorcycle's had it."

"You're very fond of it, aren't you?"

"It cost a lot, man, I'll tell you. And I won't be able to come up with the money to take it into the shop very soon."

"Is it that badly wrecked?"

The tramp let his shoulders slump in a sign of consternated solidarity, shaking his head wearily.

"You should be more careful of the hitchhikers you pick up, my boy."

Raul eyed the man with growing apprehension, gripping the lug wrench still tighter in his hand.

"Who are you?"

The man turned his back on Raul Pessoa and headed back for the highway. Before disappearing into the darkness he turned back for a minute to look at the boy once more.

"Just a tramp, my son, that's all."

And he turned back to the highway, quickening his pace.

Raul felt calmer now and went to return the wrench to the toolbox. To his astonishment, the bike was standing again, free of any damage and shining as if it had just come out of the factory. He examined the machine palpably, to make sure that he was not totally delirious. His cycle did not even show signs of having been scratched, let alone bashed in—perfect and beautiful, all seventy horsepower.

He mounted it without a second thought and started up, heading in the same direction taken by the man who called himself a tramp. He must have been Quazgaa; and the woman who tried to kill him? Some enemy being. He took off like a shot along the highway but found no trace of the tramp. As his fears began to overtake him again, Raul Pessoa headed for home.

TUESDAY, AUGUST 23

The small Bandeirantes plane had bumped along for nearly the entire flight but was finally landing at the airport in Parintins. The airport, in fact, was nothing more than a short, wide asphalt strip in a small clearing cut out of jungle and almost completely surrounded by miserable-looking shacks. As they touched down on the runway, Paulo had watched a frightened calf scramble out of the way and all sorts of domestic animals begin to scatter from the asphalt patch full of water puddles and barnyard slops. The Bandeirantes turboprop bounced once, on impact, and then rolled smoothly to a halt with a monumental racket from the reversal of the engines. The cloud accumulation and poor visibility had prevented them from having a better view of vast waters and threading lands from the air. The plane had been loaded with civil servants and small businessmen, all silent and exhausted because the flight had proved too much for them.

They set out on foot: Paulo following Vera, who knew the city. They installed themselves in a small, rather dingy hotel where she had spent most of her six months of torture. The hotel was called the *Tupinambarana* and run entirely by women. The girl at the desk must have been fifteen at most, but she was wearing a simple halter and Bermudas so tight that she seemed to have grown right into them. In reality, it seemed to be the official uniform of the complete hotel staff, who received Vera with a barely concealed indifference and replied to her questions in monosyllables. Not all of them were attractive, but the youngest guarded traces of that olive-complexioned, oriental beauty of their still recent Indian ancestors—something Paulo Veronezzi failed to appreciate and merely dismissed as so much Amazonian exoticism.

They booked the same room together—the only one in the house with air conditioning.

"I put up with the worst solitude imaginable here, Paulo."

"You might have at least sworn never to set foot here again."

"I'm not very sensible, as you've probably noticed, hmm?"

He chided her good-humoredly and kicked off his shoes. The room was completely shut; only one small window—of the type mounted on hinges to swing up and hook to the ceiling—permitted the gusts of heat to enter. The walls were painted immaculately white; the entire hotel smelled of cleanliness and cheap wax.

"Did you say anything to the hotel staff?"

Vera had already undressed, and lay stretched out on the bed, her body covered with a printed sheet stiff with starch.

"They're not very communicative," Vera replied with some bitterness.

"You mean to tell me that the legendary Amazon women are not given to the feminine art of gossip?"

"Very funny. . . ."

If people from the Amazon interior were traditionally supposed to be closemouthed and peculiar, then these women at the Hotel Tupinambarana were certainly paradigmatic of the region. Contrary to men's deep-seated belief in women's inability to keep their mouths shut, the female staff here were exemplary in their discretion and reserve. Were it not for the skimpy outfits, perfect for the heat, Vera would never have noticed the women at all, and had certainly never caught them gossiping or rumoring—an astonishing accomplishment for anyone who lived, worked or ran a hotel in the capital of intrigue of the lower Amazon known as Parintins.

Vera swung out of bed and threw herself into Paulo's arms. She kissed him lingeringly and realized she was falling for him—not in any deep way, but with the enchanting sensation of pleasure at last, after so many sad and empty months. Astonished, Paulo nearly lost his balance but responded in kind to her impassioned kisses. The two began to laugh together, aroused and not a little tired from their trip.

"What made you decide to complicate my life?"

Vera could see that he was referring to their relationship as if it were already an accomplished fact—a typically masculine mania, the outgrowth of obvious male insecurity.

"Don't worry," she chided. "A few days back in the big city will erase all this."

He failed to understand and let her get on with fondling his chest matted with hair. The silence of that hotel room was impassive. Its thin walls and the hollow, laminated door seemed sufficient to isolate them from the world. It was the city itself, however, that was silent. At noon, not a soul ventured forth in the scorching streets; everybody withdrew to the shadow of home and awaited, nearly breathless, the onset of evening when the sun would finally lose some of its power. The air conditioner, meanwhile, hummed in its niche while struggling to neutralize the moist wafts of heat drifting in through the cracks in the single window frame.

Vera was lying upon him, her heart pounding with excitement. His fingers were running lightly over her body and she felt a pleasurable frailty, a delightful slackness. Yet she also felt a slight apprehension—a fear, latent but undefined—that kept her from wholly enjoying his caresses. It was as if all of her experience were still subject to that nameless fear she had carried within her, mixed with curiosity. At first, when it had just come to her, the fear itself had thrown her into the journalist's arms. Now this same emotion had begun to subjugate even her flesh, supplanting the pleasurable sensation of his hands upon her body. She slid off him and onto the mattress, and so he turned on his side and cupped his hands over her breasts, squeezing them gently as if testing their consistency, caressing them in slow alternating rhythms. She shivered when, with the tips of his fingers, he probed her sensitive nipples. How they swelled and stood erect beneath the firm pressure of fingertips; surging proudly, he thought, from their areolae. She could feel them throbbing between his thumb and forefingers, could feel the flesh of her entire body slowly igniting. She closed her eyes convulsively and attempted to expel the fear, but met resistance and came to realize how deeply it was embedded within her, an implacable invader, firmly entrenched. . . .

She disentangled herself from him, lunging out of bed, and began to pace around the room without knowing where to set her hands. Paulo was watching her with concern; he had also sensed the fear present in the throbbing of her diaphragm and the uneven respiration as she prowled the room.

"Don't be this way," he pleaded.

But Vera was already distant and lost, defeated by the ominous sensation. That fear was like a viscous humidity seeping into her rational mind.

They surrendered to the fear and slept deeply until five in the afternoon. Paulo was the first to awaken, in a bad humor for having nearly lost the entire day without having begun to work. Vera, still exhausted, felt no desire to get out of bed. She was practically carried by him into the bath and came to her senses screaming under the icy water of the shower. They dressed on the run, and before she knew it she found herself outside with her hair dripping and her shoes untied.

The head of the Rural Workers Union was out of town, a bit of rotten luck. They did find the mayor, however, seated at home in a rocking chair and staring out at the children riding back and forth in front of his spacious veranda and pedaling like babes in toyland. He received them with a rather cool affability, and for several moments no one spoke. The clamor of the children and the trafficking of bicycles animated the unpaved street of hard clay flanked by sewer drains flowing placidly in the sun.

"So you traveled all this distance, miss, over such nonsense?" The prefect smiled with an expression of fatigued irony. "Surely Parintins has far better attractions than that."

"It's terribly important, Your Honor."

The old mayor peered at some vague point in the street, as if it were painful to endure such conversation.

"You have a very vivid imagination, miss."

"But I was right there on the docks, Your Honor. We talked, don't you remember. How can you say I have a strong imagination?"

"Miss, I've already explained to both of you that this is the first time I've heard anything about this."

"I just can't believe this! The entire community of Valéria was right there on the—"

"It couldn't have been here in Parintins. You're probably mixing us up with some other town. And that's only natural when one travels about here for the first time."

"You have to be kidding. . . ."

Obviously constrained from the outset, sitting on the edge of his chair by now, Paulo Veronezzi was becoming more and more irritated each minute. Vera's experiences in Parintins must have added up to total boredom, he thought. And the screwy dame probably spent her whole time smoking grass and tripping on idleness, imagining everything! As he watched the mayor, his own embarrassment grew nearly insupportable. The man was obviously very sure of himself, responding to her questions with cutting irony. And the mayor was only reflecting the attitude of most inhabitants of the city with respect to some hallucinated agronomist who had just spent six months preaching new agricultural techniques to be applied to the savannah from the other end of a marihuana joint. The only one not to have perceived the truth immediately was himself, the idiot!

"Look here, miss," the prefect insisted, obviously fed up with their presence, "no person and certainly no entire community fled their homes to this town in fear of this weird business you're talking about."

Vera Martins felt like screaming, or like burying her head in a hole.

"But I was *there* in the *harbor*, I *saw!*"

"People see a lot of things, miss."

"She can't be just lying," Paulo interjected, hoping the mayor was indulging in some sort of joke which escaped him.

The prefect looked straight into Paulo's eyes.

"I did not say that she was lying. What I'm saying, my dear fellow,"—the mode of address struck Paulo like a slap—"is that such events did not take place here in Parintins. It must have been in some other municipality."

"I'm simply not crazy," Vera remarked in a different tone.

Paulo turned from the mayor to observe her: she could only be just that. The mayor, in the meantime, remained perfectly calm, behaving paternally. No one could possibly dissimulate that perfectly, something Paulo judged to be too sophisticated for anyone like the prefect. He alone had allowed himself to be taken in by a whacked-out drughead with visions of flying saucers.

"But it didn't happen more than a week ago," Vera insisted, her voice breaking into sobs. "I'm not imagining things."

The mayor stood up from his chair; it was a sign for the intruders to kindly leave him in peace to watch the children playing in the street as he did every other day.

"I'm truly sorry, Your Honor," Paulo apologized in embarrassment, getting up as well.

Vera grew more and more agitated. She began wringing her hands and looking from one to the other in a fury.

"You're treating me like an idiot!" she shouted.

The children in front of the house stopped playing and stared at her.

"Take it easy, Vera." Paulo's attempt to moderate her behavior only served to increase her rage.

"You're not the only person living in this city. I'm going to come up with the truth about this even if I have to spend the rest of my life here to do it."

The mayor eyed her with condescension.

"There's no need to go on this way, miss. You are free to talk to whomever you wish; do as you like, in fact." He turned to the journalist, continuing to appeal to him for support. "I'm very sorry, Mr. Veronezzi, but I've never heard anything about this business of *Chupa-chupas*, at least around here. I've heard something of that sort took place out in Pará somewhere."

"Son of a bitch!" Vera cried, rushing off from the veranda and knocking a chair over in the process.

The mayor blushed and shook his head disapprovingly. Paulo, hardly anticipating such an outcome, stood there paralyzed. He could not make up his mind whether to stay there and apologize to the mayor or race off after Vera who was furiously leaping over puddles on her way to the harbor.

He offered a simple gesture of dismay to the mayor by way of explanation and departed on the run, catching up to Vera by the end of the street.

"You don't believe me, either," she challenged.

His irritation had reached the point of explosion.

"Enough of shooting off your goddamn mouth!"

Vera turned to him speechless.

"Why should anybody want to take the raving drug fantasies of a fly-by-night agronomist seriously?" he burst out uncontrollably.

"You're just another stupid son of a bitch—"

"I must be," he retorted. "Only a stupid son of a bitch would bother to take you seriously."

"Then go back to Manaus! What are you waiting for?"

"That's exactly what I'm going to do. You stay here and hunt for your flying saucers."

"And you go fuck yourself, you rotten bastard."

He stood motionless, listening to her spewing out an assortment of scurrilous insults.

Vera headed off along the edge of the bayou. The journalist followed closely behind. He had suddenly remembered the murdered American agent found back in Manaus. He should have brought up that particular subject to the mayor as soon as he had started denying the story about flying saucers. The death of the Adventist pastor was something concrete—the press in Manaus had already published the whole gruesome story—and the prefect would have to have offered some explanation. If Vera hadn't been making such an ass of herself, he might not have let the matter slip his mind so easily.

A breeze was coming off the water that sparkled incandescently from a dying sun now behind the perfectly lilac clouds. The journalist had no idea what he should do, and began to feel troubled by Vera, all alone, her pride wounded, intimidated by fear. And what was worse, she probably felt betrayed by him as well.

"Shall we go back to the hotel, Vera?" he suggested.

She accepted without another word, and once back at the room cried on in silence, her face ravaged by a sense of extreme futility. The egocentric manner in which women use tears certainly had the power to irritate men, but for Paulo Veronezzi the situation was becoming so bizarre, he allowed himself to sit on the edge of the bed while watching Vera sob.

Little by little she regained control, or perhaps she was simply overwhelmed by exhaustion. But she still refused to give in: bravado was one of Vera's strongest virtues.

"There *is* someone who can help us," she said finally.

Paulo actually shivered at the possibility—going after yet another witness who would turn out to know nothing as well. For Paulo, the Parintins where Vera had supposedly spent six months was evidently not this one suffocated by heat. She must have invented another which could not be found on any map—it was too fantastic.

"I have a friend," she continued, sniffling, her eyes bloodshot. "Well, not exactly a friend, just a guy I know. He works for the local radio station. You know him—he was the one who I had tape that boy's deposition. He can certainly give us a hand."

Paulo nodded simply because he did not wish to further contradict her. And the idea wasn't so bad. Whoever had taped that deposition could hardly deny what he had done, unless he was a crackpot or a complete scoundrel. And if that should turn out to happen, then something very ominous really was going on around here.

"Just tell me where I can find him," Paulo said, trying to be more sympathetic.

"I'm going with you."

"No, let me bring him back to the hotel. You stay here where you are and rest a bit, you don't have to worry."

Vera did not offer any resistance and gave him directions on how to get to the radio station. Paulo had her write down the fellow's home address as well, then set out from the hotel room, relieved at having something to do. He could no longer deal with that woman's whimpering.

"Do you believe in me again?" she pleaded as he was leaving, in a way that made him suspect that her sanity depended upon the answer he was about to give.

With no great finesse—because he had never managed to conceal what he was actually thinking—he stood staring at her from the doorway.

"I guess so. . . ."

Yet, his reply seemed sufficient.

"Don't take too long," she pleaded. "I'm scared."

"There's no reason to be afraid. Tomorrow we'll be on our way back to Manaus and you can come on to São Paulo with me."

"I don't want to go to São Paulo," she warned with a hint of rancor. "I simply want to find out what the hell's going on in this city. People can't just forget that much from one day to the next."

"Your radio friend will probably give us the answer."

Vera Martins watched Paulo shut the door without a sound, and knew that there was not a drop of truth in what he had just said. How could she expect understanding, she reflected, if her own witnesses refused to cooperate. She would never have suspected the old mayor of being such a fake: capable of outright lying, of denial with such convincing authority that he had caused even her to doubt her own certainty. And when you reach the point of doubting your own certainties, she warned herself, it's because you're so lost that the borders of reality start to grow fluid and dangerously imprecise. She could not permit him to defeat her.

Vera stayed as she was, lying on her back in bed, turning every minute or so to look at the clock. Finally, overcome by sheer nervous exhaustion, she fell asleep. The night wore on, and it was nearly eleven when she awoke. She realized immediately that Paulo had still not returned with her radio friend. Their luggage was in the same spot, and Paulo's pair of socks were hung exactly where he had left them on the back of the chair.

Her head ached and she could barely sit up in bed. Her whole body, especially the muscles of her neck, pained her; but all she craved at that moment was to get up and escape the room, run out to the street and find Paulo and her friend from the station. Perhaps the two had already gotten together and were busy rapping somewhere together, stuffing their faces full of food. Jorge, her disc jockey, loved to drink at one particular dive, out a bit from the center of town, a stinking hovel where they managed to serve a divine fried fish and a cachaça made in Pará, strong and gooey. The dirty bastards had obviously forgotten her completely.

She got up half-stumbling, splashed her face with water and left the room. Her anxiety was making her temples pound, and her eyes ached as if they had been punched. There was no one at the reception desk, only one of the girls dozing off on a couch before the phantasmagoric glow of an untuned television screen. Leaning against the wall of the lounge was the bicycle that the girl had obviously used to pedal to work.

"Can I borrow this bike for a bit?"

The semi-nude girl lifted her gaze from the television set and consented with a perfectly indifferent nod, until suddenly she observed Vera Martins with apparent alarm.

"Are you all right, miss?" the girl inquired.

Vera saw herself reflected in the mirror hung behind the reception desk. Her hair was wet and still dripping; her face, swollen and with an expression of suffering only to be found in those engravings of early Christian martyrs at a Roman circus.

"I've got a bad headache," she replied, attempting to straighten her hair a little—hopeless, in fact, because it was still so soaked that the water was running down her back and shoulders, wetting her clothes.

"You want an aspirin?"

"Do you have one? That would be great, it's really killing me. . . ."

The girl got up and went into the kitchen. She returned with some aspirins and a glass of water. Vera downed the pills, barely able to wait for the analgesic action to take effect.

She mounted the bicycle and wheeled off wobbling along the street of paved cement. The girl from the hotel shook her head disapprovingly until the strange guest had pedaled out of sight.

After bicycling for some ten minutes, she finally caught sight of the kerosene lamps that provided the only source of light for the cheap tavern Jorge generally patronized. The little bar was set off a dirt road, almost hidden among a group of giant mango trees. This was obviously not the most popular place in town. It was little more than a decrepit straw booth with a few rotting stools and a pair of tables staked into a mud floor splattered with chicken droppings.

An old woman was busy frying fish on a black-sooted skillet while a man sat pouring himself cachaças and eating his fish-and-manioc meal. He tossed the manioc into his mouth with quick jerks of the hand but chewed the fish carefully, spitting out the long, nearly transparent bones. One of those bones, swallowed by someone unused to eating such fish, might cause a lot of damage. Vera stood watching the man with fascination.

The humidity began to penetrate her nostrils and chill her hands and feet. The dark jungle seethed with millions of frogs and insects. Vera left the bike leaning against one of the two tables and walked up to the brazier reeking of fish oil. She could not escape the feeling of a tremendous loneliness, nor could she account for the fact that neither Paulo nor Jorge was there.

"Has Jorge showed up yet, tonight?"

Neither of the two paid any attention to the question, as if they were making a point of not getting involved in conversation. Vera Martins began to feel uneasy—these people were also behaving strangely to her, as if they had been imprisoned on the far side of an old and blurry mirror. It may have been a prudent tactic to ignore her, but she was not about to let herself be sidestepped so easily.

She pulled up a stool and sat down next to the bike. But it was as if she were invisible. Only the crickets and frogs, in the depths of the jungle, made any living sounds—in contrast to the crackle of frying and the hum of the flames.

Something finally broke inside her—a sort of glacial fracturing of her courage. But what the hell was going on there, she pleaded to herself, and why had she deserved such treatment from people? She began to weep; first quietly, then with a loud sobbing; uncontrollably, even though she had no tears left to shed.

Perhaps because Vera Martin's suffering seemed so genuine, the old woman finally turned her head and for the first time focused her attention on the girl.

"What's the matter, my child?" the old woman asked, withdrawing the skillet from the fire and coming over to her.

"Nothing," she replied, still sobbing, with no thread of hope that the old woman's interest could lead anywhere.

"Why are you upset, my child?"

The old woman, curiously, seemed frightened to death.

"I'm just crying, that's all."

The man was observing the two of them with the hazy look of a drunkard, his hands trembling as he held the glass of cachaça to his lips.

"What do you want, girl?"

"You haven't seen Jorge lately, have you, ma'am?"

The old woman glanced at the man, and Vera thought she glimpsed something pass between them: a look of complicity, perhaps, as if they were attuned to some secret frequency from which she was wholly excluded.

"Jorge's left Parintins, my child."

Vera could not believe her ears—this was far too much of a coincidence. Her only remaining witness prudently swept out of reach. And maybe it was no coincidence, though Jorge had often spoken to her of how he planned to leave for Manaus someday, to find a more lucrative job. Jorge had his own ambitions and no intention of simply rotting away in a town without a future.

"Would it have been a while ago that he left?"

"I believe so," the old woman replied. "He took the ferry and went off to try his luck in Manaus."

Vera knew what the ferry was: a floating tub overstuffed with river folk racked together in tiers of hammocks, like animals headed for the zoo. So Jorge had taken his chances on one of those floating disasters, to find a better life in Manaus. He had no time for phantasmagorical apparitions in the sky; he was too busy repeating the destiny of those from the interior: migration to the capital. The absence of a Jorge could be explained, but where was Paulo?

"You're a friend of Jorge's, aren't you, miss?" the old woman quizzed her.

"It's urgent for me to talk to him. I just arrived from Manaus today and expected to find him here."

"He used to come by here quite often to have some fish with me."

"Yes, I know," Vera concluded, getting up.

She took hold of the bike, having decided to head back to her hotel.

"Thank you very much, I'm already feeling much better," she added as she swung onto the seat and started to pedal off.

The road was dark, and on an impulse she circled back to the hut. The old woman and the strange man were exactly as she had left them.

"You haven't by any chance heard anything about the appearance of the *Chupa-chupa*, in Valéria, have you?" She deliberately ignored the drunkard, concentrating instead on the old woman who had seemed more accessible.

The woman shook her head negatively.

"You don't know about it, then?"

"No, my child, what is it?" she confirmed.

She's lying, thought Vera. She could not really say what made her realize that the old woman was lying, but the fact was incontrovertible.

"Don't believe those people in Valéria," the drunkard suddenly muttered.

"Why shouldn't I?"

Vera was surprised by the vehemence of his tone.

"Such people are against the government. They simply like to agitate."

"So you know something about this, after all, don't you?"

The man seemed to come to his senses and looked suddenly terrified.

"I don't know nothing, miss."

"For the love of God, tell me *what's going on?*" Vera beseeched him—an enormous courage suddenly surfacing in her, a courage capable of leading her to the doors of hell itself, should that prove necessary.

"Go away, miss," the drunkard warned her.

"Why don't you want to tell me anything! Who told you to keep quiet?"

The old woman set the skillet down on the table and started nervously wiping her hands upon her grimy skirts.

"Go home, child, it's already getting late."

"Girls like you shouldn't be wandering around a place like this, not at night," the drunkard menaced.

"You're both afraid. Come on, you don't have to be," she insisted in the hopes that something would finally give way, that at least somebody would finally admit to these apparitions.

Vera's heart pounded as she stared expectantly at the two terrified creatures.

"I already know all about it. I was here when those people arrived from Valéria. They were scared of something, something that kept being spotted out there."

The man got up, half crazed, and took the woman by the shoulders. The pale glow of the kerosene lamps scarcely illuminated the expressions of terror that were manifested on their faces once they heard what Vera had said.

"People have died, do you know that?"

But before Vera could go on, the two of them fled almost on the run and vanished into the jungle's darkness.

"Come back, please! Don't be afraid. . . ."

It was no use; the two of them had certainly fled. Vera Martin's heart seemed to want to leap out of her, as her anxiety intensified. She wanted to go back to the hotel, find Paulo and tell him that the people of Parintins were keeping silent because they were terrified— and that their fear was the one thread that could lead them to the mystery itself. It was a rather precarious thread, to be sure; epitomized by the sight of those two poor souls in total panic. Somebody with the power to terrorize people to such a degree had managed to transform a peaceful community into a horror-stricken herd. The thing was growing more and more sinister. She pedaled the bicycle at breakneck speed—a dangerous thing to do along so dark a street, but she was unconcerned with that sort of danger. She covered the distance in less than ten minutes and dashed up to her room. Things were just as she had left them. Paulo had not returned.

Anxious, but controlling herself in order not to break into tears, she went back down to the dining room and sat at a table. The hotel was asleep. Darkness still enveloped the dining hall, and only the mosquitoes seemed delighted with her presence. The combination of her impatience and the affliction of mosquitoes prompted her to commence wandering through the corridors of the hotel. The place was virtually empty of guests; many of the rooms had the doors opened and the beds with bare mattresses. She felt a desire to be far away from there; she wanted to rest. She longed for the old, dull routine; for her house in São Paulo which she should never have left. In the hushed penumbra of early morning she felt a vast vulnerability. It dominated her. It made her life a toy. Slight shivers ran through her tired, long-suffering body, and the morning dampness left her feet chilled.

She slept in the plastic-covered armchair, right in the lounge of the hotel where the girl had been watching television. But her sleep was light, allowing into her dreams all that her senses picked up from the night: distant, diffuse noises; the creaking of the hotel's foundations, linking dream upon dream in a chain of discordant incoherencies to produce one of those semiconscious and perfectly realistic nightmares.

She could not repress a scream when she felt them touch her. She opened her eyes and found herself before the woman who took care of the kitchen. She was coming from the market, and her two baskets full of foodstuffs sat on the floor beside her.

"Why didn't you sleep in your room, miss?"

The poor woman was also frightened; she had not anticipated finding her curled up like a cat in the chair, let alone that scream.

"It's still dark, isn't it?" Vera said to dispel the other's fright along with her own.

"It's four-thirty in the morning," the woman informed her.

Vera recollected that that was an hour when the harbor was normally full of people from the interior. It would be a propitious place to learn something.

"I'm going to take a walk down to the docks," she explained to the woman, getting out of the chair with difficulty.

"Wouldn't you like some coffee first?"

"No thank you, perhaps later on," and immediately she repented the refusal, for she felt an emptiness in her stomach from not having eaten a thing since lunch the previous day.

The cook disappeared into the back of the hotel, and Vera Martins ventured one more look in her hotel room before leaving. Paulo Veronezzi really had ditched her and not even bothered to offer an excuse. But the irritation that she felt was not all that extreme; for her fear was overpowering everything—a definite, clearly defined apprehension that gnawed at her will. She felt certain that Paulo could not simply vanish without a trace; unless he had been in some way detained, actually prevented from returning to the hotel. Now the only person who had, however reluctantly, allowed himself to become involved with her suspicions had been intercepted somehow. It was enough to send her crazy!

The definite certainty that something monstrous was occurring in this city could no longer be quelled. Her will was splintering apart; panic, rapidly constricting her behavior. The room was impassive, the same; just as she had left it. A wave of nausea surged up in her throat as she noticed Paulo's socks still hanging from the chair— symbols that nothing was more anguishing than impotence.

Meanwhile, in Manaus

General Pessoa was just finishing his cup of coffee, still wearing his jogging shorts from the two kilometers—Cooper style—around the square adjacent to his quarters at the Vila Militar. At the same table sat Captain Cruz, his attention focused on the morning papers which generally challenged all his powers of ratiocination—a fact he blamed on the entire journalistic profession. The biggest headlines were devoted to the impending accession of Brigadier General Bernardo Fischer to the head of the Joint Chiefs of Staff of the Armed Forces. The ceremony was tomorrow, and journalists and political insiders were full of speculations as to the possible candidacy of the brigadier general for the presidential office in the coming elections.

"It certainly doesn't please me," commented General Pessoa.

"He's a soldier with a considerable reputation. You don't like him?"

"The people of this nation are tired of soldiers in government, Captain. It's time for all of us to return to the barracks and look after our own profession, which has gone to seed."

The telephone rang and the captain got up to answer it.

"It's for you, General."

Pessoa took the phone, and what he heard left him stunned.

"My God," he moaned, his face turning white.

The captain grew alarmed at the general's appearance. He was frightened the old man might be having a heart attack. His facial expression could only be matched by some disaster: the impeachment of his friend the President of the Republic? News that his crazy flying saucers actually came from the USSR?

"What happened?"

The general took time to answer. He was still in a state of shock, as if it were too much for him to admit what he had just heard.

"My son Raul had a very close call on his motorcycle."

"An accident? Was he injured?"

"It was all very peculiar. It seems finally the accident never actually occurred. The intention apparently was to prevent him from talking to Nelson, my aide."

"Thank God the boy wasn't hurt. Motorcycle accidents can be pretty serious."

"But we've lost our offices."

"What do you mean?"

"The NCPR offices went up in flames last night. The strangest thing is that none of the neighbors noticed any sign of a fire. They only discovered the damage the next morning, when they set out for work. The house was a heap of rubble."

"Well, you can be sure the community is going to investigate the matter."

"They're already on the case but have yet to find the cause of the fire. My son distinctly recalls turning out the lights, and the possibility of a short circuit or some such thing is extremely remote."

Cruz could not imagine what kind of terrorist organization would be interested in putting a match to the offices of an organization devoted to research on flying saucers.

"You don't realize the gravity of the situation, do you, Captain?"

Cruz remained silent: no known terrorist group fit the bill.

"Why do you think I'm here, Captain?"

"To investigate these sightings of the *Chupa-chupa*, sir. And you've been a great help to us."

"Talk is cheap, Captain. I'm more of a hindrance to you people."

"You shouldn't feel that way, General. It's a pleasure to serve you."

"Perhaps you get some pleasure out of it, Captain, but the people from Second Section over at the Military Command of Amazonia don't share your enthusiasm."

Cruz did not reply, because what the general had said was the gospel truth. He himself would have preferred to be stationed on the border, investigating corruption in some commissariat or a similar assignment, to chasing around with a retired general. It was not that he disliked this surprising idealist, but all that business about extra-terrestrials left him rather dumbfounded—and he detested feeling dumbfounded.

"I'm going to tell you something, Captain: Whoever set fire to the National Center for Paranormal Research doesn't like my presence here one bit, and at the moment must be thinking they've managed quite a coup by burning up our archives."

The captain nodded, without much conviction.

"Since 1976 I've been receiving reports about the phenomenon of the so-called *Chupa-chupa*. Then during the Third Brazilian Congress on Ufology, held in '79, the subject was dismissed as not relevant to the field. The sightings did not follow the internationally recognized patterns defining UFOs. We were dealing only with lights—no report went so far as to refer to ships or crafts. The frequency of the appearances was the single disturbing factor. Even your people were investigating."

"Yes, we had some reports; but all type F, which is to say, their competence could not be verified."

"Well, I didn't attribute any importance to the subject, either, until last week. It was my buddy Nelson, an extremely meticulous researcher, who called my attention to certain peculiarities of the phenomenon."

The general opened the drawer of the table and took out a notebook with stiff binders. He leafed through its pages until he reached the section he was searching for.

"Listen to this: 'The phenomenon of the *Chupa-chupa* was first recorded in the north of Maranhão State, in 1976. From then until now it has been moving slowly up the channel of the Amazon River. It is particularly manifested in remote areas and only to impoverished people.' Nelson has managed to establish the following statistics," the general said, passing the notebook to Captain Cruz.

The figures were certainly intriguing:

98% of appearances by the *Chupa-chupa* have occurred in rural areas.

2% of appearances have occurred on the outskirts of actual cities.

75% of appearances were before peasants.

10% of appearances, to common laborers.

10% of appearances, to foresters.

5% of appearances, to educated people: professors and the like. . . .

91% of appearances have occurred in areas where title to land was under litigation.

9% of appearances, in areas where ownership was clearly established.

89% of locales visited with the phenomenon lack even basic sanitary conditions.

76% of witnesses were illiterate.

100% of locales visited with the phenomenon lack any form of medical assistance.

87% of locales visited had extremely high records of infant mortality.

92% of witnesses earned below half the minimum wage.

8% of witnesses earned the minimum wage or higher.

74% of witnesses had voted for the government in the last elections.

26% of witnesses had voted for the opposition.

60% of witnesses termed themselves Catholic.

15% of witnesses were Protestant.

25% of witnesses professed primitive forms of religious belief.

12% of witnesses claimed to have been attacked.

2% of witnesses had been hospitalized as a result of such alleged attacks.

45% of witnesses had abandoned their homes after the occurrence of the phenomenon.

80% of witnesses believed the phenomenon could be blamed on the Americans.

10% of witnesses believed it could be blamed on the Japanese.

8% of witnesses believed it had to do with the Russians.

1% of witnesses believed it to be the work of the Chinese.

1% of witnesses believed that the *Chupa-chupa* was a phenomenon of outer space, i.e., flying saucers.

Captain Cruz handed back the notebook.

"Intriguing statistics, all right."

"And Nelson has been very cautious," General Pessoa added, noting that the captain had said so out of mere politeness. "You don't really get the significance of such statistics, do you, Captain."

Cruz eyed him with a vague expression of annoyance.

"This phenomenon, whatever it is, has the potential to generate serious social unrest, Captain. It makes its appearances to the bottom of the ladder, that sector of society that has been denied everything. It might prove a crucial factor in such explosive terrain."

"We have such matters under control, sir," Cruz answered with growing irritation.

It was more and more difficult talking to these young officers, the general reflected: all very cocksure of themselves, they seemed to regard subcontinental Brazil as if she were a Caribbean island.

"I wouldn't be too sure, Captain Cruz. Not everything is under your control."

The captain sighed patiently and lowered his gaze.

"This is a big country," the general continued, "a young nation with a new civilization in the making. There are powerful forces busy conspiring in the wings."

"Occult forces, I suppose."

"Exactly, Captain. But as plain as the nose on your face."

The clearest mysteries were those that passed for normal, as General Pessoa's long experience had taught him. And Brazil was a country full of just such mysteries—so normal-looking that people tripped in the streets over such marvels every day without any awareness of the fact. Occasionally such mysteries were not so marvelous and brought shame to the nation.

"I'm going to tell you exactly why I'm here, Captain. As I told you, I didn't take this business of the *Chupa-chupa* very seriously either. The resolution of the Third Congress was enough to dissuade me. But then, last week, I suddenly had a visitor who helped me change my mind. Did you know a Sergeant Melo?"

"I know the story. A pretty sad business, wasn't it. . . ."

"It's the truth nonetheless. That boy went through hell. He was a member of the semi-clandestine arrest squads for the DOI-CODI, in São Paulo, until 1974. You can imagine what that was like. He'd been a wonderful husband and father until joining up with Major Lisboa. Then things started going wrong on the domestic front: his wife finally walked out on him, taking their only daughter, and he developed a fondness for barbiturates. They say he became a real butcher; his name made all the lists of torturers compiled after '78. He was finally sacked for exceeding even his duties, wrecking and burglarizing the homes of the subversives he had taken into custody. He went so far as to sell six cars seized in a variety of raids by our celebrated Division-of-Operations: Internal for the Company-for-Operations-of-Defense: Internal. Abandoned by the said DOI-CODI, with no further contact with his buddies in uniform, you can imagine what he became. One of the worst things that can happen to any one of us is to be denied the friendship of our fellow soldiers. We lose our bearings; we lose everything. Sergeant Melo tried to put his life back together by taking a job with a security firm, but was almost immediately fired for causing injuries to an employee he was interrogating on suspicion of theft. Melo then went on to become a pimp, for whores in the port of Santos; and soon after really hit the skids: trafficking in drugs, fencing stolen property, hustling for the white slave market in Hong Kong. By 1981, he was on his last leg when suddenly a friend gave him a hand."

"According to our information he drowned in '81, in Santos harbor."

"Not true, I'm afraid. You'll recall the body was never found."

"Right, only his clothes and identification papers. When the police checked out his room, all they found was a few grams of cocaine and some false passports for women being shipped to Asia."

"Sergeant Melo fortunately ran into a lieutenant he'd known from the Municipal Guard in São Paulo, also 'retired.' A fellow by the name of Assunção—black, powerfully built, though already in his fifties—he'd served under Chief Inspector Fleury on one of the death squads. Anyway, he convinced Melo to leave Santos and return to Brasília with him. He promised to help the fellow get his life in order. And he kept his promise. Assunção got him to some sort of psychiatric clinic from which he eventually emerged a different person. He finally converted to some esoteric religion and worked as a medium at the Valley of the Seven Moons, with a new name and a clean identity."

Captain Cruz was listening to what Pessoa had to say with a degree of skepticism. He could not make up his mind whether to give some credence to what he was saying or simply dismiss it as just another crackbrained theory of a senile old soldier. But the habit of gathering information proved the stronger impulse, and anything at all was better than nothing.

"The sergeant worked there until last week."

"Gave up his religion?"

"Disappeared. At the end of his first visit, we made plans to meet again, but he never showed up. Nelson did some snooping around and discovered that he had been struck from the list of available mediums as of the day he first came looking for me."

"Who runs this sect?"

"That's still a mystery—everyone refers to him only as the Master. The sergeant confided to me that he was very high up but couldn't, or wouldn't, tell me his name. Only a handful of the most trusted acolytes have ever had permission to see him. He's supposed to be the priest of an entity known as Sylyon—the one I've spoken about many times before, only none of you believed me."

"But high up where? Civil or military?"

"We don't know, but as a priest of Sylyon he's bound to be very powerful, whether or not he holds any office or rank—this thing is a time bomb."

"Do you actually think there's some conspiracy behind all this? Any danger to the military regime?"

General Pessoa flashed him a knowing smile.

"I think it wouldn't help a bit to tell you *what* I think."

"But we might be able to spur the intelligence community to try to discover the identity of such a dangerous element."

"I doubt it. Nowdays the Community plays messenger boy to a bunch of technocrats. The Service for Electronic Gibberish."

"But the death of the American—do you think it was this same element that gave the order to eliminate him?"

"Melo told me that in the Valley of the Seven Moons a variety of elements were at work who had had a hand in the repression—all of them converted to the sect and supposedly liberated from evil by the Master."

"Do you have a list of those elements, sir?"

"Unhappily, no. But Melo swore to me that one of the links was right here, in these sightings. He said that if I looked carefully enough into the business of the *Chupa-chupa*, I'd run smack into some of the acolytes from that sect. According to him, most of them were living at some sort of base of operations."

"But what for? What do they hope to accomplish?"

"Power! I know it seems crazy. But that's what they want."

Perspiration had totally fogged his glasses, and the general paused to wipe them. Without the spectacles it was possible to observe his two large pupils, sky-blue, which gave him a wholly unbelligerent, almost childish air. Once he put them back on, he began paging through his notebook again.

"Let me find it . . . here!" A sheet of printed paper sailed out of the notebook and floated floorward until it was finally retrieved by the general. "Here it is," he continued soberly. "This is one of the propaganda sheets from the Valley of the Seven Moons."

Captain Cruz took the sheet and perused it carefully, as he did with everything he touched. He could detect the slightest hint of the subversive, no matter how disguised it might be—one of his specialties.

The sheet read as follows:

SYLYON is the voyager. SYLYON is the ritual name of the Master. SYLYON is the final avatar. The Master is a privileged embodiment of the LIGHT. He has established contact with the planet MATRIX, the KARMIC SEAT of THE EARTH, and with a few of its ILLUMINED INHABITANTS, such as the messenger SYTAR SYN, the one embodied on Earth in João the Medium.

The spaceship of SYLYON the MASTER has visited the depths of the infernal region and was on MATRIX, a place invisible to astronomers because of its position behind the SUN.

The most important mission of those from MATRIX—superiorly evolved beings—is to preside over the passage from the Second Millennium to the Third.

SYNTAR SYN has prophesied that the final twenty years of our century will bear witness to many deaths and the launching of a new civilization.

KARMIC LAW will be abolished and only supermen will remain. There will be no more sickness on Earth and the Earth's climate will be paradisiacal forever after.

Brasília is one of the 7 POINTS of the MOON and one of the

7 VALLEYS *of the planet chosen to benefit. The others are to be found in Haiti, in Chile, in South Africa, South Korea and Formosa.*

The Valley of the Seven Moons shines on the passing of the millennium.

Glory to SYLYON, the Voyager.

"It sounds like some sort of esoteric doctrine, doesn't it, Captain?"

No particular scent of political subversion was to be detected by the sharp nose of the captain. And if there was anything to be detected, it was the precarious mental state of the author of such a doctrine.

"The passage into the Third Millennium begins now, Captain."

"It's difficult to believe all this, General. There are literally thousands of crazy sects just like this that have proliferated across the country. All of them innocuous as far as subversive politics goes."

"But this sect has already liquidated a CIA agent and who is to say what other people as well?"

"All I can promise, sir, is to seek to identify their so-called Master."

"That would already be a great help. But I must pay a visit myself to that little community where the phenomenon took place."

"You really still want to go there, then?"

"I'm afraid I do. It's not so far from here, is it? I must have a look around where the American was doing all the snooping. Mike was a professional, and would hardly have chosen the place out of love for the exotic."

Captain Cruz scratched his head resignedly and dialed a number on the telephone. He spoke with Second Section and managed to obtain authorization for the general's trip there in a single-engine trainer from the Brazilian Air Force. It would be sufficient to get him to the base in Manaus and talk to the officer of the day.

Upon hearing of his authorization, General Pessoa hurried to his room to change into other clothes and set out immediately—remembering to bring along the notebook and pack a small suitcase. The captain followed at his heels, smiling at the youthful spirit of the old man.

They took a C-14 van and headed off in the direction of the military airport. The route they had to follow was heavily congested and they were soon bogged down in the traffic, but they were in no particular hurry—at least not the captain. The orders he had were to place General Pessoa aboard the craft and return to General Headquarters.

"It's a pity you can't come along," lamented the general over and over.

"I have an important meeting at GHQ. The Americans have apparently arrived to collect the body and offer their explanation."

In the vicinity of the Japiim neighborhood, not far from the airport, a police barrier blocked the route. There were two vehicles painted with the colors of the Military Police and a gray Volkswagen from the Transit Police. Lines of automobiles waited to pass through the checkpoint, honking incessantly. Captain Cruz started to curse the local police's habit of erecting roadblocks at the worst possible hours, causing senseless bottlenecks in a city of what was otherwise light traffic.

"Don't worry, sir, whatever time you arrive there you will take off immediately," he said in an attempt to tranquilize the general.

The C-14 sat stranded in the middle of a noisy three-lane traffic jam—hemmed in by two trucks, a busload of workers from some factory out in the Industrial District, and a Belina with a couple of kids on the way to school with their mother.

The two soldiers were so annoyed that they failed to notice the two men on a motorcycle weaving their way through the rows of autos. The bike pulled up alongside the van they were in and the cyclist rested a foot on the pavement, still revving the powerful pistons of his motor. The din soon drew the attention of the two officers, and General Pessoa turned to confront a .45-caliber pistol, equipped with silencer and peculiar to the armed forces, extending from the hand of the cyclist. The weapon spat a tongue of yellow fire, at nearly the same instant the general had thrown himself forward from his seat, opening a dark and bloody hole in the right temple of Captain Cruz. The door on the passenger side of the van was suddenly opened, and the general felt the still-hot barrel of the revolver placed against his neck. The man who was seated on the rear saddle of the bike had already gone around to the driver's side and was dragging the body of the captain out of the driver's seat, dumping him on the pavement. The woman in the Belina saw the body tumble out gushing blood, and screamed with her children. Then the passengers on the bus also began to shout and get down from the bus, desperate at the sight of the captain sprawled on the pavement and bleeding to death.

General Pessoa felt only terror that his own life was about to end.

"Out of the truck and don't try to be a hero," ordered the other fellow, pressing the barrel of his weapon into the general's ribs.

Pessoa got carefully out of the van, and the two cyclists calmly led him across the highway into the oncoming traffic. The C-14 sat empty, its doors wide open, already engulfed by the curious in the midst of a more and more volatile traffic jam, while the two men forced the general into another car, an Opel, and raced from the scene. Pessoa kept looking behind, and saw policemen running from behind the roadblock toward where his companion lay dead, his brain perforated by a .45-caliber bullet.

"This is madness! You'll never get away with this," Pessoa protested.

"Shut up!" one of the men snarled back.

The general for the first time took a look at his abductors. There were three of them, bordering on middle age. Those from the motorcycle were light-skinned and blond, like immigrants from the South. The one who was driving the Opel was dark-skinned, a mulatto, and rather powerfully built. Pessoa had the impression he recognized the fellow from somewhere before.

"But what the devil do you think you're doing?" he insisted, at the same moment that he began to reach the conclusion he might finally be heading for what he had been looking for.

The answer was a blow from the butt of the gun, which immediately put him out of commission. The fugitives had no time for questions at such a moment: one of the Military Police vehicles was in hot pursuit as they sped along at more than a hundred and twenty kph.

"Watch me give them something to remember me by," said one of the kidnappers, leaning out the window of their Opel and pointing the .45 in the direction of their pursuers.

But the police saw the maneuver and sent a hail of bullets flying into the Opel, smashing windows and demolishing the rearview mirror. The blood then seemed to rush to the head of the fellow with the .45. He climbed into the backseat—practically kneeling in the lap of the still unconscious Pessoa—and began to return fire through the shattered rear window. He was an excellent shot and proved as much immediately. The first bullet tore the lid off the driver's skull. The next shot—fired a second later, the instant before the police car went into its skid and the police officers realized what was happening—blew out the left front tire, compounding the skid. The car lurched to one side and veered full-speed onto the sidewalk, running down a group of men playing dominoes at a table and crashing into the grocery store, where it finally plowed through a wall with an infernal racket of twisting metal, agonizing screams and crumbling concrete.

The marksman howled with contentment and seemed, insanely enough, to be crying. Minutes later the Opel had disappeared safely from the scene, while the neighborhood of Japiim suffered the worst traffic jam in its history.

Immediately Afterwards, at GHQ for the Military Command of Amazonia

The assembly room of GHQ was filled to capacity, and the conversations among the higher-ranking officers of the Military Command of Amazonia hummed a few decibels above normal. The room was seldom used and normally served only to receive groups of trainees from the Brazilian War College, whenever conferences were held there on the military matters of Amazonia. At the moment, however, the assembly room appeared to be far from the tranquility of those conferences perennially irrigated by coffee and seltzer water. The commanding general, about to be appointed to a new post with the Joint Chiefs of Staff, could hardly control his temper. Seated next to him, pale and tongue-tied, was Colonel Nunes from the SNI, attempting to come up with an explanation.

"You call it a routine case of drug trafficking?" the general fumed. "Then how do you explain the death of Captain Cruz—a brutal murder! And the kidnapping of that lunatic?"

"The Federal Police have been investigating, General."

"Investigating what? They're all completely corrupt! You told me the case was practically wrapped up. Wrapped up? Where are your suspects? How many people have been arested?"

"I've just spoken with Brasília," Nunes rushed to reply, the words sputtering out of his mouth almost without his even thinking. "We plan to expand the investigation to include the possibility of subversion. That way we have full autonomy and considerably more resources to bring into play."

"I don't want to hear any more of this nonsense. You're a bunch of incompetents! I'm going to order a house-to-house search. I will drag the guilty parties out from wherever they're hiding. And I don't care who gets burned in the process!"

Colonel Nunes paled still further. He could not permit anything of the sort to occur. All that was needed for disastrous political repercussions was to have the army go into the streets.

"You can't do that, General. The matter is under the jurisdiction of the Federal Police and the Ministry of Justice."

"The hell it is, you idiot, you! I want no more of your squawking, do you hear? I want silence!"

The officers' talk grew hushed and Nunes was praying to himself that the commanding general would recover his senses. But the man was already too agitated and would soon have heads rolling. And the first would most likely be his own.

"Has the lad's family been informed?"

A major stepped forward.

"Captain Cruz lived alone, sir, and had no immediate family. But we did phone Brasília to advise the family of General Pessoa."

"Who gave orders to notify that *lunatic's* family?"

"The Chief Communications Officer, sir. He said to follow normal procedure."

"Son of a bitch, doesn't anybody do anything *right* around here!"

Colonel Nunes, eager to regain the commanding general's confidence, intervened: "They should never have leaked that information to the public. It might prejudice the whole investigation."

"And you shut your mouth, idiot, do you hear? No one asked for your opinion. And be advised that I intend to strip you of your rank— and you can be sure you'll never have another promotion under my command. . . ."

The colonel lowered his eyes and slipped away from the general's side. Meanwhile, the major who had informed his commander about the call to General Pessoa's house now interrupted.

"Begging your pardon, sir, but the Americans are here and they're already waiting in your office. The meeting is supposed to begin in twenty minutes."

The commanding general strode out, accompanied by various intelligence officers. The colonel, with his injured pride, was busy hiding his fears behind the cover of a magazine until the other snapped his fingers:

"You too," he beckoned over his shoulder.

Nunes tossed aside the magazine and followed the cortège. The commanding general's office stood at the opposite end of the corridor, some five meters from the assembly room, a distance that the colonel traversed a few steps behind his colleagues while ruminating additional excuses and rationalizations.

The two American officers, both of whom spoke an elegant *madrileño* Spanish, were savoring the reheated coffee from GHQ with no sign of distaste. When the commanding general walked in, they stood up and saluted. The major assigned to the commander's office made the introductions.

"Major Carson from the Office of Consular Operations," he announced with an outstretched hand to indicate one of the two Americans: a portly fellow whose sweat had already soaked through a starched collar and left twin stains under the armpits of his navy blue jacket of synthetic fabric.

The commanding general shook the fellow's hand vigorously without compromising the gravity of the situation.

"Major Miller from Administration, at Andrews Air Force Base," the aide continued, indicating the thin officer with bald head and graying mustache who wore a jacket a good two sizes larger than his physique.

Both the Americans were obviously nervous, and behaved with a formality that suggested how disagreeable this meeting was for them.

Colonel Nunes had a file on each one of them:

Major Donald Carson, chief of Center for Operations, in Montevideo. The man was almost respectable because Uruguay implied respectability. Corruption down that way did not normally descend to the barefaced decadence of Saigon under the American occupation, where the major had directed an intelligence network specializing in economic matters and become a popular figure among the riffraff of Cholon with its casinos, feverish whorehouses and profitable traffic in opium. Uruguayan corruption was restricted to the upper echelons of power: the spartan offices of the various ministries, the expensive hotels of Carrasco and the luxurious dwellings along the Rambla Sur. Such refined corruption was not his cup of tea, and Carson generally contented himself with making a few hasty deals of little worth among his Paraguayan connections. He stuck to facilitating such transactions as trafficking in a couple of small light planes, via the flat pampas of the frontier—a transaction involving a smug general from Paraguay, ignorant as an ass but the owner of several stores in the duty-free zone of Puerto Stroessner and of a hotel in Asunción, both traps for the unwitting tourist. This same general operated a half-baked smuggling racket in electrical appliances between Brazil and Paraguay, as well as a pathetic ring of car smugglers; and he sometimes served as a link for couriers making the southern connection in the Bolivian cocaine market. Out of either sheer blockheadedness or simply a total lack of geopolitical sensibilities, this Paraguayan general would never take the slightest interest in the anti-Communist obsessions of his colleagues, whether these were Brazilians, Chileans or Uruguayans; and he considered the present regime in his own country to be a pillar of democracy. He never tired of repeating as well that Paraguay was a country apart: wretched as an Indian, enigmatic as a Chinaman, and thus immune to the political insanities of its neighbors. It was this general who had alerted Carson to the sinister goings-on in Brazil— with the aid of Chileans and Uruguayans—purportedly to introduce a Third Millennium. Carson, however, had failed to take the information very seriously—particularly because his informant, from a lack of interest or intelligence, had not bothered to pursue the subject in greater detail. With the death of the CIA agent, the major's interest was rudely reawakened.

The other American was a less familiar figure, and Colonel Nunes surmised he must have made the trip out of professional obligation.

Major Gwyneth Miller, head of Special Section for Consular Operations, CIA, Andrews Air Force Base. Miller had a brother in Brazil, an element long suspected of being a CIA operative, although he had always managed to be discreet about his activities. The brother was the owner of a small travel agency specializing in tours of the Southern Cone. It was a lucrative business and the brother spent a good part of his time accompanying excursion groups to Argentina, Uruguay, Paraguay and Chile. The tours were generally organized to satisfy the growing consumer fever of the middle class. The differences and fluctuations in currency values allowed his business to take advantage of favorable exchange rates, and he profited by it. One of the lesser-known activities of this Mr. Miller was to serve as a courier to move foreign exchange out of the country on behalf of a select group of clients from the middle and upper echelons of various state and federal offices. His agency had its main office in Rio. The major's brother was sixty-two and had been in the business since 1952. He had come to Rio in 1950, and his Brazilian son, age thirty, was at Annapolis, learning how to fly one of the Mirage jets used by the Brazilian Air Force.

The activities of the various intelligence branches from the U.S. were far from precariously managed in South America. Since 1979, the pulse of U.S. intelligence—whose chief area of interest at the moment was an explosive Central America—emanated from Montevideo, Uruguay, spreading its tentacles across the entire subcontinent as far north as Southern Panama. Almost all of the present staff had been there from the beginning, having arrived from Chile on the heels of the freeze in relations between the two countries. In November of '79, the Chilean government had been ordered by a U.S. court to indemnify the Letelier and Moffit families to the tune of four million dollars. The news was greeted with shock and indignation by the Chilean military; and once the realization came that the capital investments of Lan-Chile Airlines might be expropriated to pay the damages, violence erupted. Four agents from the staff of consular operations were forcibly detained by the DINA and subjected to harassment and humiliation. Stripped and beaten, they were dumped in a woodland park along the Mapocho River. The trade office which had served as a front for intelligence operations was stormed, one

predawn morning shortly thereafter, and the two night watchmen—
Chilean militiamen moonlighting for the Americans—were murdered
in rather barbarous fashion. Papers were strewn all over the place and
the offices fouled with human excrement. Central quickly decided to
transfer its operations to the serenity of Uruguay, and the Chilean
"trade" office never resumed the same level of importance, even after
the election of Ronald Reagan and the subsequent declarations of
renewed friendship by Secretary Haig, in 1981.

This was why Colonel Nunes pondered the presence of Major
Miller in Brazil. It was a sizable honor for a mere dead agent who,
the Americans insisted, had been working there on his own, to be
thus retrieved by the most important intelligence figure in the field.

The commanding general, with his head slightly tilted, listened
once again to the official excuses that had already circulated *ad nau-
seam* through all the ministerial offices in Brasília, cognizant that
they were no more than a formality. The illegal presence of a foreign
agent in the country was a concept that did not even enter his mind—
after all, this was an ally. What the general most desired at the moment
was to be freed as quickly as possible from the entire mess, in order
to return to the tranquility of his chessboard.

Once the Americans had finished with their protocol of apologies,
the general breathed a sigh of relief. Soon the meeting would be over,
at last!

"Sir," Carson addressed him, as if reading his thoughts, "there's
just one more matter to be discussed."

The commanding general shifted impatiently in his chair. Major
Miller opened a leather attaché case and lifted out a brown manila
envelope, handing it over to Carson.

"We've already shown this material to our colleagues in Brasília,
General," Carson went on to explain while removing a few photographs and several typewritten pages from the envelope, only to pause.
"I'd like to make certain that the officers present have clearance to
review classified information. . . ."

The commanding general assented with a wave of the hand, in no
mood to continue much longer with a meeting that had already dragged
on endlessly, to his way of thinking.

"You may speak freely, Major Carson."

"A man was kidnapped from a hotel in Brasília, last Sunday. I
don't know if you are aware of the fact?"

The general shook his head: "It's not my area, Major."

"We've already been informed. It's an agent from the KGB. We still have no idea what he was doing in Brasília; or why he was kidnapped, for that matter."

It was Nunes who had just interrupted the conversation, producing another disaster—the commanding general shot him a glance that clearly evinced an impulse to have him court-martialed.

"Well, we've got some photographs," Carson went on. "One of our men was in the hotel parking lot when they came out with the guy. A real piece of luck. We had no idea he was going to witness a thing like that."

He handed the photographs to the general, who after examining them cursorily passed them around among his junior officers.

"Do any of you gentlemen recognize either of the kidnappers?"

The officers kept silent. Perhaps they really did not recognize the two men—they were rather young officers. Yet Nunes knew very well that pair of lunatics making those obscene gestures at the photographer from the CIA. Nonetheless, he decided to keep his mouth shut; he had already stuck his neck out dangerously far, and in a single hour seemed to have earned the eternal hostility of the principal military authority of the entire Amazon region in return for the favor.

"It would certainly be possible to identify them by checking our files," said the general in such tone of voice as he hoped would avoid any hint of inferiority before the Americans or, for that matter, his general staff. "If the major would care to leave the photos with us, we could easily have the answer in a few hours. That is, if it's of interest, obviously."

The American took the photographs and papers back and stood up.

"No. It's not our problem in any case. If the Russians want to find their man, they're the ones that should have to worry about it, don't you agree? We have enough problems of our own, not to worry about those of the Communists."

The Americans laughed, but their merriment was not shared by the Brazilians. The disparity in sense of humor was too great, and the way the Americans wielded their Spanish made for even more dubious understanding.

"The body has been duly prepared for shipment," the commanding general's aide-de-camp informed the two majors. "You may pick up the coffin from the cargo terminal at the municipal airport whenever it suits you, gentlemen."

Major Carson also stood up and thanked the aide, then took his leave of the commanding general. The laconic Miller shook hands

with each officer in turn, then exited from the room followed by the
junior officers and their general—this last now in a more expansive
mood. Only Colonel Nunes, still in his chair, remained behind.

Once the Americans had disappeared from view—now led in turn
by the retinue of junior officers working for the general—Nunes stood
up and began to rummage through the dispatches piled upon the desk.
It was virtually a mechanical gesture of pure habit—an instinctive
snoop, he never missed any opportunity to pry into matters that did
not concern him.

"What the hell are you doing over there at my desk," the commanding general shouted out of nowhere, causing Nunes to jump back
in surprise.

"Sorry, I had no intention of—"

"Out of here, at once!" barked the general.

Nunes headed swiftly for the door.

"Colonel Nunes!" the general yelled after him.

"Yes, sir!" Nunes turned about and saluted.

His commander replied curtly in kind and then lowered his hand
ferociously.

"What did you have to tell me?"

"It's about those photos, sir."

"The photos? Don't tell me you knew about them as well?"

"It was the first time I laid eyes on them, sir."

"So, what about them?"

"Two of the men, sir. The kidnappers . . ."

"Some sort of fifth column, obviously—so what?"

"They're already dead, sir."

"What?"

"That's what I said, sir: Dead. . . . Both of them died a long time
ago—they simply cannot have kidnapped that Russian."

The commander sat down slowly into his chair. A craving for a
good belt of Scotch was welling up in his dry throat.

"Would you care to explain yourself, Colonel. And don't let your
imagination run away with you."

Nunes stepped back into the office and closed the door behind
him. The soft carpeting made the room seem suddenly cosier, although
the clash of colors still diminished the effect.

"I knew the both of them, sir. I even attended a funeral for one
of them."

"You went to his funeral and now he's back grabbing KGB agents
off the streets of the federal capital?"

"That's what I can't understand either, sir."

"Then find out what in hell's going on . . . that's what you're paid for! Dig up the fellow's grave if you have to. But I guarantee it won't be him you find in it."

"The fellow's name was Tobias. He was a corporal in the Military Police of Bahia, a simple guy and a decent soldier. He was part of the team that liquidated Captain Lamarca; worked in the Marine Corps Center for Information. He died in 1978, drowned off Itaparica, an unfortunate accident. He was spending his leave from CENIMAR with a girl friend and decided to go fishing. It was no easy task coming up with the body—the fish had done quite a job on it."

"You actually saw the body?"

"No, they returned it to the family in a sealed zinc coffin. Apparently the sight of it was none too pleasant. The coffin was buried in Salvador—I myself made the arrangements. The mother still gets his pension."

"What kind of country is this," the commanding general wondered aloud, obviously innocent as to the originality of his question.

Colonel Nunes left the office with the impression that he had already been shot and was merely on his way to meet the wrath of the Creator.

WEDNESDAY, AUGUST 24

Vera's entire body felt as if it had been through the mill, and the feeling put her in a murderous mood. If the mayor had only suspected her state of mind, he would not have continued to sit like that at his desk with a leer on his face, flanked by the two flags of Brazil and Amazonia like a plaster bust in some patriotic store window.

She had been wandering about the port in the midst of the throngs of river people wielding baskets and crates of fish, with the continual impression that Paulo Veronezzi was about to emerge unexpectedly from some crowd or other. Her intention had been to sock him with all her might, right on the jaw, in order to teach him to pay greater heed to her innermost fears. But Paulo had not appeared; it was as if he had vanished, forsaking her like the skin of an orange; and now she was helpless, completely drained by fear, by this paranoia of constantly imagined threats. There were eyes glued to her everywhere, following her, watching her every move.

The sergeant from the Military Police walked charily into the mayor's office, his face swollen from alcohol and sleeplessness. He was Indian, stocky, with the broad shoulders and heavy hands of a true peasant, and his polite drawl did little to couch the violent temper he barely held in check. He commanded a detachment of twenty-five recruits, and every one of them considered him the absolute master of law and order in the city. He traveled about in a brand-new jeep equipped with a radio through which he communicated with head-quarters and he sported a nickel-handled .38-caliber revolver in his belt. The latter he used rarely, and then only to shoot buzzards in order to demonstrate to would-be hoodlums his capacity to knock off any numbskull fool enough to play macho with him. In general, his watchdog behavior was restricted to rounding up a few alcoholics by the scruffs of the neck and dragging them off to the can by dint of sheer brute force, or to walking into any rat-infested whorehouse along the banks of the river with the assuredness of those who have been anointed with the mark of absolute authority.

Vera had previously spoken to the sergeant on only one occasion. The fellow had treated her courteously, looking the other way with respect to her habit of smoking joints on public thoroughfares—his subservience to class suddenly coloring his normally impervious, Indian demeanor: a fact which greatly amused her. The effect of her being a federal employee was to lend her, in his eyes, something akin to superior rank—an effect which the sergeant now demonstrated upon entering the mayor's office by suddenly straightening up and saluting.

"Sergeant," the mayor began tiredly, "you haven't by any chance come across a kid from out of town, a journalist supposedly, while on your rounds last night?"

The sergeant shook his head to say no without otherwise abandoning his rigid posture, or the look of subservience etched into his dark face.

"At ease, Sergeant," ordered the mayor as an afterthought.

The Indian relaxed finally, assuming the familiar posture of limp shoulders which he had adopted from karate films.

"He was visiting Parintins," the mayor continued, "in the company of Miss Martins, here; and now he's disappeared."

"No one disappears in Parintins," the sergeant corrected.

The mayor nodded contentedly. He was not about to allow this woman to cause any scandal in his municipality, even if she were some kind of federal employee.

"That's precisely what I've been trying to explain to her," agreed the mayor. "Her fellow, this journalist, apparently left the hotel at nightfall."

"He was going to look for the disk jockey from the radio station," Vera attempted to explain, feeling an uncomfortable acidity rising in her stomach.

"You mean Jorge? But he's gone to Manaus, ma'am," the sergeant informed her. "Didn't you know?"

"That's what I've since been told," she replied, almost out of inertia. "I went everywhere looking for Jorge, but it seems that even his family has left town."

"As I've told you, miss, all of them went to Manaus."

"What's the journalist's name, ma'am?"

"Paulo, Paulo Veronezzi," she told the sergeant. "He works for the magazine *Isto É*. He arrived with me yesterday, on a TABA flight from Manaus."

The sergeant continued to regard her as if she were the minister of agriculture in person. His wrinkled uniform was too large for even his stocky figure and the sleeves bagged over his wrists.

"There are many places in Parintins where a man can go to forget about life," the sergeant suggested timidly, immediately regretting that he might be causing the lady some sort of embarrassment.

The mayor had the opposite reaction, and took delight in the sergeant's observation. What he desired was simply to extract the problem at its very roots and be rid of this bitch. Most likely the sergeant was right—the guy was probably dead drunk in some bar or sleeping in the arms of a waterfront whore.

"A young bachelor has a lot of possibilities at his disposal around here," affirmed the mayor, accentuating the word *bachelor*. After saying so, however, he felt he might have gone too far. "I'm sorry, miss."

"It doesn't matter," Vera replied.

She could hardly claim to know Paulo very well. In São Paulo, recently, she had run into him once or twice on weekends at some bar. It could be very possible that the dirty lout was busying himself in one of the stinking hovels that floated in the shit and garbage where twelve-year-old girls offered themselves for half a bag of flour. Occasionally she had walked past such houses and seen grown men hanging on to ragged little girls, trying not to fall on their faces with drink. It was hard to imagine Paulo—so full of his scruples and damned self-sufficiency—in one of those sordid holes, much less surrounded by children bought at the lowest possible price of degradation. Such customers were generally riverines, as toothless and hungry as the prostitutes themselves, but who now and then would splurge their earnings on such sinister bartering of affections and other forms of gratuitous violence.

To picture Paulo Veronezzi among such people was difficult to imagine. Even the little intimacy that she had shared with him told her he was incapable of going that far.

"What I can do," offered the sergeant, "is take the Jeep out and have a look around town. Who knows? He might turn up."

Vera eagerly accepted the offer and the mayor expressed a sigh of relief. At least while she was with the sergeant, she would leave him in peace.

They headed off on their search of the city, and the Jeep's bouncing finally awakened Vera from her lethargy and exhaustion. They stopped at a cafe near the cathedral and the sergeant spoke a few soothing words in an attempt to calm her down. He had a great deal of experience under his belt, in dealing with nearly every walk of humanity; and in his simplicity he had the unerring capacity to comfort. Still, Vera's fears continued to dog her, threatening her good sense and driving her to desperation.

When they stopped back at the hotel, they discovered that Paulo Veronezzi had yet to return there. Vera could no longer bear the socks hanging from the chair and took the opportunity to thrust them into the journalist's suitcase.

In a little over an hour they had made a complete circle of the city. The sergeant, showing extraordinary patience, continued to quiz passersby as to the whereabouts of a young journalist from out of town. No one had seen him, however, and finally there were no leads left to follow, at least of a kind the sergeant felt appropriate to explore with a lady in his presence.

"I just don't understand it, ma'am. Nobody can hide himself this way in Parintins. Your fellow must have left town."

"He wouldn't have done that, I'm sure. His bags are still in the hotel where he left them. And so is his ticket for the return flight."

"Maybe he took one of the ferries. You have a boat leaving for Manaus almost every hour of the day, ma'am."

"Do you think that could be it?" she wondered out loud, also trying to convince herself in the process. "But why would he take the ferry?"

"He probably just got fed up with being here. You have a lot of folks who don't like this part of the world, ma'am. I've known people from the capital who can't stand to spend even a single day in this place."

He stopped the jeep at the edge of a steep bank. Down below, forming a small cove, the river elbowed its way inland and then continued on its course, leaving behind a small harbor of calm waters. Three floating hovels, with their zinc roofs gleaming in the sunlight, were nestled into the cove.

"Let's go have one final look down below there," the sergeant suggested.

They had a difficult time of it descending the steep trail that, worn into the moist clay, led them down to the floating huts. The huts themselves were actually makeshift shops built of old planks, already rotting out, where practically anything was sold. The owner of the nearest one met them on the boarding plank and offered a hand to help Vera make her way along the narrow, slippery bridge.

The sergeant took off his kepi and wiped the beads of sweat gathering at his brow. The owner quickly poured a glass of beer for him and then waited to see if the young stranger would also join him.

She declined: she was so queasy, a glass of beer would be the last imaginable straw.

"Do you think I might have a guaraná?"

The man served her with a tall well-iced glass which he took out of the only appliance to denote the existence of an industrial civilization in this part of the universe: a white, brand-new freezer running quietly.

"Did you see a boy from out of town in this vicinity last night?"

"I closed pretty early last night—went to a relative's wedding," the storekeeper boasted.

The sergeant grumbled something to himself and emptied his glass.

It was then that Vera noticed the leatherbound notebook: a small, rather beat-up pad that Paulo always carried in the back pocket of his jeans. She picked it up reverently and opened it, recognizing at once the primary-school calligraphy that had always been the greatest humiliation to her journalist friend's ego.

"Whose is this?" she asked innocently, pretending not to know; but her heart was pounding as the owner of the store reached out to have a look.

"I don't know, miss. Some customer probably forgot it here."

"You've no recollection?" Vera persisted.

"I think it might have been somebody's from out of town," the merchant confirmed without seeming to trouble himself about his previous evasion.

"He's the one we're looking for," Vera commented in the most casual voice she could muster.

"But he left town already," explained the shop owner.

"That's not possible," Vera objected.

"No, he did, miss...he took a lift from a launch that was tied up here last night. And he was with another fellow."

"What fellow?" the sergeant interrupted.

"I don't know, some kid or other. How should I know?"

Vera cursed and tossed the notebook into the murky waters of the cove. The sergeant was about to thank the storekeeper when Vera interrupted.

"Do you know where they were headed?"

"I don't know, miss. It was a private launch."

"So you see, he did go away, ma'am. I told you as much. The poor fellow probably couldn't take any more of this place."

The sergeant had said this with the air of a mission completed.

Later that day, already aboard the Bandeirantes flight soaring peacefully above the Amazon River, visible beneath the fraying clouds, Vera Martins was attempting to assemble her thoughts. She had lost two days in Parintins, in utter futility, and Paulo had abandoned her without explanation. By the time the plane was preparing to land at the airport in Manaus, she no longer troubled herself about her friend's inconstancy, nor about those damned appearances of the so-called *Chupa-chupa*. She was in a hurry to finish her report and bill the Ministry of Agriculture for all her expenses.

Clutching her travel bag, Vera Martins entered the arrivals hall of Ponta Pelada Airport, where domestic flights had their own terminal although they shared the same runways with the Air Base. The airport itself was quite busy at that hour, and she paused to run an eye over the headlines of the papers racked in the newsstands. The subject was invariably the assumption by Brigadier General Fischer of the command of the Joint Chiefs of Staff of the Armed Forces of Brazil and his likely candidacy for the Presidency of the Republic. The brigadier general was to assume his new post on the following day, and every paper had recorded the fact in bold type, since it was the first time in years that the post would fall to an officer from the Air Force. But a few papers from Brasília likewise gave front-page coverage to the bizarre kidnapping of the director of public relations for the Moscow Circus, also suspected of being an agent of the KGB.

She walked hurriedly over to the taxi stand, to queue up for the trip back to her apartment and the reward of a good night's sleep. It was then that a young man wearing an unbuttoned shirt and a pair of Bermudas called her by name, motioning her to come over and join him in his office. The fellow was smiling affably and she had the impression of knowing him from somewhere, but this might have been merely the result of what were fairly common features.

Vera stepped into his office and, before she could even ask what the young stranger wanted from her, she suddenly heard a shot and everything went black.

WAR OF THE WORLDS

Classification: 01/06/M

FROM: Col. Alfredo Nunes e Silva
TO: Departmental Chief of Central Operations SNI

Brasília, August 26, 19...

Dear Sir:

The present report has been prepared at the request of General Alacir Pereira Bastos, the distinguished Commander-in-Chief of Amazonia, in order to chronicle on behalf of the National Service for Information the bizarre events that took place on the twenty-fifth day of the present month—the date of the assumption of the post of head of the Joint Chiefs of Staff of the Armed Forces by Brigadier General Bernardo Fischer—and which would appear to us to represent, as paradoxical as it may seem, explicit attempts on the part of certain occult forces to interfere with the process of democratic liberalization set into motion by the President of the Republic.

The enclosed evidence has been pieced together as a series of narratives. The resulting material contains considerable lapses, in addition to exhibiting at times an excessive degree of subjectivity—this from the fact that we have been obliged to examine the said events from the point of view of that of an indirect witness.

Should there be any further questions regarding the enclosed matter, we remain, of course, at your complete disposal.

Respectfully yours,

Col. Alfredo Nunes e Silva
Operational A/02

Report to the Department of Central Operations

Prepared by Col. Alfredo Nunes e Silva, A/02

Table of Contents

1. The Edge of Unreality
LOCALE: São Borja, Rio Grande do Sul
SOURCE: Seldom Reliable

The vicar of the Cathedral of São Borja, Father Noel Rezende, was celebrating the seven o'clock mass that morning when he was suddenly attacked, during his sermon, by something malevolent but invisible. The arms of the said vicar were twisted violently, behind his back, and his face became horribly contorted as if he were suffering terrible pains. At the same instant he was lifted into the air and hurled to the floor of the church, before the astonished eyes of a small gathering of the faithful.

The mass was suspended and the father carried hastily into the parish residence, where he was succored by a second priest and by two lay sisters from the Order of Earthly Pastures.

In the parish house, however, the thing manifested itself once more by throwing stones at the rooftop and scrawling slogans on the walls outside. The slogans, in red ink, repeated the familiar anti-Communist catchwords. At the same time that such events were occurring outside, the vicar suffered additional vigorous slaps in the face, which left marked abrasions on the flesh confirmed by a doctor through subsequent examination.

Father Noel Rezende has been a notorious figure in the progressive wing of the Catholic Church and has already provoked a number of disturbances to the public order with subversive intent.

We determined that Father Noel Rezende had also been under our surveillance since November of 1981, when he organized a march through the town to protest the ousting of the subversive Miracapilo. Our division in Rio Grande do Sul has already collected on file and on tape a series of objectionable sermons by the same Father Rezende impugning the honor of the Armed Forces and the dignity of the Commander in Chief of the Republic.

2. *Ritual in Botucatu*
LOCALE: Botucatu, São Paulo
SOURCE: Fairly reliable

Celina Matos and her husband, Roque Lane Matos, unemployed textile workers, came for assistance to the local Workmen's Compensation Office of the INPS, at five o'clock in the morning. For the past six months Celina had been suffering from some sort of illness and had tried, unsuccessfully, to obtain an appointment. On this particular morning when the couple arrived, they discovered a line already formed by some two hundred contributors.

Roque Lane thereupon drew a circle on the ground and began to intone some sort of devotional incantation. Celina lit a portable coal stove and initiated the burning of incense while wielding in the other hand a five-pointed star that she uplifted in a variety of directions in accordance with instructions from her husband.

Within a short time the spot was invaded by apparitions descending from the spiritual plane. Roque Lane thereupon commenced to plead with these entities that they assist his wife in her quest for an interview by bringing a doctor to that particular branch of the INPS. The spirits replied that they would do so provided the couple wait on that same line for a period of thirty days. The husband and wife accepted contentedly, because they were people of great patience.

Yet something went awry with the ritual and Roque Lane was the first to realize as much. There had been too many spiritual entities present at the site, a number in fact that far exceeded that which might have been expected from his prayers. The additional intruders suddenly began to invade the consecrated circle and a few of them even became visible to the other contributors standing patiently on line.

Celina, terribly frightened, threw herself to the ground and covered her face. Roque Lane, meanwhile, desperately recited the protective incantations, fearing at any moment an actual assault by the intrusive apparitions.

The body of Celina was discovered on the line by a television reporter. Her husband had disappeared. Doctors subsequently confirmed starvation as the *causa mortis* to the unfortunate Celina Matos.

3. Aliens Among Us
LOCALE: Angra dos Reis, Rio de Janeiro
SOURCE: Fairly reliable

Felisberto Ramos, a technician from Nuclebrás, was leaving the twelve o'clock shift at the Angra I nuclear reactor, heading for his residence in the city, driving a company-owned Volkswagen. He was not especially tired, because the shift had not been a very busy one; and he followed the highway with reasonable attention and no apparent physical discomfort.

When he was about ten kilometers from his house, he saw his fiancée Suzana Caldas walking by herself along the highway. Judging her behavior to be rather unusual, and annoyed with the recklessness of the act, he pulled over to the side of the highway and ordered her to get in the van, with a gentle reprimand.

The fiancée remained silent, as if bowing to the ill-timed outburst of her suitor, until suddenly she started sexually provoking him— something that was not her habit, decent girl that she was from a respectable family. At first, this only increased Felisberto's irritation, whereupon she augmented her techniques of seduction and he began to yield. After all, Suzana was a very beautiful girl with a stunning figure, and before he realized what was happening she had totally undressed and commenced to engage in activities he had never even suspected were possible.

Two hours later, Felisberto awakened by himself, half-undressed at the side of the road. Suzana had vanished with the company van, in which—by the merest chance—was stowed a sealed metal container filled with highly contaminated radioactive iridium. Felisberto managed to thumb a ride and to be driven directly to his fiancée's home—certain that she had decided for some reason to play a prank on him. But Suzana Caldas had never left the house that day, and had spent the entire morning in the kitchen with her mother. The van had obviously disappeared.

Felisberto Ramos lost his fiancée, and Nuclebrás continues to follow the efforts by state and local authorities to locate a missing Volkswagen van with its shipment of iridium.

4. Ships from Outer Space
LOCALE: Avenida República do Chile, Rio de Janeiro
SOURCE: Absolutely reliable

The president of the National Household Finance Bank, Mr. Marcos Loureiro de Guimarães, informed his principal advisers in strictest confidence that the data pertinent to their intervention in the affairs of the Golfinho Thrift and Loan Financial Group, as well as the documents establishing the illicit nature of the financial dealings of that same group, had disappeared from the memory bank of the computer—siphoned off by two spaceships of unidentified origin which had landed on the roof of the main office of the bank during the night of the 24th and morning of the 25th of the present month. The said spaceships, classified as of German origin—"kraut fireballs"—by the night watchman, had emitted a kind of spout that connected itself to the computer, thus erasing the above material from the memory of the data bank without the said maneuver's having any other effect upon the computer.

The original documents themselves, filed in the vault for safe-keeping at the accounting office, likewise vanished without any visible signs of a break-in.

The case against Golfinho Thrift and Loan was eventually dropped for lack of evidence.

5. *Hazy Residential Neighborhood*
LOCALE: Lago Sul, Brasília, DF
SOURCE: Absolutely reliable

The Minister of Planning left his residence in an official vehicle of the ministry—license plate no. MP-0008—which was often put to private use. In the vicinity of the Península Sul, the said vehicle and its occupants encountered a dense haze which the chauffeur decided to attempt to penetrate.

The minister, rather intrigued inasmuch as that type of fog was not a very common sight in Brasília, commented on the fact to the chauffeur. The latter replied that he suspected the haze might in fact be smoke from some sort of fire, perhaps even a forest fire somewhere far off from the Plano Piloto but carried there by prevailing winds. At that time of the year the scarcity of rain often provoked such incidents.

Minutes later, when the car emerged from the haze the minister realized that he was no longer in Brasília. Instead, they found themselves at 1000 Madison Avenue, in New York City, where he took advantage of the mysterious circumstances to sign a new letter of intention with the International Monetary Fund.

His Excellency returned by plane to Brasília, the following day.

His chauffeur is still interned at Bethesda Hospital in the Psychiatric Pavilion, with his condition diagnosed as psychosomatic catalepsy.

6. *Voices Recorded on a Tape*
LOCALE: São Félix do Araguaia, Goiás
SOURCE: Generally reliable

An agent and informer in the employ of this service, the farmer Rubião Gonçalo, had just finished taping a lengthy subversive assembly of peasants and homesteaders organized by the notorious Bishop Dom Pedro Casaldáliga in the sacristy of the diocese with the intent to perpetrate yet another of his anti-democratic, Communist-inspired plots.

Returning to his house, Rubião Gonçalo immediately sat down to play the tape for the purpose of recording the contents on paper, in accordance with the agent's manual of instructions. Whereupon he was shocked to discover that the tape had failed to record any part of the discussions, although he had thoroughly checked out all his equipment beforehand and was absolutely certain that his machine was not defective.

Eventually, to the great relief of this operative—one of our most competent agents in the area—the same tape was discovered to have registered faint murmurings, a succession of vague grunts and whisperings. Upon closer examination, it was discovered that the voice was actually the operative's own mother, recently deceased. The voice confided that she did not have much time to tell her son everything she would wish, but warned him to stay on the path of righteousness.

Rubião Gonçalo took a long vacation and was last seen inside a macumba tent on the outskirts of Salvador, in Bahia.

7. *Visit to a Subterranean World*
LOCALE: Carajás Project, Pará
SOURCE: Reliability yet to be ascertained

Yojimbo Nakashima, an engineer from the Akugatawa Mining Company engaged in geological exploration for the Carajás Projects, claims to have been led by two female Parakanā Indians to a species of underground kingdom. According to the Nipponese engineer, events unfolded as follows:

At the principal entrance the Indians removed his canvas hat.

At a second entrance the Indians took off his shirt.

At a third entrance the Indians removed his trousers.

At a fourth entrance the Indians took off his socks.

At a fifth entrance the Indians removed his watch.

At the sixth they removed his eyeglasses.

At the seventh door the Indians pulled down his shorts and he entered a luminous, vaulted passage that one of his female companions called: "Land Where Nothing Changes."

Yojimbo Nakashima is currently attempting to organize a religious sect at the site of the Carajás Project.

8. Tale from Beyond the Grave
LOCALE: Brasília, DF
SOURCE: Absolutely reliable

I still get chills up and down my spine whenever I think about it. This event happened to me, and I would not have believed it if I had not personally participated in the strange affair.

Two agents from the CIA showed me on a certain occasion several photographs of the kidnapping of a known KGB operative. This was during a meeting of the general staff of the MCA. The CIA agents were seeking identification of the two kidnappers photographed in the process of taking the Russian to a parked Volkswagen and, once surprised, making obscene gestures at the camera. I remained silent, but I recognized the two of them. They are dead. I am prepared to swear under oath to the fact.

One is Corporal Carlos Tobias, from the Military Police of Bahia. Corporal Tobias died of a drowning accident, off Itaparica, in 1978. The other is Lourival Ribeiro, a civilian but also an operative on the interrogation team from the DOI-CODI, in Rio de Janeiro, at least until 1974. A rich man, the son of a notorious Communist, he studied for several years in the Soviet Union, where he learned to speak Russian fluently. He died of electrocution, from a bolt of lightning that struck his apartment in Tijuca, in 1980.

But there they were—alive as can be—carrying off the Russian. The CIA took photographs, and photographs don't lie.

9. Enigmas from the Anavilhanas Islands
LOCALE: Anavilhanas Islands, Amazonia
SOURCE: Fairly reliable

The director of the Internal Revenue Office in Manaus, Mr. Antonio Bittencourt, is in the habit of going on fishing trips, accompanied by his friends, all along this conjunction of islands set in the middle of the Rio Negro, not very far from the Amazonian capital. On the 24th of this month, while stretching out his long weekend with a few local businessmen and two officers from the army, this same director of Internal Revenue had a rather bizarre experience.

From the outset of these excursions he had begun to notice the existence of a species of mirage, whenever his boat would approach one of those islands. The mirage offered the illusion of a wall of imposing skyscrapers, cathedrals and lights, as if there were a great metropolis on the island. A scientist eventually explained to him that this was merely the effect of the reflection of light projected by the city of Manaus.

Nevertheless, this particular night he was unable to sleep, thinking about it, when a huge yacht approached his own vessel. Supposing it might be some friends of his, Mr. Bittencourt made ready to receive the visitors on board. But the yacht floated past, apparently empty, and he himself was suddenly struck by a powerful beam of light that left him momentarily blinded.

Now, the same Mr. Bittencourt suffers from a compulsive desire to pass insiders' information on to his investor friends concerning any intended adjustments in the exchange rate of the dollar—something he stoically bears with a contrite heart. A doctor in the city, consulted surreptitiously, has diagnosed his condition as "Tourette" Syndrome.

10. Journey through Time
LOCALE: Esplanada dos Ministérios, Brasília, DF
SOURCE: Generally reliable

Upon his arrival at the office that morning, the Minister of Labor was surprised by strange noises and knockings emanating from his office desk. The sounds gradually became so insistent that he was forced to cancel the visit of a group of industrialists from the Northeast.

One of his advisors, who frequented certain mystico-religious circles that seemed to be springing up all over the Federal Capital, decided to attempt to enter into contact with the apparition purported to be provoking the noises—noises the advisor classified as the typical manifestation of a poltergeist.

Through a simple code—one knock on the desk meaning *yes;* two knocks, *no*—the advisor actually managed to communicate with the supposed entity. It proved to be the ghost of a union leader who had disappeared during the ill-fated Osasco strike, back in 1968, but who continued to attempt to participate in the labor politics of the government.

The remains of this union leader were eventually discovered by the police in the dead archives of the ministry—exactly where the spirit had told them to look. The Minister of Labor felt deeply moved by the deference shown by the ghost of the union leader in still seeking an audience with the proper authorities despite the fact that he no longer inhabited this vale of tears. It was proof positive of the proper management of a ministry.

11. Instances of Spontaneous Combustion
LOCALE: Rio de Janeiro, São Paulo, Belo Horizonte, Porto
              Alegre
SOURCE: Reliability yet to be ascertained

Testimony of one Adroaldo Costa, 55 years old, widower, owner
of a newsstand in Belo Horizonte, as related to the Department for
Political and Social Order—acronym: DOPS—in Minas Gerais:

"It was still before dawn when I arrived to open up my stand. The
air was brisk and all I was thinking about was the moment when the
cafe on the corner would open up so I could have a shot of brandy.
As the cold was beginning to get to me, I climbed inside the newsstand
and lay down, curled up on my piles of stock. I sell everything: papers
from the capital, papers from other states, and all the usual magazines
with a national circulation.

"I lay there for a while, checking the time occasionally. Soon the
delivery truck would be by to dump the bales of newspapers from
Rio and São Paulo. I think I must have dozed. When I woke up again,
it was to the smell of something burning; and the newsstand was filled
with smoke. I was terrified, but I still managed to push out the awning
in front. All the men's skin magazines, like *Playboy* and *Status*, and
others that were even more raunchy, were licked by flames. The
newspapers from the alternative press, such as *Pasquim* and *Tribuna
da Luta Operária* had also ignited.

"It was a tremendous loss. I didn't see anyone; the stand was
closed and there I was, inside. I don't know how it happened. I think
it was God's punishment."

Nearly identical accounts have been heard by various special de-
tectives in Rio, São Paulo and Porto Alegre, each time they have had
to take depositions from the proprietors of newsstands where subversive newspapers and pornographic magazines had been consumed
by spontaneous combustion.

12. A Ghost in the Barracks
LOCALE: Fort Príncipe da Beira,
                 Rondônia
SOURCE: Fairly reliable

The soldier Moacir Palhares was on guard duty, armed with a rifle, just at the entrance to the arsenal at Fort Príncipe da Beira. He was a peaceable young man with a good disposition who followed orders. He enjoyed all the confidence of his superior officers in that faraway outpost of the frontier.

On that particular day an unaccountable event was going to blemish his career forever. At nine A.M., as he was walking past the arsenal, a Lieutenant Colonel Paiva was shot at virtually point-blank range by Private Palhares and died on the spot. There was no sign of any altercation, nothing; the soldier had simply pointed his rifle and fired at the officer.

Immediately thereafter, as if overtaken by an acutely violent paranoia, Private Palhares went running through the outbuildings of the fortress, firing on everything that moved. He gravely wounded a Sergeant Pereira, shot out various windows, killed the regiment's mascot dog and finally committed suicide with a bullet through the heart.

While racing madly through the fort, he had repeatedly shouted that his orders had come from the deceased Marshal Castelo Branco. Apparently, the ghost of the fondly revered marshal—first President of the "Redemptive" Revolution of 1964—had appeared to him by the doorway of the arsenal and ordered him to institute a cleanup of the armed forces.

Two other privates, whose names have yet to be confirmed, as well as an unidentified female, had also seen the ghost of Marshal Humberto de Alencar Castelo Branco drifting through the same fort.

13. A Case of Warlocks
LOCALE: Guarulhos, São Paulo
SOURCE: Fairly reliable

A team of Reconnaissance Operatives "Tobias de Aguiar"—acronym: ROTA—were on routine patrol through the streets of Guarulhos when they spotted a suspicious-looking gathering in the vicinity of a bakery. There were actually three suspects, two of them black, one white, who immediately attempted to flee. The ROTA vehicle gave chase along an unpaved street, but the suspects escaped into a boat yard, forcing the officers to continue their pursuit on foot.

After several hours of an intense manhunt, these very capable officers from ROTA—viciously maligned by a press that has been thoroughly infiltrated by Communists—managed to surround the suspects in an abandoned house. But imagine their shock when, from inside the house, there emerged three enormous black mastiffs with bloodshot eyes and gleaming fangs to attack them. Horrified, with no other choice, they fired upon the savage dogs, which only were killed after some half an hour of gunfire. Two of the policemen were injured with leg bites, and the sergeant who had directed the operation suffered gluteal lacerations.

When reinforcements finally managed to break into the house, the suspects had vanished, and instead of finding the three mastiffs where they had fallen, the police came upon the bullet-riddled bodies of three warlocks.

The Committee for Justice and Peace, a subversive organization of the Archiocese of São Paulo, thereupon began distributing a flier whose purpose was to turn the people against the forces of law and order. The flier claimed the three deceased warlocks were simply innocent metallurgists with no criminal records.

14. Enigmatic Death of a Collaborator
LOCALE: Cascadura, Rio de Janeiro
SOURCE: Generally reliable

Ludovico Silveira, an employee of TELERJ, our agent and collaborator since 1980, was victim of a yet-to-be-explained fatality. Ludovico worked in maintenance at the phone company and was also responsible for wiretaps requested by our intelligence branch in Rio. Lately, however, he was also arranging a few private taps with a view to earning a little extra on the side to add to his daughter's dowry— she was about to be married.

Ludovico was attacked by two men, in his words "dressed like frogmen," in the lavatory of a bar in Cascadura. He had been having a few beers with some friends when, naturally enough, he felt the need to relieve himself. He had gotten up from the bar stool and walked to the lavatory where two figures suddenly materialized—he had not noticed anybody coming in behind him and obviously the enclosure was too small a one for anybody to pass unnoticed, not to mention anyone dressed as a diver.

One of the two then seized Ludovico, immobilizing him, while the other pulled down his trousers, rubbed a cotton swab with disinfectant on his buttocks and administered an injection. Then both of them immediately disappeared.

No one believed Ludovico Silveira, even when he arrived at the emergency room of the hospital where he was not attended and subsequently died of a pulmonary edema. Ludovico's wife confessed to Colonel Jorge Lopes, of our network in Rio, that those same men dressed as divers had approached her in the Disco Supermarket and made obscene proposals.

15. *The Enchanted Bookie*
LOCALE: Botafogo, Rio de Janeiro
SOURCE: Seldom reliable

Silvino Paixão, alias "The Spigot," a bookie for the illegal lottery rackets in Botafogo, received a strange visitor last year while fulfilling a promise on the steps of the Church of Nossa Senhora da Penha. It was a very "with-it" sixteen-year-old girl whom he ended up taking to a motel on Avenida Brasil, where they spent some unforgettable hours together.

Wishing to have some additional sessions with the sweet little number, "The Spigot" asked her for an address which, at first, she did not seem to want to divulge. But the arguments of love were more persuasive and she ended up giving in. It turns out that the address she gave him was of the cemetery in Caju, where "The Spigot" went to grave no. 1178, dug in October of 1982, housing the remains of a Francinete Suely da Silva, typing student and part-time "crooner" at the Chanticler Club, on Marechal Hermes, fatally shot twice in the head by her lover.

The bookie Paixão had nearly forgotten the bizarre incident when, on the 25th of this month, the deceased Suely appeared to him in a dream. The unfortunate soul pleaded with the bookmaker that if he would begin to contribute ten percent of the take from the daily lottery to the coffers of the right-wing ruling party, there in Rio, it would—she guaranteed—have the same effect for her soul as countless masses.

"The Spigot" has already begun making the said contributions.

16. Goalie for the All Stars
LOCALE: Flamengo clubroom, Rio de Janeiro
SOURCE: Absolutely reliable

Saulo Marques de Moura, medical student and goalie for the Flamengo Junior Division, is one of the most frequently mentioned athletes for the next all-star team to play in the World Cup match.

On the 25th of this month, Saulo woke up with his body covered by strange marks. The Flamengo physician examined him and concluded that it was merely some sort of dermatological inflammation. He ordered the athlete to be confined to his room.

Around midday Saulo was discovered by his teammates in a kneeling position but levitating about a meter off the floor, apparently in a trance. The marks on his body had turned into bleeding stigmata. Tuta, right end and a devout Catholic, immediately recognized the wounds of Jesus Christ.

Saulo Marques de Moura, according to the police blotter, was heavily involved in drug trafficking and had posed naked for the gay magazine *Adam*.

17. Teleportation
LOCALE: State line, between São Paulo and Minas Gerais
SOURCE: Fairly reliable

The highway patrol located a group of twenty-five children, all unclothed and half-starved, gathered at the side of the federal highway that marks the boundary between São Paulo and Minas Gerais.

Subsequent investigation revealed that the children were residents of the National Foundation for the Care of Minors—acronym: FUN-ABEM—in São Paulo, from where they had mysteriously vanished. The directors of the orphanage at first suspected that there might have been a massive flight from the institution, but they soon concluded that it was the result of something far stranger. The children eventually confided that they were already in bed that night when a very intense light suddenly filled the entire dormitory. No one attempted to react in any way, and in fact, the enigmatic light seemed to have hypnotized them all. An unknown force then drew them from their beds and they experienced something akin to flying. A sort of powerful wind, meanwhile, tore their clothes from their bodies.

When the highway patrol came upon them by sheer luck, they were obviously terrified. The light had abandoned them in the dark, distant locale without explanation.

18. Spatial Anthropology
LOCALE: Brasília, DF
SOURCE: Absolutely reliable

Colonel Helmut Zucchini, head of the Council for Research and Study at the National Indian Foundation—acronym: FUNAI—was one of the most brilliant graduates of the National Intelligence Institute and the ex-chief of security at United States Steel Company. He recently reported being sequestered by the crew members of a ship from outer space, while on a visit to the Xingo National Park.

The crew members—creatures of some sixty centimeters tall, dressed in green uniforms with a kind of triangular badge on the right shouders—took him inside their craft where they examined him carefully in a kind of flying laboratory. One of the tests taken was a sampling of his blood, resulting in the absolute verification of the colonel's Aryan identity.

Afterwards, the extraterrestrials passed on the methodology of this last test to Colonel Zucchini himself and he is currently making good use of it in the identification of the various indigenous populations.

By means of this technique, bequeathed to FUNAI by a civilization far superior to our own, Colonel Zucchini has already unmasked a number of hoaxes perpetrated by subversive priests from the Indian Missionary Council, along with Communist anthropologists.

One of the examples of its extraordinary success has been the discovery that the so-called Xuxuruku Indians, who were improperly inhabiting territories belonging to the Santa Sofia Reforestation Enterprise, Inc., in the north of Maranhão, and consequently producing enormous social tensions, turn out actually to be members of the Negro race—descendants of the fugitive slaves from the old sugar cane plantations.

19. *The Vampire of Curitiba*
LOCALE: Curitiba, Paraná
SOURCE: Fairly reliable

Terezinha Letão Schmidt, graduate in philosophy from Unisinos, Rio Grande do Sul, was appointed through competitive examination to work as a censor of public entertainment in the Department of Federal Police. According to the account of this diligent public servant, on the 25th of this month while her husband happened to be away visiting relatives, she was attacked in their apartment by a man measuring nearly two meters in height and muscular as a weightlifter.

This is what transpired, as related by the victim in her own words— duly expurgated in order not to give offense to morals or decency:

"I was in the arms of this adorable vampire who kept running his fingers over my throbbing. . . . My hands delicately surrendered to the damp body of the vampire. And when for the first time I touched his . . . it was already hard and pulsing with lust. It was a much larger . . . than my husband's. He mounted me and thrust his . . . into my . . . piercing like a hot arrow the most secret depths of my pleasure. His movements were fevered, revealing a supernatural anguish that left me begging for more and more and more! It was then that I felt the explosion of his . . . within my . . . followed by a spurting shot of . . . there in the depths of my. . . . When I thought that he was about to stop, he rolled me over on my stomach, parted my . . . and into my tight . . . forcibly inserted his. . . . I fainted from the agonizing pleasure, feeling the hot breath of the vampire on my neck. To say that I surrendered to the pleasure of it is to give you only the palest idea of . . ."

20. Another Instance of Teleportation
LOCALE: Shipyard of the Akutakawa Corporation, Rio de
          Janeiro
SOURCE: Absolutely reliable

Mr. Frederico Ponte, chief engineer of the Transport Division at
Petrobrás, reported that on the morning of the 25th of this month
while he was conducting a routine inspection of the Petrobrás terminal,
along the Rio docks, he witnessed with total astonishment the disappearance from before his very eyes of the tanker *Anaconda*. The
tanker was currently under lease to that authority and had been dam-
aged in a storm off the coast of Africa. As Mr. Ponte explained it
after piecing events together, the said oil tanker actually evaporated
from the spot with the entire crew on board, only to be found several
hours later in a shipyard of the Akutakawa Corporation, where it had
suddenly materialized before the startled eyes of a variety of witnesses.

The oil tanker was left at that location for repairs, even though
the normal process of competitive bidding for such services had not
taken place, due to the unaccountable phenomenon which continues
to defy explanation. The president of Petrobrás admitted that this was
not the first time that the inexplicable has plagued the goods and
services of that public authority.

TOP SECRET

Classification A1/01

DECREE FROM THE MINISTER IN CHIEF OF THE NATIONAL SERVICE FOR INFORMATION (SNI)

The Minister in Chief of the National Service for Information, General José Rebello de Roswell e Campos, in accordance with the legal authority invested in him, orders by the present administrative decree, which decree shall become effective as of the date of its publication in the *Diário Oficial da União*, that Colonel Alfredo Nunes e Silva shall be reassigned to duties on the General Staff of the Armed Forces and relieved of duties as an operative of A/02 at the disposal of this service.

Published and decreed.

Brasília, August 26, 19 . . .

Gen. R.I. José Rebello de Roswell e Campos

Minister in Chief of the SNI

To the Department of Central
Operations for immediate
implementation.

TELEX 103/000B
CECOEXGENERALSTAFF
MCAOFFICE
08/26/19 . . .

CONVEY DISMISSAL COL NUNES FROM INTELLIGENCE
FUNCTIONS STOP SAID OFFICER TO RECEIVE IMMEDI-
ATE REPEAT IMMEDIATE PSYCHIATRIC TREATMENT STOP
DANGEROUS STATE SCHIZOPHRENIA USUAL COMMU-
NITY PSYCHOLOGICAL STRESS STOP URGENT INTERN-
MENT IN MILITARY CLINIC MAXIMUM SECURITY STOP
ORDER TOTAL BLACKOUT INCLUDING IMMEDIATE FAM-
ILY STOP

> CORDIAL REGARDS
> BRIGADIER GENERAL FISCHER
> JOINT CHIEFS OF STAFF
> ARMED FORCES

END OF TELEX
ZZZZZZZZZZZZ

FORBIDDEN PLANET

STILL THAT SAME WEDNESDAY OF AUGUST 24

"Something on your mind, old boy?"

Father Wender was poised on the edge of the bank, dressed only in shorts and gripping the handle of his hoe, his bare chest bathed in sweat. Paulo Veronezzi continued to stare out at the murky brown river, lost in thought. He had arrived in Valéria the previous night and until now had not managed to talk to anybody. He felt cheated.

"I have to head back," he answered finally. "Too much to do."

"But you haven't seen anything yet."

Paulo shrugged. "Well, is there anything to see, Father?"

Wender set down his hoe and crouched beside the journalist.

"Your presence here is extremely important. For goodness sake, you're the first journalist to set foot in this community."

"When do you think I can leave for Parintins?"

"The moment you like, my son."

They sat there watching the river flow by. The deceptive calm of the Amazonian landscape had the effect of a spectacle that hypnotizes through its very monotony.

"Have you been here a long time, Father?"

"A fair bit," the priest replied, his blue eyes sparkling with humble pride. "It's a rather different place than where I was born."

"You seem to have adapted pretty well."

"At least I've tried. . . . They're a very simple people, very close to nature. What amazes me about life here on the Amazon is the uncommon religiosity of the people. A religiosity that's very different, say, from your Northeasterner. People here are less festive, more ritualistic. It's as if the grandeur of nature and Indian traditions had combined to create a stark, unaffected liturgy."

But Paulo Veronezzi was hardly interested in discussing theology.

He was still feeling guilty about his abrupt departure from Parintins and wondering what Vera might be doing in his absence, given his inexplicable disappearance. He had not even had the opportunity to leave her a message, some sign that he was all right and simply setting out for Valéria. After a futile hunt for the radio announcer Vera had told him about, he was on the point of returning to the hotel when he was suddenly approached by a boy on a bicycle.

"Mister, you want to know more about those lights?"

The boy looked frightened and had spoken in almost a whisper.

"Mister, if you do I can take you there."

He had hastened after the boy to the floating pier where a boat was waiting with a crew of three men. They were amiable-looking but, for some unknown reason, had insisted on leaving Parintins at once. If he should like to go with them as far as the community of Valéria, he would have to make up his mind to depart immediately. They had not time for him to return to his hotel or leave a message for Vera.

Paulo's curiosity got the better of him, however, and he had climbed aboard.

"Why didn't those men want to be seen in Parintins, Father?"

Wender smiled, his heavy peasant hands wiping the sweat from his head of straw-colored hair.

"They were frightened of the mayor. He's been bought off somehow and has forbidden them to return to Parintins."

"Bought off by whom?"

"Don't you know?"

"I don't know anything about it, Father."

"What time is it, my son?"

Paulo checked his watch, annoyed at the heat that only provoked further indolence, making it impossible to put one thought after another.

"It's eleven o'clock."

"Let's go back to the church. Everybody from town is to be there for a meeting to discuss these matters."

They got up, and the journalist ambled along beside the priest feeling worn-out. His shirt was bathed in perspiration and clung uncomfortably to his body. They entered the sacristy, and Wender took a knit shirt that was hanging from a nail and slipped it on. The majority of the peasants were already in the church and murmuring in hushed voices.

"I'd like to know one thing, Father. What was that Adventist pastor really like?"

Wender scratched his head hesitantly.

"It's difficult to talk about a brother of the faith."

"It's not his faith that interests me, Father."

"I know that he was murdered. He suffered a horrible end. May God grant him salvation."

"Rumor had it in Manaus that he was connected with the CIA."

The priest turned and stared straight into Paulo's eyes. A momentary hint of suspicion colored his expression, as if he were still wrestling with the idea of revealing to this reporter what he felt about the matter.

"Pastor Gary did not seem to be very versed in the Scriptures," he began. "For the first week or so after he arrived he was very cordial to me and seemed quite open and aboveboard. Then slowly he seemed to change, to the point of acting more recently like one of those insufferable fundamentalists."

"What do you think happened?"

"As I say, he didn't seem terribly familiar with the Scriptures, which is most peculiar for an Adventist pastor. I first noted his shortcomings during a conversation we were having at a party. Ever since, he was careful to avoid my company."

"He probably didn't want any more lessons in the Bible."

"I dare say. The worst of it, though, was the way he began attempting to arouse hostile feelings among his flock against the Catholic segment of the population. It made me worry, I tell you. What is basic to these people is a sense of fellowship and unity. The last pastor gave his full support to any efforts on behalf of the community, to whatever Pastoral gatherings we were able to organize among us. He always participated—debating, yes, but always in a spirit of solidarity. A true Christian. . . . I was very sorry to see him leave us when he took ill and had to return to the United States.

"Which was when this new pastor showed up?"

"He arrived a month after the other's departure. And within two weeks of his arrival, everything began to go sour: the community divided against itself, Pastoral efforts reduced to a handful of Catholics."

"Was that when you started having suspicions?"

"I began to have terrible doubts. He was so rudimentary in his attitudes of faith and he was spawning very divisive feelings among the community. I finally went to Parintins to make a few inquiries. What information I was able to obtain about him revealed a very foggy past with too many blanks."

"Where did you get your information?"

"I spoke with friends of the Church—one has to be very cautious. The Americans seem to fear us even more than they fear the Communists. The Rockefeller Report is very blunt about the Church's opting for the poor."

"So you don't really think this Gary fellow was a pastor at all, do you?"

"I don't think he was a true Christian. Whenever he went to Parintins, he would visit houses of ill repute. I heard this from a variety of people in the base communities. Perhaps it was only human frailty. We all have our failings, but there was much that was odd about his behavior. He had what must have been extremely expensive videotape equipment, for example. He went around filming almost everything."

"Even the *Chupa-chupa?*"

Wender nodded silently, to confirm the fact.

"What actually troubled me wasn't so much that, nor even the fact of his frequenting prostitutes. What disturbed me was the kind of disruptive behavior he manifested here in the community."

The priest shook his head to himself and then proceeded to the Church, followed by the reporter.

"It's time to get our meeting under way," Wender explained to excuse his sudden haste.

The benches in the tiny church were nearly all taken by the farmers and their families. They stopped talking the moment they noticed the priest enter, along with the stranger. Wender went straight to the altar, kneeled, then began to offer a prayer aloud as a kind of invocation for the meeting to follow. Paulo, meanwhile, went to find a place on one of benches, among the gathering.

Wender stepped down from the altar and pulled a stool up in front of his flock.

"I want to introduce you all," he said, at the same time signaling the journalist to stand up, "to a friend who is here to visit with us today. Paulo Veronezzi is a reporter from the magazine *Isto É*. He is going to do us a great service by publicizing our struggle and denouncing the problems we face here to the entire nation."

Paulo stared awkwardly at the peasants. What the devil was going on? What in the world was he doing standing there in the midst of some peasants' rally out in the Amazon jungle? And why was this fool Wender so ridiculously exaggerating his position as a journalist?

One of the younger peasants among the group stood up to talk.

"My name is Pedro. I'm a farm worker. I live here in the community," he said, directing his speech to the embarrassed reporter.

Wender noticed that Paulo was still on his feet and motioned him to sit down. Obviously the poor fellow had never taken part in a popular assembly before.

"I will try to explain a little about our situation," Pedro continued, "so that our brother here can begin to understand what has been happening in Valéria. If he or any other of you don't follow something, just speak out and I will try to clear up any doubts."

The gathering murmured approval.

"Our community has confronted a great number of problems lately," he began. "We are all landowners, here. Our ancestors, the first to arrive in this place, did not trouble themselves with titles and deeds in order to register their holdings—they worked the land, and lived all around here without any trouble. But now things have begun to get complicated for us. First came the fishing boats which started motoring about the lakes that we had always fished and soon destroyed everything spawned there, depriving us of our basic source of food. These boats would let out a fine fishnet across the lake and drag out everything at once. Sometimes they would catch a school of *branquinha,* but then come upon a school of *jaraqui* and dump their first catch back into the lake, squandering God's bounty. The waters were awash with their rotting carcasses, a pitiful sight. We started to organize our community with the help and encouragement of Father Wender. We sent a committee to Parintins to ask the mayor to institute protective measures against such boats, but he did nothing. He simply told us that matter did not fall within his jurisdiction but rather lay within that of the federal IBDF and SUDEPE. So we drew up a letter and sent two representatives to Manaus to meet with the respective forest and fish-and-game agencies. But again we got nowhere, since these agencies are filled with people who simply talk a lot and do nothing. Since the fishing boats continued to despoil the lake, we organized an activist group to take matters into our own hands. We closed the mouth of the lake and kept watch until the next fishing boat appeared. We ordered the boat to go back, but its crew simply laughed in our faces and proceeded to cast their nets. At that point, we boarded the vessel from canoes and, armed with shotguns, cut their nets loose. Afterwards, we let them leave. They returned once more, with an official from the IBDF to tell us that we were breaking the law since the nets were private property, and that the agency would be forced to call in the police if we didn't stop immediately from molesting fair competition. But none of us were frightened by all that talk and they left the lake in peace."

"They never showed up again?" Pedro asked.

"No, brother, they didn't. And we thought that the matter had ended and we could relax finally. But the beginning of this year, some Japanese engineers arrived and told us they were here on orders from the government with a contract for oil exploration. They showed us a pile of documents. At first we tried to welcome them, but then things began to heat up. These Japanese insisted that we would have to leave here because the land had been granted to them. They promised to pay us some kind of indemnification for our crops and our homes, but they told us they could only give us till the end of August— this month, brother—to clear out for good. We held a meeting of the whole community and voted not to leave, but rather to legally challenge the Japanese assertions. Father Wender actually traveled to Manaus for us and took the matter to court with a plea of *usucapion*, but the court denied his plea. The judge claimed that the land had already been deeded to the Japanese firm in a risk contract and there was nothing more to be done. It was then that these mysterious lights began to appear, frightening everybody. The Adventist pastor warned us that we should not go against the government because that was the same as going against Jesus's teachings. But we are too attached to this place to leave—we were born here, although everybody is scared to death of the *Chupa-chupa*, which comes at night to give terrible electric shocks to people."

"Have you actually gotten close enough to see the *Chupa-chupa* yourself?"

"Thank God, no. I've only seen it from a distance. But there are others here who have."

At this point a middle-aged but still strong-looking peasant with straight black hair stood up.

"My name is Carlos. I'm also a farmer who lives here in the community. I've seen the *Chupa-chupa* myself from a distance, when that huge fire burned its way across the river. But last week it attacked my youngest son, nearly sinking the canoe he was in at the time."

"Almost everybody here has seen what they call the *Chupa-chupa* at one time or other," the priest observed.

"And what about you," the reporter asked. "Have you seen it?"

"The *Chupa-chupa* seems pretty canny about which people to choose. I never happen to be around when it decides to put in another appearance. I've even tried to keep vigil; I've done it for nights on end, waiting and waiting; and nothing. I no longer lose sleep on that account."

"So you all think it has something to do with the Japanese?"

The same Carlos hastened to answer.

"It's the only thing that it could be. Before they came, nothing like this ever happened here. It was when that company began telling us the land belonged to them that this crazy light started showing up as well."

"It is a curious coincidence, isn't it?" the priest concurred.

"This business originates right here in Valéria, and it's being done to frighten us off. When we sent that committee to ask the mayor for help, some of the members refused to even return here because they were so terrified. They abandoned their holdings and went off to find a new life elsewhere. That's what this Japanese company wants: to have us give up our land."

The idea was convincing enough, the reporter reflected. A flying light that can somehow give electric shocks to ingenuous peasants might just be the perfect tactic to clear out the whole area. But the peasants from Valéria weren't proving quite so ingenuous. They had organized to look after themselves and refused to be intimidated so easily. What would be the final end of all this?

"What does this light-thing look like?" Paulo asked aloud.

"It's like a ball of fire," Carlos answered. "Sometimes two or three of them come together."

The priest was beginning to get impatient, seeing how the reporters were becoming more interested in the *Chupa-chupa* than in the problem of his community.

"The *Chupa-chupa* is hardly the most important issue," he interrupted. "It's real, of course, but not terribly mysterious for all that. It obviously appears to receptive people, those who are truly desperate, without even sufficient food to eat. The wretched circumstances of most people here make it easy for them to 'see' things or for someone to arrange it so they do. If you were ever to undergo half the hunger that many of these people endure, you would be wandering about with worse visions than the *Chupa-chupa*, I can tell you."

"But if it really is a trick of the Japanese to get these people off the land, I have an idea they'll be changing their tactics before long. The *Chupa-chupa* hardly seems to be producing the desired effect."

"Thanks to our organization," Pedro confirmed. "If enough people get together, they can face the Devil himself, God forgive me."

"And the Adventist pastor? What were the circumstances of his disappearance?"

A silence descended upon the gathering. People's memory of the pastor was still quite vivid and there was no wish to revive the torment of families split apart over the fundamentalism he espoused.

"You must understand, brother, that it is forbidden to any one of us to even enter the area where the Japanese are working. The Pastor Gary dared to do so, attempting to film their activities. He came back out of there with no problem, but vanished that same night and was never seen alive again."

"Where did he disappear from?"

"From his home. He had eaten dinner and was listening to the radio until about eleven. Then he went to bed apparently, but the next morning the bed was the only place that was still in any order."

"And the rest of the house?"

"Turned upside down. And his camera equipment was gone."

"And it was an eerie night," Carlos added. "The *Chupa-chupa* was sighted about ten times, causing quite a stir."

"Have any of you seen what kind of work the Japanese are engaged in?"

The response was negative, but it was clear that the mere mention of the Japanese brought fear to the entire gathering.

"They explode bombs out there," Pedro explained.

"The noise is tremendous—no one goes near the place," Carlos continued. "Our biggest fear is that they will decide to drop the bombs on us if the *Chupa-chupa* doesn't accomplish the job."

The gathering withdrew into silence once again, a pall descending upon the whole climate of the meeting, producing an atmosphere dank with sweat and terror.

Even later, after the meeting had drawn to a close and he was having lunch with Father Wender, Paulo Veronezzi was still intrigued by at least one question that came to mind over this grisly affair. If the priest had obtained his information about the American pastor through the channels of the Church, why had he not made use of those same channels to denounce the present situation?

"I can imagine what you must be thinking," the priest interrupted, reading his thoughts. "You must realize, however, that I have no concrete proof that these lights are being produced by the Japanese. The only certainty is the inevitable expulsion of these people from their own lands. And unfortunately, the problem and its exposure must pass through the diocese of Parintins, where we have a conservative bishop of the old school of faith who has done everything possible to curtail my efforts here in Valéria."

"So you need the help of the press. . . ."

"Exactly! Once we found out that you were in Parintins, our hopes were suddenly revived. A magazine like *Isto É* is not the same as some small press from Manaus entirely in the hands of huge enterprises operating in the area. There have been journalists here from the state capital in droves, but none of them have done anything. Those papers are not about to tackle some enterprise that takes out full-page advertisements boasting of the progress they're bringing to the Amazon."

Paulo's thoughts suddenly returned to Vera Martins and the need to get in touch with her finally. She was a very nervous woman and he had no idea how she might behave in the face of his inexplicable disappearance. At the same time, he had to help these people somehow, just as she had tried to tell him. He had yet to decide whether the subject was a viable one for the magazine. Certainly the alternative press was no option, given the rapid decline of its market over the last few years, depriving such subjects of the only space available in the complicated editorial process of the politics of democratization.

"I know it won't be easy, my son," the priest acknowledged.

A lot more difficult, Paulo mused, will be explaining his disappearance to Vera Martins.

Meanwhile, Thirty Kilometers Outside of Brasília

The meditation room reeked of the smell of an unwashed body because it had become Pavel Aksentyevich's prison cell in which he slept, ate, and reflected upon his solitude. No one had permission to say a word to him. The waiter entered and exited mutely with his trays and two men appeared now and then to sweep the floor and remove the garbage without so much as a glance at the prisoner.

So far, the Russian had been unable to fathom the interest which the head of this sect of fanatics seemed to nurture in his regard. But the possibilities were not too encouraging.

The door opened and Brigadier General Fischer walked in, full of his habitual tics and breathing asthmatically. The old creep was dressed in his field jacket with a revolver in his belt and his face seemed flushed with excitement.

"I expect our illustrious guest has been treated in decent fashion?"

The Russian did not bother to reply, behaving somnolently, with that vacant air of a prisoner who has accepted his fate. His slender fingers toyed absently with the wrinkled lapels of his jacket.

"We have managed to bag a precious prize," announced the brigadier. "It is sad to think that we shall have to rid ourselves of him."

Pavel shrugged indifferently.

"Well, you're in all the papers, my friend: congratulations!"

The Russian suddenly felt a chill. At this stage the embassy people must be hopping mad, just dreaming of the opportunity of taking him by the neck and making him pay dearly for such carelessness.

"You're not even going to thank me?"

A crystal vase rose into the air and went crashing to the floor.

"Is that the way for a Communist to show his appreciation?"

The brigadier general drew his revolver and fired. The bullet whistled past the Russian's head and ripped through the back of the sofa, exposing stuffing and metal spring.

Pavel's face went white and his body stiffened.

"I know one way to make things levitate," the general warned.

He returned the weapon to its holster and, with a suddenly more amiable expression, went over and sat beside the prisoner still frozen in shock.

"In another two days this country will be ready to enter the next millennium."

Little by little, Pavel Aksentyevich relaxed again but was determined to pay no further attention to this crazed officer.

"This has to be a nightmare," Pavel said to himself aloud.

The general gave him a few encouraging pats on the shoulder.

"What is this, comrade Aksentyevich? Losing hope? That's supposed to be the weakness of materialists, giving up so easily."

"What the hell kind of country is this!"

"Now you're not being very original, my dear comrade."

"What you're attempting is madness. There isn't the least social foundation for such a transformation."

"We shall see about that."

"The United States will never permit it in any case. You'll find yourself surrounded by U.S. Marines the moment you attempt it."

"The America of today is a demoralized nation. They've allowed themselves to swallow the subliminal propaganda of you Soviets. They've been reduced to total decadence by drugs and pornography."

"But they still have lots of money—and soldiers."

"I too have soldiers—and money."

His sickly breathing grew more rapid and his eyes seemed about to leap from their orbits as his hands fluttered in the air.

"I have remained a faithful signatory to the Protocol for Survival. Many of those who signed have since betrayed, letting perversion of one sort or another take hold, but there are still those of us who remain firmly committed to its articles of faith."

"Pinochet, for example?"

"He happens to be one of my most devoted followers. He was Attila, lord of the Huns, in a previous incarnation. He has returned to us to redeem himself and to raise his Karma. In the past he was representative of the barbarous Asiatic hordes that nearly destroyed our superior Occidental civilization. But this time he has come to redress the balance, to command the front line of invasion in the war against the barbarous Asiatic materialism that wishes to dominate the world. This is the true significance of the Third Millennium: the final victory of our glorious civilization against a Communist atavism."

"In my country they would have already had you put away."

"They might have here as well. That's precisely how our sickly democracy defends itself, crippling those who would bring enlightenment."

The idiotic conversation was beginning to tire the Russian. He would have a thousand times preferred the discourse of any political commissar in praise of the growth in production of sugarbeets on some *kolkhoz* to sitting there being forced to listen to the imbecile theories of his captor.

"I think you should listen rather carefully to what I'm saying, comrade."

Pavel Aksentyevich closed his eyes and sighed wearily.

"I've managed to gather an excellent group of acolytes," the brigadier continued incessantly. "All them wholly faithful to the principles of Sylyon. Some have already traveled to Chile and Uruguay to offer courses of instruction and propagate the faith."

"What is the Protocol for Survival?" the Russian asked with burgeoning interest.

"You are not permitted to know that, comrade," the brigadier general replied with a perverse intonation.

The hum of the air conditioner weighed heavily upon the room's silence.

Brigadier General Bernardo Fischer recalled to himself that hotel back in Punta del Este, from those fondly recollected days of 1972. Winter had emptied the beaches of the crowds of tourists, and only a few sober-looking men in formal attire—charcoal gray jackets and dark ties—populated the corridors and restaurant of the hotel. They were the military chieftains of nearly every country in Latin America—powerful men, responsible for some of the most profound political transformations their countries had ever experienced. And all of them were united by a single preoccupation: the inroads of Communist subversion throughout the entire continent, an advance that had been regarded with negligence, at times the connivance of politicians and even a few industrialists, not to mention ample sectors of the intellectual world and of the Catholic Church.

In a conference room carefully screened for security, they gathered to debate, deliberate, exchange ideas and establish programs. There was General Juan Moreno, head of the Joint Chiefs of Staff in Argentina and responsible for the liquidation of a recent Communist uprising in the city of Córdoba. There was Colonel Garcilaso Aguillera, Commander in Chief of the National Guard in Nicaragua, heroically combatting the criminal subversion of notorious Communists in the pay of a Castroite Havana. Many other names equally expressive of the crusade against Communism could be found on the roster of those listening with absorption to all the discussions: men like General Pilar Mexa, from Ecuador, president of the Latin American Anti-Communist League, or like the representative of the government-in-exile of Cuba, Captain Demetrio Simpson, his legs paralyzed by the terrible tortures he had suffered at the hands of Fidel's jackals.

And the meeting had not been in vain. The idea of a protocol was quickly and unanimously approved. They were already too habituated, as military men, to being the butt of the inconstancy of politicians. For the time being they might be the heroic saviors of the threatened fatherland, yet once order was restored and tranquility reestablished, voices would arise to accuse them once again of being criminals, torturers, enemies of human rights—it was the same old story. In order to avoid such repetitions, the protocol was drawn up and signed, assuring that whoever might be threatened by any new wave of irresponsible liberalism would receive the ready assistance of the remaining signatories.

Four years later in the United States of America, there arose to the seat of power a vacillating peanut planter. His reckless politics of the defense of human rights—even for subversives—shook the confidence of the hemisphere and led Latin America's northern neighbor down the path of total demoralization. In many countries across the Americas, the locusts of liberalism returned to ravage institutions and one was forced to witness various individual signatories to the Protocol suddenly beating their breasts and intoning professions of democratic faith. Even some who had been known for the diligence with which they frequented the interrogation chambers were seen to condemn what they called lowly, criminal elements.

And the results were everywhere apparent: countries like Brazil heading down the road to Communism; instability in countries like Peru, Venezuela, Colombia; scandalously Castroite governments in Nicaragua and in the Republics of Guayana and Suriname; revolutionary war in El Salvador, Honduras and Guatemala. In the midst of this apocalyptic tableau stood only the unassailable rock of Chile, and the power of Sylyon, invoking the right to set into motion the Protocol for Survival.

"You are still quite naive, brother Aksentyevich."

"I am a citizen of the Soviet Union."

"And an agent of the KGB."

"What do you want me for?"

"Nothing against regulations, I assure you."

"I hope you won't endanger my health—I've a very sensitive constitution."

"No need to worry, as I've already told you."

If he did not exercise the utmost care in his choice of an explanation with sufficient substance to placate his superiors, Pavel Aksentyevich felt certain that the wiser alternative would be to adhere to the sect of Brigadier General Fischer. Pavel's own wife was not the most agreeable sort of creature and he could not count on his brother-in-law to lift a finger on his behalf. If there was to be any possibility of coming out of this bizarre affair alive, then the best course was to manage some very concrete proof, some incontestable bit of evidence to the effect that the insanity of Brazil had the potential of affecting world order.

"Come with me," the general ordered.

The Russian followed him with all of his senses on the alert. A pale light illumined the corridor until suddenly his eyes felt the blinding intensity of sunlight. The sky, very clear and very blue, without a cloud, disoriented him completely. He had lost all notion of time, and the circular space of the amphitheater, with its immense statue of Sylyon overshadowing the lines of the faithful, kilometers long, left him vacantly serene, with a sense of inertia that threatened his very consciousness.

The numbers of people and the silence disturbed him. At the end of each spoke of the amphitheater, dressed in a long pale blue toga and seated upon a cement throne, was a consecrated medium who cured or at least mitigated the sufferings of the credulous masses lining up each day with millions in gifts, seeking hope and a rationale for their existence.

The Russian began to fight off the lassitude of his days of confinement, allowing the grandeur of the spectacle to distract him from further temptation toward unreality.

"I would give anything not to be here," said Fischer.

Pavel turned to the general and was astonished: instead of at a soldier in fatigues, he found himself peering at a slender, aged figure dressed in black, his face made up with a thin covering of plastic mascara that made him seem like an actor of some Japanese Kabuki theater.

"What?" stammered the Russian.

"My real dream was to have been in the cavalry," Fischer explained, "but I've always been afraid of horses. I can never relate well to animals: dogs spring at me to bite, and horses—"

"Yes, what about them?"

"Horses are extremely sensitive creatures—almost spirits like those of our own Karma. They bolt whenever I approach. I can't even visit the President of the Republic without creating problems."

"The President?"

"Yes, he adores horses and seems to have some secret link to the beasts. He also gets nervous whenever I approach him. He has actually forbidden me—discreetly, of course—to visit his Granja do Torto ranch, though he spends most of his time there and has ministers and friends over for the weekend. But the last time I was there I provoked a positive panic among his thoroughbreds."

"Well, I never liked horses either," Pavel confessed. "There are a few rather odious trained horses in the Moscow Circus. They've learned to dance to the musical strains of the 'Internationale,' and the number seems to me to smack of dissidence. The trainer is a Ukrainian Jew."

"At the same time I can't complain too much about this problem I have with animals. It turns out to have catapulted me into the most modern branch of military service: the Air Force. At least in this branch I haven't run up against the aristocratic vices of the Navy or the feudal traditionalism of the Army."

"Yes, it was the Argentine Air Force that played a crucial role in the Malvinas War," the Russian acknowledged.

"We could blitz London if we wanted to—we have the necessary resources to do it. I examined personally the Vulcan bomber that our fighters intercepted; it's an obsolete weapon. Our equipment is far more sophisticated."

"How, for example?"

"Atomic-powered flying saucers."

The Russian laughed, imagining that Fischer was joking.

"You don't believe me, eh? You have the idea only you or the Americans are capable of weapons research?"

Pavel decided to keep his mouth shut.

"Let's continue our walk," the brigadier ordered him politely.

They strolled through the midst of throngs of people, heading toward a collection of low buildings just beyond the steps of the amphitheater. It was a veritable patio of miracles, the whole panoply: people on stretchers, in wheelchairs, assisted by family members, from every racial group and socioeconomic condition. Brazil was an incredible country, Pavel reflected.

"You see that woman over there?" Fischer resumed, pointing a finger.

The Russian observed a well-dressed woman of middle age, in dark glasses and heavy mascara.

"She's the wife of the president of the Ford company here in Brazil. She comes every month to seek the advice of our mediums."

They finally made their way to the section of low buildings, after many pauses in the midst of the crowds. Mediums came up to kiss the hand of the Master. There were the faithful trying just to touch the hem of his clothes and women kneeling in his path so that he might bless them like some holy bishop.

"Here is our center for spiritual ascendance, Sylyon's school for the illuminated."

The entrance plaza was jammed with adolescents, and Pavel Aksentyevich began to perceive that Sylyon had little taste for females.

"Are there no women studying here?"

Fischer paused and took the Russian by the arm.

"Sylyon is all: female and male. He is the beginning and the complete cycle."

Pavel felt a trajectory of pain surge through his arm, emanating precisely from the point where the general's fingers had locked upon him.

"Sylyon has chosen men to serve him here on Earth. It is in homage to the principles of evolution. As you no doubt know, the masculine sex has evolved merely to satisfy natural selection—it is the expendable sex and, for that very reason, the more developed one."

Still in the grip of the painful pressure on his arm, the Russian was led to an elevator and thereafter through a series of empty rooms to a perfectly normal-looking office with busy typists and clerks poring over bureaucratic papers. Everyone stood up to greet the Master and then sat back down to his work.

"Our administrative center . . . Here we have at hand more than fifty million addresses of the faithful, scattered across the nation and spreading as far as Chile and Uruguay."

Pavel was unable to focus clearly upon his surroundings, as the pain in his arm grew nearly unbearable.

"Sit here," Fischer told him, thrusting him into a chair.

He found himself before an executive desk filled with books and papers. The brigadier general took his own place in the large, stuffed revolving chair that was on the other side of the desk.

Relieved finally of the pain, the Russian scanned his surroundings. There was nothing exceptional about them; he seemed to be in an ordinary public administrative office with merely a notably excessive preoccupation regarding fire prevention. But there on the desk in front of him, his trained eyes suddenly encountered an amazing document. It was a map of South America with specific sites marked. At first he imagined the sites to be nothing more than the locations of branches of the sect; but upon reading the text he felt a strange emotion take hold of his senses. The map indicated the various sites of secret, small-sized atomic energy plants for the separation of plutonium from pure uranium. Each of those reactors could produce a few precious grams of the least expensive material involved in the production of an atomic bomb. Just within Brazil itself, Pavel Aksentyevich counted fifteen reactors. Two of them were located right here in the Valley of the Seven Moons.

At a Private Prison Cell, Somewhere in Manaus

General Pessoa was crouching at one end of his cell, breathing like a cornered animal. The heat was unbearable, even though they had taken nearly all his clothes from him, leaving him only in his undershorts. The total absence of windows, plus the small door with a nearly perfect seal—like a freezer—prevented him from entertaining any notion as to how long he had been there or whether it was day or night. Yet, those were hardly his major preoccupations at the moment. A maddening headache together with a bodily sluggishness provoked by the high temperature obliged him to struggle against both somnolence and a feeling of faintness. He knew that if he should give in to the temptation to sleep, hypnotically powerful as it was, he might very well lose his way down a path of no return. In this circumstance of physical depletion to which he found himself now subjected, together with exposure to the implacable temperatures, to fall asleep would be simply a prelude to comatosis—not to mention death itself. And General Pessoa had no wish to die.

He was familiar with this kind of torture. His instructors at Fort Bragg had called it an invention of the English: a method that left no visible traces of physical violence on the body of the prisoner and the goal of which was to reduce the victim to a vegetable state, stripped of any will. The English method, however, had seldom achieved popularity in Brazil, where it was generally considered to be too soft to be used against the subversive scum of the earth, as well as unnecessarily time-consuming. If political prisoners were not subjected to something on the level of a human meat-grinder, then arrest seemed hardly worth the effort to the powers that be.

The fact of this method's being employed in his case was a clear sign that they merely wished to humiliate him. Had the purpose of the kidnapping been to obtain any information, they would have already hung him upside down from a "parrot's perch" and administered enough electric shocks to light a lamp by merely inserting the plug into his nostrils. From the moment he came to his senses, he had been trying to evaluate his plight. He had yet to be interrogated, and the pattern of behavior on the part of his captors recalled the antiquated methods of the seventies. A sense of total impunity, as well as the arrogance of connections to high places, was evident in the comportment of both those men on the motorcycle and even in that of the driver of the car. Besides which—and this really intrigued him—his abductors had felt no compunction about apprehending him on a public thoroughfare in broad daylight nor about assassinating a high official of the army in the process—and an officer from the intelligence community at that, which was rather astonishing.

The last thing he recollected was the agglomeration of the curious around the body of Captain Cruz and a vision of the police running toward the scene of the crime. If, in fact, the police themselves—at least those policemen—did not actually have a hand in the operation. His kidnappers were somehow familiar to him, with recognizable faces and gestures, but he could not pinpoint where he had seen them before. The entire action of the abduction passed through his head with the same moldy impression of a *déjà vu*. Until his thoughts were suddenly interrupted by the dry click of a door being unlocked. It startled him, and he scrambled to his feet, leaning against the humid wall to ward off the sudden vertigo that blurred his vision and quickened the beating of his heart. His vision, however, swiftly adjusted to normal.

Two men shoved a handcuffed girl into his cell. They were the same two who had overtaken him on the motorcycle, but now they were dressed in suits and ties; and perhaps because they had washed and shaved, they looked more distinguished and less aggressive. They removed the handcuffs and hurriedly exited, locking the door once again behind them.

The two prisoners stood immobile, indecisive, without exactly knowing what should be done next. It was General Pessoa who, remembering his state of undress, took the initiative to break the impasse.

"Kindly excuse my state of dress," he said blushingly as he instinctively lowered a hand in a gesture of modesty.

The girl herself was hardly in a condition to go out into the street with impunity, since she was entirely naked. She stood there with one arm across her breasts, and with the other attempted to conceal her dark pubic hairs.

"Where are we?" she managed to plead.

"In a prison, I imagine," the general replied.

The girl's eyes were deeply bloodshot, as if she had been crying for a considerable time, but there were no visible signs of violence on her body to indicate that her captors had molested her in any way.

The first inference to be drawn by General Pessoa from the presence of the girl in his cell was that he had been mistaken in his original suppositions. This was no English system of torture, nor were his captors trying to break him psychologically. The prisoner must be kept in total isolation, without companions—especially female companions—for the method to take effect.

Yet the certainty that he was not being subjected to English methods offered him no advantage. And the presence of a female prisoner—aside from breaking the norm, she was completely nude—left him totally ill at ease. Nearly to the point of causing him to wish for isolation and its more concrete menaces . . . a feeling that seemed to be shared by the young prisoner before him.

"Have you been locked away here for very long?"

"I don't know, child. I've lost all notion of time."

Although naked, the girl was wet with perspiration.

"I don't feel very good," she managed to say before dropping to her knees and falling into a swoon.

The general raced to her side and managed to prevent her from hitting her head on the concrete floor. He began to examine the girl, and his concern turned into a realization of what a lovely woman she really was. He smacked her cheeks gently, attempting to revive her. The girl responded vaguely; the blood commenced to flow more vigorously through her livid cheeks and her eyelids fluttered to life as if still under the effects of some soporific.

"Feeling a little better?"

The girl could not get beyond moaning incomprehensibly. She stared at the general as if imploring him to explain what was happening to her. Pessoa shifted her body to a more comfortable position, resting her head upon his thigh. She was breathing more easily now, and more vigorously, an indication that her condition was not too grave for the moment.

They remained in that position for a time, which grew long and fatiguing for the general. Their captors, meanwhile, gave no additional sign of their existence and had yet to bring them food or even water. The girl awoke finally, with lips dry and chafed and her face swollen from sleep. She stared up at the general without expression, but Pessoa's experience told him she was probably suffering from that pathetic fear common to prisoners who have fallen unexpectedly into confinement.

"Have you been kept here very long? . . . Who are those men? . . . What do they want?"

Pessoa lifted a hand as if to put a halt to her questions and to indicate his lack of any certain answers.

"I'll try to answer your questions as best I can, one at a time," he told her.

"Forgive me," she answered, timid and defenseless. "My name is Vera, Vera Martins, and yours?"

"My friends call me Pessoa."

"Pessoa?"

"That's right, I'm a retired general from the army, Vera."

"My God, you're a general? Then what are you doing here?"

"The same as you, I imagine."

"They picked me up at the Ponta Pelada Airport."

"That's funny," the general remarked, "I was abducted while on my way to that same airport, expecting to fly to Parintins."

"Parintins! What were you going to do in Parintins?"

"Do you know Parintins, child?"

"I was just coming back from there when they picked me up."

"Do you work for the government?"

"I have a job in the Ministry of Agriculture."

"Were you on any special assignment for that ministry, in Parintins?"

"I spent six months there," she confessed, eyeing him dubiously— unsure as to whether she should confide in the old general what her purpose had been in returning to that little town on the lower Amazon.

"Well, that's where I was headed when I was taken from my car."

"On your way to Parintins . . ." she reflected.

"That's right, child, and I'm beginning to think that these people have some objection to our familiarity with that town."

Vera said nothing more. She still could not make up her mind as to whether to trust this blue-eyed general who regarded her with such paternal concern. But she had to admit that her cellmate somehow inspired her confidence.

"I wanted to visit the locale where some UFOs had been sighted recently—what the locals were calling the *Chupa-chupa,*" Pessoa confided with complete equanimity.

The explanation had been offered so candidly that at first Vera gave it no importance. Then it slowly dawned on her that this Pessoa was speaking of the very thing she wished to conceal.

"You too!" she confessed in surprise.

The general regarded her with curiosity.

"Don't tell me that you . . ." He discarded his question the instant she nodded her head.

"I had gone there with a friend, a journalist. I wanted to find out what was going on. But my friend vanished without a word and nobody wanted to tell me anything. Even the mayor attempted to convince me I was crazy."

She fell silent as the tears poured down her cheeks.

"Everything's going to be all right, child."

"I'm afraid they might have done something terrible to Paulo," she offered by way of explanation.

"Paulo?"

"My friend, the reporter. He's disappeared."

"He's probably being held somewhere, like us. But they won't do him any harm."

"How can you be so sure?"

"We're not completely unprotected," he replied, with confidence radiating from his vigorous features that belied his age. Immediately, however, his expression changed to a scowl and his blue, beadlike eyes squinted with preoccupation. "Vera, tell me something. How did you get here? I want you to try and remember everything. Did you recognize anything that might indicate where we're being held?"

She shook her head no.

"I don't know what help I can be, sir. I think I was drugged. I heard a shot and everything went blank. When I came to, I was blindfolded with a kind of mask and strapped onto one of those hospital beds, the kind with wheels. They rolled me around for a while and then removed the blindfold. I found myself on the other side of that door. It looked like the entrance to a freezer; all the walls were white. I glanced around quickly and saw one other door, the one they had used to enter the hall. I was still in a daze while they stripped me and then brought me in here. They made no attempt to conceal their identities—you saw that much for yourself when they came in."

"And that's all you saw? Nothing more?"

"Look, I was on my way back from Parintins. I walked into the airport lounge and was about to go out and find a taxi. Some fellow called me by my name and then I heard a shot. That's all I remember. . . ."

"Did you get to see any of the UFOs?"

"No, sir, I stayed in town, and the sightings occurred in a more distant community. But I was a witness to the panicky arrival of people from the area and I saw the manner in which they were treated by the mayor."

"As far as I can tell, you have about as much to do with this business as the man in the moon," the general observed with characteristic good humor.

"But what is going on there, General? Is it some secret project of the army?"

"No, my child. These are very likely authentic sightings of actual UFOs."

"Real aliens?"

"No need to feel so surprised. UFOs have been entering into contact with us for many years. I've personally had more than one encounter."

Vera Martins sat down and eyed the general. She was unable to tell if this was just some additional joke on the part of the old officer or if she might be locked up with a lunatic. Once again, fear took hold of her and she felt close to tears. Maybe this wasn't a prison after all. How could she tell she wasn't being locked away in some psychiatric clinic where her fantasies commingled with reality in such a way as to make her unable to tell the difference.

"You don't believe that, do you, Vera? Well, it doesn't matter."

She backed off from Pessoa, dragging herself along the concrete floor. The notion of lying naked in the same cell with a lunatic disgusted her. She had already read too many denunciations concerning the treatment of patients in Brazilian mental hospitals, though she had yet to come across the least reference to the practice of interning patients of the opposite sex in the same cells.

Then, on an impulse, she reached out with one hand and pinched the general's leg with all her might. Her sharp nail dug into the flesh, which was real, not an illusion—a fact confirmed by Pessoa's letting out with a howl and jumping up from the floor.

"What in hell did you do that for, girl?" His leg was stinging, and he ran his hand over the welts left by her nails.

"I only wanted to find out if you were really real, General Pessoa."

"Well, I am," the general said with irritation. "You have some nerve thinking I'm a product of your imagination."

"I'm sorry. . . ."

Pessoa muttered to himself and proceeded to examine his wounds.

"You have very sharp nails there, Miss Martins."

He continued to regard her with caution, to make sure she remained where she was and did not begin to reveal some other sort of strange behavior.

"You're not Sylyon, are you?"

It was Vera's turn to stare at him with a growing certainty that she was locked up in a mental asylum.

At the Bus Station in Brasília

Buses were rolling in and pulling out with few passengers aboard. At that hour the station became a hangout for nighthawks, beggars, homosexuals and prostitutes. Near one of the escalators, a group of policemen stood talking while some ragged-looking kids were racing back and forth, shouting to each other in an outlandish simulacrum of child's play.

Young Raul Pessoa and his colleague Maurício were ambling through the midst of this amalgam of nocturnal fauna so common to the great urban centers of the world. No doubt they would have preferred to be in some other, more desolate locale confronting the most savage of extraterrestrials. The two youths were attracting the attention of homosexuals, who now and then approached them, asking for a light, inquiring about the time or making some other play. The two boys found themselves compelled to light cigarettes and listen to solicitations in hopes that one of those hustlers might turn out to be whomever they were looking for.

Earlier that afternoon, soon after their having learned about the abduction of Raul's father, somebody had phoned Banco do Brasil and asked to speak to Maurício. A voice filled with panic, talking in barely a whisper, had pleaded with the young lawyer for a rendezvous somewhere as soon as possible. At first Maurício suspected a hoax; it was not unusual for one of his colleagues to phone him up with fantastic stories in a strange voice because they knew of his interest in flying saucers—a common enough obsession in Brasília. But the voice made it clear to Maurício that he knew about the general's abduction, and warned the lawyer that the old man was in great danger. Finally taking the call seriously, Maurício had listened more attentively as the man scheduled a meeting with him for that same night, at the bus terminal, where the stranger would deliver an extremely important document into the lawyer's hands. The voice claimed to also know Maurício, and over the latter's objections insisted that he shouldn't worry, because he had only to appear at the station, as if intent on catching a bus, and he would be met there.

Then Raul Pessoa had insisted on accompanying him. His friend had already planned to fly to Manaus on the following day and felt that perhaps this meeting might shed some valuable light on the whereabouts of his father.

Now, however, far from acting naturally, the two of them wandered back and forth from one end of the station to the other—ill at ease, and turning their heads at every second like two neophyte lawbreakers. Twice already, they had been asked by policemen to produce identification, and the constant propositioning by homosexual hustlers began to irritate them.

They decided to have some coffee, and went over to the cafeteria. Standing at the counter together, holding scalding cups, they slowly sipped their coffee, desperate to have done with their nocturnal adventure.

"I guess the call must have been a phony," Maurício confessed, exhausted.

But Raul would not accept the idea, for no one else had any knowledge of his father's kidnapping and the voice had clearly referred to the fact.

"It's been a long time since I've come here at night," he said, attempting to talk about something distracting.

Maurício looked around him. The bar served all night long, and behind the heated glass case an assortment of fried dishes and boiled eggs boldly displayed their venomous nutritive values—invitingly daring one's Karma to pass from this plane to the next in a matter of minutes.

"It seems that whore over there has got your number," Raul bantered, interrupting Maurício's reverie.

The lawyer turned and noticed the horrendous-looking woman smeared with mascara and sporting a huge blond wig, batting her eyelids with their outlandishly overextended eyelashes.

"That's no whore," Maurício confided, observing her Adam's apple as it rose and fell in the throat of the supposed female. "He's a transvestite."

The two began to laugh embarrassedly as the creature lolloped over to them swinging a shoulder bag.

"Hello, dumplings, feeling a bit lost?" the creature warbled in a falsetto voice.

Raul turned to face the transvestite, while Maurício—his courage failing him, or perhaps his sense of human decency getting the better of his sense of humor—leaned on his elbow and covered his eyes with a hand.

The jaunty-looking waiter, a young black, paused to observe with growing amusement.

"You're Maurício, aren't you?" the transvestite observed, nudging the lawyer's back with her bag. "Come along, boys. . . ."

The two of them put some money down for the coffee and stumbled after the transvestite, confident in their flustered embarrassment that the entire fauna of the bus terminal were now the spectators to the drama.

They headed toward the North Wing of the city, in the direction of the Teatro Nacional, making their way along the upper level of the roadway. There was not another living soul to be seen outside at that hour; all activity had ceased beyond the perimeter of the station.

"Thanks for coming," said the transvestite.

"We were beginning to think it was a hoax," explained Maurício, still not entirely at ease with the situation.

"I'm Melo, Sergeant Melo," the travesty introduced himself, dropping the falsetto.

The two young men stared in bewilderment at the curious figure in his blond wig and smeared mascara, who broke into a smile now as he offered his hand.

"An amazing disguise," Raul confessed, extending his own hand to great the sergeant.

"It's no disguise, dumpling. I trick here every night."

"What?" Maurício stammered.

"That's what I said. I'm free, I've come out," he explained, returning to the falsetto for a moment. "Now that I'm dead I can do whatever I want."

The youths were more confused than ever.

"To all effects, I'm a dead man," the sergeant continued. "After I left the DOI-CODI, I felt totally abandoned and very nearly did give up the ship. The army has considered me dead since 1981, when I supposedly drowned off Santos. But I've always been a homosexual. And what better place to meet young boys than in the barracks?"

Sergeant Melo took a turn in his high heels and completed the gesture with a wide flourish of his arm.

"Ah, the barracks! Full of terrified recruits subjected to rigorous discipline. In the flower of their youth: eighteen! And every size and shape imaginable: mulattos, whites, blacks, blonds, tough, shy, muscular, skinny—I had only to choose. Never did one of them dare to refuse the protection of yours truly, the ballsy Sergeant Melo."

The two young men grew more embarrassed, biting their lips and not knowing what to say. Melo was enjoying the shock value of his performance before these naive two who, come to think of it, might have made wonderful recruits.

"They were the happiest years of my life," he reflected with malicious amusement. "Nothing like a well-lubricated adolescent joint dipping in and out of my petty officer's ass. Nothing to compare with that nowadays, roaming around all hours of the night. The youth of today have been wholly corrupted by drugs, and those studs will do anything to get out of serving their country."

He cleared his throat and dabbed the few tears that threatened to escape down his cheeks, making the jet eyeliner run pathetically down his nose. He opened his purse and took out a small yellow cardboard box. He slipped the box into the astonished hand of the lawyer and clacked off in the direction of the bus terminal again.

"Don't you dumplings ever forget that Melo is dead," he reminded without breaking his stride.

"But what is this?" Maurício shouted after him.

"A little present for General Pessoa," he cooed, disappearing into the night and wielding his spiked heels with baroque dexterity.

Maurício handled the box with care. It was not at all heavy and looked to be a container of photographic film, only a bit larger.

"Let me have a look at that," Raul insisted.

His lawyer friend handed the box over with obvious relief, and the general's son proceeded to examine it more closely. Finally, he opened the lid. Inside the box, wrapped in lead paper, was a roll of microfilm. The two of them eyed each other apprehensively.

THURSDAY, AUGUST 25

A very sleek-looking microbus rolled along the modern asphalt pavement, snaking smoothly past forested areas dotted by majestic factories whose gleaming facades touted all the famous international brands in microchips and electronic software. The young guide next to the driver (both employees of the Superintendency for the Freetrade Zone—acronym SUFRAMA— in Manaus) was narrating with a mixture of tenderness and rapture the technological miracles that were supposedly transpiring there regardless of the fact that they were surrounded by one of the largest still virginal rain forests in the world.

The two passengers peered out from the microbus, and only distractedly followed the indications of their guide, like tourists who had discovered too late that they had taken the wrong excursion. Yet, from time to time one of them did take out a pad and scribble down a few notes. To the guide, they had been presented as North American industrialists in the micro-electronic field who were pondering possible investments in the region. The fact of their being North Americans certainly had a positive effect on the enthusiasm of the guide, especially since they had the bus entirely to themselves at the specific request of the superintendent of SUFRAMA—a privilege normally reserved for only the most important officials, military chiefs, foreign dignitaries, and international executives bearing the highest recommendation from the Ministry of the Interior.

The seeming nonchalance of these particular two was attributed, by the guide, to their being North American and already accustomed to far more advanced technological centers. It was a different matter when it came to governmental officials or company executives from some neighboring country or from the African continent. Such visitors were generally enthralled, especially the Africans, which lifted his professional pride a few notches; and he even detected a certain envy on the part of Latin Americans.

"We're now entering a sector still under development," he announced to the pair of sightseers.

The driver slowed his vehicle down, and the two businessmen could see clearly that no factory was yet operational there. Although much of the infrastructure was already in place, the presence of the jungle was evident all around, having simply been mowed down and thrust aside by enormous bulldozers.

"Which sectors of the market do these new enterprises represent?" asked one of the Americans, the fatter and more somnolent of the two.

"We have eight new enterprises," the guide expounded with the pride of an impresario. "Three from electronic games, one from plastics, one in TVs and three in calculators."

"Mostly entertainment, then," the other concluded.

"Exactly," confirmed the guide. "The expansion of the entertainment industry is noticeable even here in the Zona Franca, our freetrade zone in Manaus."

The entrepreneur nodded his head as if the answer had satisfied him. In reality, he felt totally indifferent. Carson knew that the information presented by the guide was nothing but propaganda. The microchip industries geared to entertainment hardly proved their expansion by the fact of their sprouting up here in the middle of a tropical rain forest. The truth was merely that the native workers were as unorganized and naive as the guide himself, to the point of accepting jobs that people from the more advanced industrial societies now refused—and for a pittance, to top it off. Carson thanked his God for the existence of naive natives, and sat back to peer out at machines dragging down mammoth trunks of trees.

The microbus was now circling a Japanese installation whose plant was still under construction, and Carson nodded imperceptibly to his companion Gwyneth, whose reply also went undetected by the enraptured guide. The terrain of the plant was muddied and clawed by tractors, and protected by a high fence of barbed wire. Some twenty meters to the other side of the fence was the factory itself, still unplastered, with doors boarded up by old planks crusted with cement and used formerly as scaffolding.

Gwyneth leaned against his window and, without looking at the plant under construction, adjusted his tie with its old-fashioned clip in the shape of a diamond-studded pin. He repeated the same gesture several times during the circumnavigation charted by the microbus along the outline of the peninsula encompassing the Japanese installation at the southern end of the Industrial Park. For this particular piece of property was situated precisely on the strip of land that formed an isthmus within the southernmost loop of asphalt pavement bounding that end of the park. It was a rather poor location, Gwyneth thought to himself, to use as a hideaway for concealing prisoners.

The factory had every appearance of being abandoned, with no construction workers around. Not even a watchman seemed to have been hired by the company.

"Did that firm abandon construction?" Gwyneth inquired with a look of mild curiosity.

The guide was reanimated by the burgeoning interest of the Americans.

"No, the project has actually been expanded. The request for authorization has already been forwarded to the Zoning Council and is awaiting approval. Work is to resume once the authorization has been filed."

"You can't hold down those Japanese," Gwyneth commented.

His host agreed, but did not seem to share the American's sympathy for the project.

"They're a complicated people, the Japanese," he concluded.

The American gave up attempting to fix his tie and turned his full attention to the guide. The lad seemed to have something on his mind.

"Those Japanese behave rather arrogantly," he confessed finally. "They won't hire blacks or Indians; only white employees. Not an easy task—you gentlemen must know what most people are like around here, everybody has some mixture or other. They had to bring in people from outside."

Very convenient, Carson was thinking.

"But with the kind of money they have, they can afford the luxury," their host concluded.

The microbus pulled away from the plant site, heading back onto the main road to return to the office of the superintendency. The tour had already proven invaluable to the two agents from the CIA. The pretext of collecting the body of a dead agent did not stick with the Brazilians, but Carson and Gwyneth were hardly troubled by the fact. On the contrary, the trip was finally turning out to be useful—thanks to the present superintendent of SUFRAMA, a veteran of the intelligence community and an old collaborator with the agency in Manaus.

The previous night, the two Americans had received a touching homage at the offices of SUFRAMA: a closed dinner party followed by a most profitable chat that extended into the wee hours of the morning. The impulsive superintendent had even shared the files of his agency's Security Division, with a cordiality that for a long time the Americans had not seen in Latin America.

"I've been keeping an eye on this company for quite some time," he had boasted to them, inviting them into his office. "The name of the firm seems innocent enough and was probably chosen to avoid drawing undue attention to itself. It's called Video Games of Manaus, but it turns out to be a subsidiary of the Akutagawa International Corporation—one of the twenty largest conglomerates of Japan. I began to look into the firm once I discovered that the same economic group had taken a venture-contract with Petrobrás to explore for petroleum. Quite a coincidence, eh?"

He turned to rummage through some papers on his desk until he found a corrugated plastic portfolio closed by a zipper.

"This'll interest you. The Akutagawa Corporation is controlled by a right-wing extremist group in Japan. The stockholders are descendants from a long line of Samurai warriors, and their principle executives are ironclad traditionalists. In 1970, one of them forced his way into the Tokyo office of American Express and committed hara-kiri. The group openly finances a number of right-wing councilors in the Diet, and here in Brazil they make large monthly contributions to the sect of the Valley of the Seven Moons, whose headquarters are located in Brasília."

He took some photographs out of the portfolio and passed them to the two Americans, one by one.

"This one here is the executive director of Video Games of Manaus. His name is Júlio Ogima, a nisei from the state of São Paulo."

The Americans examined the photo with rapt attention.

"There he is again, to the left of the other gentlemen."

Mr. Ogima was pictured next to five gentlemen dressed in suits and ties, all lined up in front of a C-47 transport plane without any marks of identification.

"Where was this?" Carson queried with emphasis.

"Right here in Manaus, at the air base, only two weeks ago. I showed this photo to Colonel Nunes, from the SNI, and he was quite intrigued. Three of the men are from Chilean intelligence. They made an unscheduled landing there, and then proceeded on to Valparaíso."

"And the other two, have they been identified?"

"Regarding those two, the mystery seems to be growing. According to Colonel Nunes they are German engineers. But, officially, they have never been to Brazil—the training took place in Cologne."

"Japanese, Chileans and Germans: an interesting brew," Carson mused.

"We've been trying to come up with more information on the two Germans, but thus far have drawn a blank: both apparently nostalgic Nazis; that's about all."

He took out another photograph: Mr. Ogima was now standing in front of the entrance to the plant under construction, welcoming the same two Germans who were climbing out of an Opel.

"Recognize the car? It's the same one they used to kidnap General Pessoa, in an action that ended with the death of Captain Cruz. Both the model of the car and the phony license plate coincide with the ones reported by the police. This photo was taken two days before the abduction. The car was found abandoned along the Manaus-Itacoatiara Highway, completely stripped. A report of the theft of the vehicle has since been filed by a Mr. Júlio Ogima.

There could be little doubt that something more than the simple production of electronic games was set for that factory.

"I took care," continued the superintendent, "to look into the flight pattern of that airplane in the photo, with its special list of passengers."

"And what did you manage to come up with?" The Americans smiled at the quality of his devotion to the service.

"The C-47 without registration as to country of origin had requested permission to make an emergency landing at Iquitos, in Peru. It was having problems with one of its engines. The Peruvian authorities granted permission to land, and the plane was subsequently isolated to a corner of the runway. But nothing goes by unnoticed in Iquitos; it's a small city and the airport rather precariously located. Everybody was talking about the C-47 and its emergency landing just as soon as the incident had occurred."

"And the Peruvians actually confirmed that it was a Chilean aircraft?"

"A garrison from the Peruvian Army cordoned off the plane, and the captain went aboard to talk to the crew. The craft sat for nearly five hours on the runway because the Chileans had to wait for a part to be brought from the base at Arequipa. The Peruvian captain reported that he had spoken to agents from the DINA aboard the craft."

"But that sort of thing must be fairly common down here, one country's helping out another in the area of military intelligence."

The superintendent shook his head and broke into a smile.

"That was the dream of the seventies: a wide and deadly-efficient network of repressive forces stretching across the entire continent and swooping down on wherever Communist subversion reared its ugly head. The notion was that all of us ought to collaborate in the defense of our traditions and of Western Civilization. But the internal rivalry of Latin America is still great, much greater than the perception of the problems of global geopolitics. The truth is that each one of these countries wants to be the greatest."

The two Americans concurred with their host's line of reasoning without masking the disdain they felt for such petty rivalries among those dying of hunger.

"You gentlemen are no doubt aware of how the Chileans and the Peruvians detest each other. They spend most of their time trying to think up new ways of pulling the rug out from under each other. The Peruvians' hatred stems from the fact that Chile took away part of their country, back in the War of the Pacific. When Chilean troops entered Peruvian territory they acted the way the Chileans always have: with brutality, violating women, executing civilians, committing the most barbarous acts. The Chileans are the most brutal creatures on the continent, and I wasn't surprised by what they did in 1973. It's for this very reason that I consider the Chileans one of the few peoples left with the capacity to defeat the Communist menace."

"But they do assist each other, nevertheless," Gwyneth remarked.

"At times, and reluctantly. I was told that during the five hours the Chileans spent at Iquitos, the Peruvian joint chiefs of staff sat there without knowing what to do. They couldn't decide whether to help out or to invade the plane and seize the men from the DINA on charges of espionage. One general suggested that they should lend assistance but at the same time plant a bomb aboard so that the plane would explode in flight."

"The Chileans must have had some idea of what a tight spot they were in, don't you think?" Carson suggested.

"Obviously, they refused to leave the plane. They had to hold out in that boiling heat and without water. They told the Peruvian officer that they had been on their way to a protocol visit in Brazilian territory, at the invitation of the Brazilian Air Force. An evident lie—what they were doing was flying clandestinely. I even checked with the general staff, and Air Force Security assured me that no such invitation had been issued."

"What happened then?"

"The plane left without food or water and entered our airspace. Air surveillance along that part of the frontier is rather primitive—it's a favorite route for contraband, and the military units we have stationed close to the Colombian frontier are essentially waterborne and infantry. So the plane ended up landing here in Manaus, and somehow our Mr. Ogima found out and went to the airport to welcome its passengers. According to the report from the FAB's general staff, the plane and its crew remained there only the amount of time it took to resupply, then departed for the return trip, with Valparaíso as their destination."

The two Americans had begun to realize their mission was not turning out to be so simple.

"I have a strong suspicion," continued the superintendent, "that the two Germans remained here in Brazil."

"To manufacture electronic games, no doubt," Carson proposed ironically.

The three men chuckled together like discreet entrepreneurs who had just uncovered a slight flaw in the competition. And when night fell, that following day, no one would ever have suspected that the two workmen in greasy monkey suits and muddied construction boots clomping methodically through the Industrial Park were the same aloof Americans who had been chauffeured along the asphalt avenues in a deluxe microbus. Soon they would reach the cover of the Japanese installation, and Carson pleaded with God that he would still be in good enough shape to demonstrate once again that his obesity merely couched the surprising agility of the hippopotamus ballerinas in Walt Disney's *Fantasia*.

Meanwhile, at the Military's Urban Sector in Brasília

A long line of high-ranking officers, politicians from the ruling party, and industrialists from various states of the union was inching forward along the red carpet ritually spread out upon the impeccably waxed hardwood floor of the Armed Forces' GHQ. All of the guests, with expressions that varied between curiosity and the wish to please, were stopping, a few seconds each, to shake the hand of the new head of the Joint Chiefs of Staff of the Armed Forces—Brigadier General Bernardo Fischer—who had just assumed office after having read to the gathered dignitaries one of the most impressively sonorous orders of the day in recent memory.

The journalists, confined behind the velvet roping that ran from post to post along the fringes of a vast Persian carpet, pressed forward and jostled one another in their attempt to register all the solemnities down to their most ambiguous and secretive connotations. The Colortran spots behind the TV cameras and the explosion of flashbulbs illuminated the grand salon, as reporters noted every detail, every gesture, every remark dropped in the midst of the murmur of conversations. Telex machines in stuffy editorial rooms were already receiving—letter by letter, as transmitted by the Brazilian News Agency—the stunning text of the entire order of the day ceremoniously articulated by Brigadier General Bernardo Fischer. And at almost the same moment, that same order of the day was being read to all the military quarters of the nation, instilling the solemn words of the new head of the Joint Chiefs of Staff into the consciousness of even the humblest soldier.

This twenty-fifth day of August—the day chosen by the President of the Republic to mark the passage of command—was one of the most cherished dates among all the ephemerides of the nation's military history. Since 1955, every twenty-fifth day of August has commemorated Military Mascot Day, to honor that sector of nature so dear to the innumerable corporations and barracks of Brazil: the small animals that have not infrequently performed like true soldiers. Who can fail to recall the courageous bitch named Mimi, the famed female basset hound of the Marques de Caxias who, early one morning in the midst of the Battle of Cerro-Cora, alerted her master—at the time, head of our glorious armed forces—of a treacherous sneak attack by Paraguayan soldiers against the Brazilian encampment: thus saving the life of our greatest patriot, though she herself perished under the barbarous blade of an enemy sabre?

The order of the day, concise and full of suggestive poetic flashes, spoke of the fidelity and capacity for sacrifice of such mascots. Some political commentators, it is true, took this as a veiled warning from the new military chief to those who might demonstrate too much impatience as to the pace of the return to political democracy, as well as to those greedy entrepreneurs who did not have the foggiest idea what sacrifice or fidelity actually meant. In opposition circles, however, the same order of the day was interpreted to be a rather somber threat, since it alluded to things plotted at night and in a spirit of betrayal, which were nonetheless forever denounced and rooted out by the humblest of soldiers, even those denied a soul or the power of reason.

Earlier in the day, before going to GHQ where he was to assume office, the brigadier general had paid another visit to the weary agent of the KGB, suggesting he might want to follow the ceremonies as they were being broadcast on TV. Any pretense of sociability between the two, however, was becoming more and more strained.

"Don't you think that the President chose a rather inopportune day for your investiture of command?" the Russian commented dryly, awaiting the brigadier's reaction.

"Why, just because it's Mascot Day?"

"You were the one who told me that you detested animals."

"It's true, I can't stand them."

"But you're about to take office on the very day that's dedicated to their memory."

"It's Sylyon who's responsible for the choice of day."

"Well, I see he has a sense of humor."

"It has nothing to do with a sense of humor," the general growled. "Mimi the basset hound was the reincarnation of Julius Caesar."

"Oh, now I understand."

"No, you don't understand."

"On the contrary. In the Soviet Union, our armed forces also celebrate a mascot day. And the pet thus honored is a mutt named Iskra. He belonged to Trotsky, but no one remembers that any longer. Iskra died in an ambush staged by White Russians, in 1918. According to an old manuscript of the period, the dog was the reincarnation of Ivan the Terrible."

Fischer stormed out as if he had heard an insult. Once he returned, he planned to fix that impertinent Russian's wagon. For the moment, however, he had to concentrate his energy on avoiding the jitters and not combusting spontaneously in the midst of the ceremony.

At the Diocese in Parintins

The bishop, wearing a filthy worn-out cassock, was seated at his desk. He spoke with measured tones: those of a pastor to his flock, perhaps simulating prudence, but in a spirit that was manifestly intolerant.

From the moment that he had first entered the bishop's office, Paulo Veronezzi had sensed the explosive quality of the clergyman's character. The old Capuchin with his long white flowing beard was already a kind of venerable patriarch of the city, having baptized and married practically all the living Catholics in Parintins. His conservative stances, though motivated as they were by tremendous generosity and a Tridentine spirit, he hid from no one. His intolerance, however, was reserved specifically for the excessive political involvement of priests like Father Wender, of the so-called "progressive" Church; while his generosity manifested itself in the form of old-fashioned paternalistic charity, which had the power to seduce a naive flock at the same time that it reduced problems of the world to the ready optic of an article of faith.

"Father Wender is still very young," the bishop was explaining to the reporter. "He lets himself be ruled by certain passions characteristic of such innocence."

"But what can you tell me, your excellency, of the kinds of problems he is faced with there in his community?"

The bishop smiled knowingly, his gray, brilliant eyes fixing on the reporter.

"I have thought a great deal about the problems of Valéria. That community has been around since the beginning of the century; an interesting story. Have you heard of the Savage Rebellion?"

"That took place in the eighteen-hundreds, didn't it?"

"It began in 1832, in Belém. Eventually it spread throughout the entire Amazon. Little by little it transformed itself into a species of indigenous movement. Here in Amazonas, the 'Savagery' dragged on nearly to the end of the last century. Only the rubber fever finally succeeded in putting out the flames ignited by the rebellion. More than half the population here in the lower Amazon died during the conflict. Valéria was founded by two families of white peasants who had decided to flee the bloody assaults of the 'Savagers.' They struck out for the frontier, and gradually the region prospered in terms of population, though it has never risen above its misery."

"I thought they were descendants of Northeasterners. . . ."

"The lower Amazon was never much affected by the rubber boom.

The Northeasterners settled principally along the upper rivers of the Western Amazon region. Here the population is nearly all a mixture of Portuguese and Indian—the typical mestizo and the Amazonian *par excellence*."

"But that's all coming to an end now."

"It has to, my son. Look, the projected installation and utilization of petro-exploration technology will inevitably foster new realities. There's already three and a half million dollars of capital invested here, and with it comes the creation of two hundred new jobs. This is the kind of project that can lead our people out of isolation and the economy from stagnation. It's a thing I've always dreamed of, if you want to know the real truth of how I feel."

"But what about the people themselves? Has anybody asked them what they want?"

"You are also young, my son. The people wouldn't know what to answer. To live under these primitive conditions of the Amazon enfeebles the mind. You young ones educated in the city don't appreciate the fact; you romanticize the lives of such people. I should know, as I've dedicated my whole life to serving them. When I first arrived here, back in 1953, the people were living in the most abject state of promiscuity. The cases of incest alone—of fathers impregnating daughters, of sons impregnating mothers—were monstrously common. Isolated the way they were, they had begun to forget that they were even creatures of God, endowed with souls. They had come to behave more like animals of the jungle. Good Lord, how it tormented me!"

"And what's going to happen to those people in Valéria?"

"They will have the opportunity to find jobs connected with the project, earn more money, leave the past behind."

"And lose their land in the process. . . ."

"Those of them who may wish to continue tilling the soil will easily find another place to do so: the Amazon is vast."

"They don't seem to share your optimism."

The bishop flustered.

"It is Father Wender who doesn't share my optimism, as you call it. It was he who actually impressed upon their minds the notion that this project is something sinister."

"You think then, your excellency, that these people are incapable of deciding what's best for themselves?"

"They are good Christians; humble, simple people. But they are easily swayed. Father Wender was a brilliant student of theology; he might very well have accomplished a mission of the greatest significance in his preaching of the Gospels. Instead of this, he has chosen to ensconce himself in the jungle, imperiling even his own bodily and spiritual health. Do you know, my son, that Father Wender has already been hospitalized twice because of malaria? He refuses to look after himself properly, forgetting that his health is also a Divine gift."

"Father Wender told me that he feels he is spreading the Gospel in the manner it was meant to be done."

"I know . . . I am quite familiar with the thinking of Father Wender. For him, spreading the Gospel means carrying the good news. Up to a point he is correct. But the good news, as he sees it, entails a negative characterization of the efforts being made to lift this land out of its poverty and stagnation."

"As I see it, progress at any cost is hardly good news, your excellency. And Father Wender, at least, regards it as a manifestation of sin. The good news is rather that people can influence their own destiny; they can organize and develop strength enough to prevent the propagation of sin."

"What you say in your innocence, my son, is but an age-old manifestation of vanity."

"Vanity?"

"Father Wender behaves more like a Beghard, one of the Poor Brothers in the Order of Saint Francis."

"I know nothing of Church history your excellency."

"Let me explain, then, if only to demonstrate to you that the Church is not as intolerant as it may have been in the past. The sect of the Beghards, which spread across Europe in the fourteenth century, adhered radically to the rules of Saint Francis of Assisi. Among other heresies, it claimed that man needs no more than what is necessary for survival, as much in matters of food as with other earthly goods. They denied any possibility of progress for man, which is the most sublime, magnificent manner of praising God. As with certain priests nowadays, they called the house of Peter—the Church of God!—an evil prostitute and a great perversion. Pope John XXIII, after much meditation, ordered in 1322 that the heretical activities of the Beghards be investigated. By 1323, one hundred fourteen heretics from that movement were burned by the Inquisition."

"And what can your excellency tell me about these strange lights?"

"The *Chupa-chupa*, my son?"

"Father Wender seems convinced that it's something cooked up by the Japanese."

"The Japanese are equally mystified, my son. They were here with me, oh . . . about a month ago, soon after the first appearances of the thing. The object also made several sweeps over the site of the project itself."

The bishop paused to open a drawer and take out a yellow Kodak envelope, from which he extracted several photographs the size of postcards which he spread on the desk.

"These photos were taken by the head of personnel, with an Olympus Pen."

Paulo leaned over the desk to examine each photograph. They were black basically, but each one of them depicted strange luminous designs, sinuous streaks similar to twists of reddish neon signs.

"That is your *Chupa-chupa*," the bishop said, self-satisfied. "Various aeronautical authorities are investigating."

"Then you believe that they are—"

"As thou knowest not what is the way of the spirit, even so thou knowest not the works of God who maketh all," replied the bishop, citing a passage from Ecclesiastes.

Yet the supposed proofs of a Divine science were rather dreary at best. The photographs clarified nothing, and Paulo leaned back from the desk in disappointment. They could just as easily be crude hoaxes. The shots were amateurish, and the images barely focused. The photographer had capped his ineptitude by using too low a setting, and the results had the character of a vulgar abstraction.

Paulo handed the stack of photographs back to the bishop with a feeling of having thoroughly wasted his time. What was happening to him, he wondered. Why hadn't he taken any initiative? Why was he allowing this scholastic idiot to lecture him this way? Through the mayor, at least, he had learned a bit about Vera's desperation over his disappearance. But it was not Vera's desperation that troubled him . . . What irritated him so was the feeling that his own professional capability—something he had thought already proven long ago— was in some manner being put to the test again. And what had he really come up with so far? A banal case of conflict over land titles, like so many other thousands of such incidents occurring daily throughout the nation.

"The Lord has mysterious ways," said the bishop, musing over a photograph of the supposed UFO.

The bishop's reflection only increased the sensation in Paulo Veronezzi that his presence was superfluous there. He stared out of the office window and noticed a group of boys playing soccer in a field just behind the church. The sun was burning, but even so, a small audience of the curious was accompanying the match in little groups under the scattered shade of trees surrounding the hard-clay playing field. Paulo felt like one of those spectators: in Parintins, cooling in the shadows, confronted by a struggle whose larger significance escaped him, but of such doubtful import as the result of that soccer match among boys of the parish.

"And the Protestant pastor?" he finally asked.

The bishop looked up from the photograph with an air of distinct displeasure.

"Poor man," he replied. "I was outraged at the news."

"Had you ever had any contacts with him?"

The bishop shook his head:

"He was against Ecumenism—a very narrow-minded fellow, despite the unusual habits for an Adventist pastor."

"So Father Wender told me," Paulo admitted with the sudden intuition that the trail of the Adventist might just prove to sweeten a little the otherwise savorless investigation. "Your excellency is obviously cognizant of the fact that the pastor might have actually been a CIA agent?"

The bishop laughed indulgently.

"It wouldn't surprise me in the least, if it turned out to be true. All American missionaries are generally suspect in that regard."

"Your excellency is also a foreigner," Paulo ventured provocatively.

The bishop eyed the reporter rather nervously.

"Italy has a terrible secret service. And I can assure you that the Vatican takes no interest in activities of such a nature."

"Do you think he really might have been CIA?"

Getting up from his desk full of papers, the bishop signaled the close of the interview.

"It's hardly a question to address to me," he concluded with a flourish toward the doorway of his study.

The young reporter chanced no further remarks. He took his leave rather hurriedly, but carried with him the gratifying impression of having finally discovered the missing piece of the puzzle. He would no longer have to search for something to fill the three vacant hours that separated him from his departure by plane to Manaus. And to his delight, he calculated that he would, by the following morning, bright and early, already be landing in São Paulo.

At the Vila Militar in Manaus

The orderly waddled into the dining room and placed the tray in front of Colonel Nunes. There was something about this private, a cunning in the eyes and the veiled expressions typical of Indians, that deeply irritated the colonel. The orderly had been assigned to him two days ago, replacing an old mess corporal who had served him for more than fifteen years but was finally abandoning the barracks to marry his sweetheart and open a tavern. This damned mestizo, who had joined the service not two months ago, turned out to have some sort of good connections with the head of the general staff in the Military Command of Amazonia, and had practically been shoved down the colonel's throat—leaving the job as caretaker of one of the general's private ranches in order to bedevil his life of a bachelor colonel. Nunes's wife had refused to follow him there to Manaus, when he was transferred a while back from Pernambuco.

"Chow good today, *Coronel*."

Nunes acted as if he had not heard the confidence and lifted the cover off the tray, upon which a dark roast meat sat steaming in a reddish gravy. The piece of meat was truncated, a sign that the orderly had already tested the same before serving it. Since he was still alive, the colonel thought he could assume it wasn't poisoned. Nunes was not a paranoid, but that kind of reasoning helped him to come to terms with the eccentricities of his new orderly.

The private proceeded to open a bottle of beer and empty the foamy liquid into the colonel's glass. At least the beer had not been subjected to the personal scrutiny of the mestizo. It was a drink that seemed not to appeal to him. Apparently he preferred much stronger brews, like the whiskey and the cognac the colonel normally kept in the living room and which had mysteriously taken to evaporating under the Amazonian heat.

"*Coronel* no hungry?"

The meat appeared to be made of Styrofoam, and Colonel Nunes chewed it stoically, recalling with some sadness his wife's desertion. With every meal he would reflect once again on her powers as a cook, though his matrimonial nostalgia abruptly ended there. His wife had recently filed a suit against him for divorce, one in which she demanded eighty percent of his property and fifty percent of his income.

"Where does this food come from?"

"From mess hall," the orderly replied. The *coronel* would not give him a "lousy cent" toward the maintenance of the house. Even the burned-out light bulbs failed to have replacements, and it was not surprising that the colonel's chin showed palpable signs of having been shaved in the dark.

"*Coronel*, yesterday fellow come look for you. . . ."

Nunes stopped chewing the Styrofoam long enough to place his knife and fork down on the plate. He wished to either starve to death or obtain forgiveness from the commanding general of the MCA.

"Fellow say I be careful, you one sick *coronel*."

"What are you saying?"

"He tell me you psycho," the orderly insisted, withdrawing toward the door to the kitchen at a prudent distance from the colonel. "No offensive, sir, but man, he say you going crazy . . . screwy! He say that . . ."

Nunes spit the meat out onto his plate and coughed. He gulped down some beer, shaking the glass in his trembling hand. "Who was it came here, soldier?"

"No say name, but he Japanese."

"Japanese? And you let him into the house, soldier?"

"No way, *Coronel*. Me too smart. He stay outside front door, don't even ask to come in. Just ring bell and ask to see *coronel*."

Colonel Nunes was ready to bet what was left of his pay that this was just another dirty tactic from his wife's legal counsel. She had hired a feminist lawyer who seemed to enjoy coming up with the most diabolical methods for peeling his flesh to the bone. All she needed now was to have him declared insane to be able to pick his bones as well.

"This Japanese fellow—he leave anything? a note or anything?"

"No sir, say he come back."

The colonel got up and left the house. He took a stroll around the block and managed to find the sergeant in charge of security for the Vila Militar.

"I want you to do me a favor, Sergeant. Yesterday some Japanese fellow came looking for me at the house. Unfortunately, my orderly is still wet behind the ears and never even managed to get the guy's name. Check the roster of visitors here yesterday, will you?"

"A Japanese fellow, you say, sir? The problem is, the register doesn't list the nationality of a visitor," the sergeant informed him with a salute.

"At ease, Sergeant. It's not important. Tell me, were you the one on duty here yesterday?"

"Yes, sir. But I don't remember having seen any Japanese."

Nunes took the roster of visitors and went through it himself. The Vila Militar had had very few visitors the day before—just the normal flow of the Vila's inhabitants, a few salespeople who had obviously tipped the sergeant, and the usual suppliers.

"And what about this 'Ogima' here?" he said, pointing to the name. "Did you think he's Swiss or something, Sergeant?"

The sergeant looked down at the name and ignored the veiled rebuke from the colonel. The guy was going bonkers anyway—everybody knew that, and he wasn't going to be the first sergeant to stick his neck out and tell him so.

"Maybe he was let in when I was away from my post," he offered instead. "I had to leave twice yesterday, sir. I don't know what to do half the time about Major Rodrigues's pet monkey over there. The little critter keeps breaking off the leash—loves to sneak into the latrines and squeeze all the toothpaste. He's already wrecked Colonel Ramos's den."

Nunes handed back the roster, after having quickly memorized the address written in by Mr. Júlio Ogima. The probability of its being a false address was rather high, but it wouldn't hurt to check it out. He walked back to his house, took out his .45 revolver and tore off from the Vila Militar with the tires of his Volkswagen burning up the asphalt. The hunger pangs he felt drove him to press more and more speed out of the car, and he kept flooring the accelerator with rage.

The address turned out to be in the vicinity of the university, and the colonel did not even take the trouble to read the bronze plaque, half hidden by the foliage, that indicated the purpose of the building. He slammed the brakes right in front of the two-story edifice painted white, and his car was immediately surrounded by a team of muscular men wearing the white dressing gowns of medics.

The colonel had barely managed to open the car door when he found himself flailing his feet, harnessed in a straitjacket, and forcibly carried into the building. The men tossed him into a padded room and he sat meditating what possible new forms of persuasion his wife was clearly masterminding in order to turn him into a beggar. But his thoughts were immediately cut short by the entrance of a physician— or so he seemed, dressed as he was in white, carrying a black leather satchel and sporting a stethoscope around his neck.

"Don't be afraid," the doctor whispered.

Nunes had to limit his reply to several gruntings from behind the cloth gag in his mouth.

"You've fallen under the wrath of Sylyon!" the physician warned him in a hushed voice.

Curving his body, the colonel managed to kick the doctor with all his mute strength, catching him with both feet in the chest. The unexpected assault caused the man not only to lose his balance but to tear off the gag from Nunes's face in the process—nearly taking the colonel's jawbone with it. The doctor went flying across the room, while Nunes bellowed with pain.

"Take it easy, will you!" cried the doctor, panting from shock and massaging his ribs to attempt to alleviate the ache. "I'm here to help you. . . ."

The colonel continued moaning and moving his jaw like a demented feline in an animated cartoon. The doctor took off his face mask and cautiously observed Nunes's contortions.

"But you're dead," Nunes suddenly exclaimed, halting the movements of his jaw to observe the other more closely. "You're no doctor. . . ."

The man raised a hand to plead with the colonel to calm himself, while he himself got up on his knees, finally recovering from the fall. If the room had not been padded, he might have fractured his skull.

"Of course I'm not a doctor," he confirmed readily.

"But you're dead."

"That's precisely why I'm not," he agreed, still massaging his chest.

"What the devil are you doing here?"

"I'm here to save you . . . repaying an old favor."

The man sat back down and opened the satchel. He took out a glass and a half-bottle of whiskey.

"Want a swig?" he offered.

The colonel rotated his jaw one final time, running his tongue over his teeth to make sure they were all still there.

The man downed a healthy shot of whiskey and refilled the glass. He held the glass up to Nunes, who drank it down voraciously, choking in the process.

"You have no idea of the pile of shit you've walked into," the man remarked.

Nunes finally remembered: In 1972, he had shelved charges of insubordination brought against a captain who was serving in the DOI-CODI, in Rio. The captain, against the specific mandate of his superiors, had raped a political prisoner. She turned out to be the only daughter of a powerful industrialist well connected in military circles. The accused captain, thanks to the colonel's intervention, was allowed to leave the army without a dishonorable discharge. But he could not adapt to civilian life again and eventually committed suicide, in 1975, turning on the gas in his apartment in Belo Horizonte.

"Sylyon saved me," the man said by way of explanation, seeing that Nunes already recognized him as that same Captain Palhares who had committed suicide.

"Who is Sylyon?"

The captain stared at Nunes incredulously.

"Then you don't know? But we don't have time for explanations now."

"Is there a Japanese man living here?"

"You mean Ogima. You know him?"

"He's been looking for me. . . ."

"We have to get out of here. They want to put you out of commission! They've already murdered Captain Cruz, so it won't cost them anything more to kill a colonel."

"Why are you helping me like this?"

"Let's just say that I discovered I don't buy it anymore."

"Buy what?"

"Just forget it for now so we can get out of here. . . ." He paused to take a thick Kraft envelope out of his medical satchel and thrust it at the colonel. ". . . Guard this carefully. It belonged to the American whom these boys decided to get rid of as well."

"How can I guard anything wrapped up in this straitjacket."

"Sorry, Colonel . . ." Palhares began to help him out of his confinement while filling him in on his plan to escape the place.

If Colonel Nunes had taken the trouble to read the bronze plaque at the entrance to the building, before getting out of the car, he might have discovered just in time that he was parked in front of the Center for Psychiatric Cure and Meditation Through Zen—one of the subsidiaries of the Akutagawa Corporation.

Still in Manaus, a Few Hours Later

Paulo descended from the plane at Ponta Pelada Airport, carrying his travel bag and attempting to appear as nonchalant as a tourist on holiday. Yet, he did not succeed in concealing his excitement. It took all his self-control not to run to a public telephone and put in a call to the magazine in São Paulo. Inside his knapsack of imitation leather was a large envelope crammed with papers and photographs, so fascinating to behold they had more than restored the professional excitement he had missed since long before the abrasive days spent in Parintins.

He had been received coldly, even hostilely by the Adventist missionaries. Yet, despite his reception by them, he had walked away with the irrefutable evidence that the American really had been working hand and glove with the CIA.

The house of the missionaries stood in an out-of-the-way locale like some well-kept country cottage wherein a typical American family, imbued with pioneer spirit, hid itself from mosquitoes behind the window screens while brandishing the Puritanical ethic like a shield against the underdeveloped promiscuity of the Amazon.

The journalist was met by the couple's children: two light blond boys who spoke perfect Portuguese and led him to the back of the sun-drenched veranda where their mother, a woman approaching forty, was putting up preserves of regional fruits. The pastor was out for the moment, and the wife had some difficulty in making herself understood in Portuguese.

The conversation moved all too quickly along, and Paulo barely had time to interject his questions. But during the short time of their conversation, he noticed, through the window screen, the figure of another woman, most certainly a native, trying to observe discreetly what was transpiring on the veranda. He judged her to be a servant, most likely, and sought to keep his attention fixed on the wife of the missionary, who was already gesturing anxiously to the doorway and ordering her sons to see the prying journalist out of the house.

Paulo did not argue; he about-faced and followed the youngsters out the door.

"She's waiting for you over there," one of the boys announced, pointing to the dirt road that would take him back to the outskirts of town.

"Who is?"

"Esmeralda," the boy proclaimed by way of explanation, already turning to head back to the cottage, bounding after his brother who had run on ahead.

Paulo walked with his attention fixed on the tall trees and thick vegetation that bordered the trail of damp earth imprinted with the double treads of the pastor's Jeep.

It was then that he caught sight of the young woman still waiting for him, half hidden by the huge trumpet trees. She was a childlike mestiza, not more than fifteen, with dark almond eyes that offered him the same enigma as the girls of the hotel. Dressed in clothes given her by the missionaries, she had the appearance of a curious anachronism in her long sleeves, buttoned-up collar and skirt hemmed below the knees. In her hands she held some sort of package.

"Were you a friend of his, mister?"

"You could say that," Paulo lied.

She began to weep. The tears rolled silently down her oriental cheeks with no sobs or melodrama, only pure emotion that escaped all context.

"He knew that they wanted to kill him," the girl explained as she walked along beside him. "But you took so long to come, I wouldn't have been able to bear it much longer."

"It wasn't easy to get here," the journalist told her, to keep her talking, lest she become frightened.

"Those heathens are the children of Satan," she said, turning to nod back at the cottage. "If the Missus found out I was here talking to you, she'd punish me awful bad. Well, she can beat me all she wants; I'll never open my mouth to her. Mr. Gary always told me not to confide in people like that."

"What were you to this Gary?"

She smiled and her dark eyes suddenly sparkled behind the tears.

"His woman."

"Yes, I thought so."

"He took me away from La Peruana's place. You understand, don't you? I started working at La Peruana's the beginning of this year; then Mr. Gary showed up. He paid about ten contos to take me away from there. He liked me a lot—he said that I was like a daughter to him."

"You lived with him in Valéria?"

"No, he told me that it was too dangerous there. I was staying here. Mr. Gary rented a small room for me."

"Did he ever tell you what was going on in Valéria that was so dangerous?"

"No, when he would come here Mr. Gary would want to relax. He didn't like to talk about work. But then the heathens found out about how he was coming here now and then to see me. They came after me to say that Mr. Gary was also a heathen and shouldn't do that. But Mr. Gary wasn't a heathen, I know that he wasn't. He was a man like yourself, mister."

"When was it you saw Mr. Gary for the last time?"

"Over a month ago by now. He came and stayed just with me, didn't leave my room. I would go out and get his meals and everything for him. I think the heathens were already after him."

"Was it then that he admitted to you that he was in danger?"

"Yes, one night with me in bed he told me how they wanted to kill him. He said I mustn't be afraid, nothing was going to happen to me. But I was still afraid and I didn't want him to go back there."

"But he had to go back, wasn't that so?"

She hugged the package and stood still.

"I never saw Mr. Gary again. One day a young boy showed up from Valéria with this, saying Mr. Gary wanted them to give it to

me. He told me Mr. Gary had disappeared. He told me I must hide
this package until a friend of Mr. Gary's showed up."

"Have you shown the package to anybody else?"

"No, mister. I already knew that Mr. Gary was dead, something
told me that. I hid the package so that no one would see. His friend
was going to show up and then I was going to give it to him . . . to
you."

"Not even the heathens know about it?"

"They are the ones who must never be told. They came to my
room and took me here. At first they acted nice to me, but now they
treat me awful bad."

She kissed the package and handed it to the journalist.

"It's yours now, it's what Mr. Gary wanted."

"Do you need anything?"

"No, I was only waiting for Mr. Gary's friend to appear to do
what was necessary. Now I'm free to look after myself again."

"What will you do?"

"Go back to La Peruana's."

The airport terminal was quiet, and Paulo Veronezzi made his way
easily to the taxi stand. As he exited from the arrivals hall, he noticed
somebody trying to gain his attention. He paused to see who it was,
and the young fellow, who might have been an airline employee,
beckoned him into his office. He started heading in that direction
when two men intercepted him, dragged him out of the arrivals hall
and shoved him into a waiting ambulance.

The ambulance drove off with screeching tires, and Paulo found
himself bouncing from one side to the other, barely able to balance
himself on the stretcher latched to the metal floor of the vehicle. His
bag got loose for a moment and he rolled over to recover it, gripping
the side of the stretcher. Then he lifted his head to try to see outside,
but the windows were toward the top and frosted. He had no idea
where or why they were taking him.

He managed to tie the shoulder strap of the bag around his waist
and began to inch his way toward the door. Should he succeed in
opening it, he might be daring enough to leap out the back, at the
right moment, since whoever was driving was either suicidal or insane.

Everything had happened so fast, there was little time to think.
Jolted about on the stretcher, certain that escape was too perilous at
the moment, he tried to remain alert and ready for the instant when
the ambulance would pull over. It might prove his only chance to
regain his freedom.

The ambulance drove madly along for nearly half an hour, but then finally came to a smooth halt. The back door was opened and his two abductors surprised Paulo still clinging dizzily to the stretcher, like a tenacious rodeo cowboy on the back of an unbroken bronco.

"He drives that way because he's a little off his rocker," apologized one of the two, gesturing with a thumb at the other.

The journalist climbed slowly out, fearfully testing the ground with his feet as if he doubted the law of gravity. His captors observed him with crazed expressions.

"You *are* the reporter, aren't you?" The one who asked him was partly dressed in military uniform, but the cap with a soft-drink logo on the crown belied such identity.

Paulo Veronezzi kept silent.

"You think we've got the wrong man?" the other asked.

"I'm Colonel Nunes," one of them finally said to introduce himself. "This is Captain Palhares, but he's already dead."

"And my friend here has gone nuts," Palhares warned, looking far too healthy for a corpse.

"Seriously, don't be frightened," the colonel said more soberly.

"I'm not frightened," the journalist replied, more frightened than he would admit even to himself.

"You work for *Isto É*?"

"I do. Why?"

"One thing at a time," the dead captain suggested.

Colonel Nunes stepped forward and took Paulo by the arm.

"Are you still in one piece, my boy?"

"I think so. . . ."

"They nearly had you," the colonel added, smiling triumphantly.

The captain, dressed in white like a hospital orderly, took a quick look around. They had parked the ambulance in a huge abandoned lot filled with the remains of old automobile wrecks.

"They can't find us here," he concluded.

"Who can't?" the journalist inquired.

"The acolytes," confided the captain. "Not to mention the no-good marshal who's after the colonel's tail. His wife is divorcing him and seems to want everything including his—"

"Enough of my private affairs, Captain."

"Sorry, Colonel."

"Dead men aren't supposed to talk so much, Palhares."

The journalist was about to ask another question when the two of them suddenly signaled him to be still. The chopping of a helicopter grew more and more audible, and the two officers rushed to take cover under the rusty shell of an old bus. Paulo, his reflexes still a bit dazed, was the last to find protection, under the carcass of an Impala.

The helicopter made a low pass over the junkyard and then leaned off beyond a copse of buriti palms. Nunes raced out of his hiding place to the ambulance and opened the front door. He scurried back to cover with the bulky Kraft envelope under his arm.

"They're already out looking for us," he shouted.

"But they don't know where we are, I guarantee you that," Palhares boasted, climbing out from under and brushing himself off. "I wouldn't be surprised if they think *you're* still back at the clinic."

"I wouldn't be so sure," the colonel said gravely, appearing to be truly close to a state of nervous collapse.

The journalist came out of his hiding place and went over to the side of the ambulance. The captain came up behind and put his arm around Paulo's shoulder.

"If you'd like to know the reason for what we're doing, that's easy enough. The colonel over there is an old buddy of mine. He got me out of a tight spot. Just because I had tried to hump a subversive who turned out to be the daughter of some hotshot, they were about to fry me. But the colonel saved my ass."

The colonel came over with the envelope.

"You recognize this, son?"

Paulo looked at the package and instinctively slapped his hand against the bag that he had tied around his waist. The envelope the colonel was holding up before him was identical to the one the mestiza had given him back in Parintins.

"I have one that looks exactly the same, in here," he said, looking down at his waist and immediately repenting having done so.

"Show me," the colonel ordered.

"Why should I?"

"Give it to me!" shouted Nunes, losing all patience.

The journalist had no alternative. He took out the other envelope and handed it over to the colonel.

"Then we *have* got the right person, thank God! I was afraid we'd made a mistake. Look at this, Palhares. It's no accident that they wanted to get hold of him."

Unexpectedly, he handed both envelopes back to the reporter.

"Take good care of that, son. It's more explosive than a stick of dynamite."

Paulo smiled in astonishment and quickly stuffed the two envelopes into his bag.

"You've never seen us," Nunes warned him, "you understand?"

The two officers got back into the ambulance and backed it out of the dump. Before leaving the journalist behind in a cloud of dust, the colonel had time to shout:

"I want to read it all in the next issue of *Isto É*, you hear me!"

Ten hours later, Paulo Veronezzi landed at Congonhas Airport, in São Paulo, with the text of his story entirely drafted and his editor—without shedding his habitual apathy—actually waiting at the exit with a car from the magazine. The American who had lost his head in a Manaus slum was still going to make a lot of people pull out their own hair in the weeks to come. As he had suspected from the very beginning, you didn't have to come up with an extraterrestrial to have a close encounter in Brazil.

FRIDAY, AUGUST 26

For the two agents from the CIA, the wait ticked on toward midnight. Carson had stationed himself at one end of the isthmus but still in proximity to the factory pavilion. At the opposite end, well to the front of the building, Gwyneth lay concealed in a clump of high grass. The distance between them was somewhere in the range of a hundred fifty meters, and they communicated with each other using small walkie-talkies made, ironically enough, in Japan. It was pitch dark except for the mercury vapor lamps on tall cement posts illuminating the pavement that wound its way through the Industrial Park. Each agent carried a magnum .45 and two hand grenades. Not far off, hidden in the shadow of a giant bulldozer being used to dig the foundation for a nearby factory, sat a vehicle with phony plates supplied by the superintendent of SUFRAMA.

Expecting events to unfold at any moment, they crouched in the wet humus of sparse, rotting jungle and watched for the least sign of activity within range of the plant. The factory itself was well lit, not only by reflectors illuminating the institutional plaque naming the site, but also by spotlights above the pavilion and a single weaker light on a short lamppost at the edge of a pile of asbestos tiles. There seemed to be no one in the factory, not even a night watchman, which only served to heighten the sinister aura of the place. Perhaps the Japanese were relying upon some form of alarm system or electronic surveillance. Yet, the analyses of material brought back from their bus tour, including photos taken by Gwyneth, had produced no evidence of TV cameras, radar or any other surveillance apparatus.

Shortly after midnight, however, a large, late-model gray Citroen van appeared down the road and soon pulled into the factory drive. A man got out and opened the front gate without demonstrating any undue concern. The van entered and parked directly in front of the entryway to the building, whereupon a group of five men climbed out and filed swiftly into the factory. Given the purposefully calm and methodical behavior of these new arrivals, the Americans began to suspect that something had gone wrong; that someone had sounded the alarm, leaked the information that the hideaway was no longer safe, that they had better transfer the prisoner to a more secure location and evacuate the plant.

Gwyneth was the first to make his move. He crept along on all fours through the jungle, heading off toward the vehicle they had left parked in the shadow of the bulldozer. Carson, keeping an eye on the van, imitated his partner's move. The two of them met back at the car to review the situation. Each was certain only that he could no longer predict the outcome—but neither one was daunted: they were accustomed to facing the unforeseen.

Hidden in their car, they watched while the same five men filed out of the plant. Two of them bore something on their shoulders, canvas sacks, rather large. A man might fit perfectly inside one of those sacks. But there were two, which meant the presence of more than one prisoner. The Americans felt confident that, besides General Pessoa, they had had the good luck to stumble on the missing KGB agent as well.

Once they were all in the van, they drove off. They did not speed away; they simply took to the road at a comfortable 60 kph, then a bit faster, heading in the direction of the city. Helped by the winding configuration of the Industrial Park, the two Americans tailed the van easily without being spotted. The Park was set upon a number of hilly inclines through which the vehicles snaked their way toward the city.

Carson occasionally glanced at his partner, intrigued by the presence of the still mysterious second prisoner. Gwyneth, who had no doubts about its being the Russian from the KGB, nodded with excitement and tightened his grip on the wheel.

Meanwhile, inside the van the two sacks, guarded by men armed with INA submachine guns, writhed and twisted while emitting muffled cries. In the front seat sat the driver and two others dressed in dark blue monkey suits and knitted caps. They were armed with .45

automatics, of Brazilian Army issue. Though they seemed calm, they were on the verge of panic, ready to explode at the slightest hint of trouble. The two in the front seat next to the driver kept peering out at the landscape with evident anxiety, turning every minute to look behind them. Still, they did not notice they were being followed by the Caravan.

The two bagged prisoners continued to struggle. Vera, on the verge of suffocation, felt the rough canvas lacerating her naked body. General Pessoa, gagged and humiliated, feared a heart attack. When they were being led out of their cell—in reality, a room designed to test electronic equipment under controlled temperatures—the prisoners had felt only relief to have escaped that ovenlike atmosphere which had reduced them to little more than slabs of human meat bathed in perspiration. Yet, they resisted like crazed animals once it became apparent that they were to be dumped into canvas sacks. It took brute force to make them acquiesce to their fates. The general, who had already suspected they would not remain indefinitely at that location, was the most difficult to convince, despite his age. He was infuriated by his jailers' refusal to say even a single word in his presence. Yet, the sight of the girl's being slapped around made him finally listen to reason. Still, now it was he who twisted and grunted the most from inside his sack. And unfortunately, the two men guarding them were taking pleasure in his discomfort, knowing he would have to endure his predicament for some time to come.

The Americans, however, soon surmised that the trip was going to last awhile, once the van turned off in the direction of the Manaus-Itacoatiara Highway. Carson opened the glove compartment and took out a road map, carefully studying the route they were about the follow. If the van did not suddenly pull off to some ranch or farm along the way, but proceeded as far as Itacoatiara, the trip promised to last some four hours. He glanced immediately at the gauge for the gas tank and was relieved: they had enough fuel to last a lot farther. The highway was unlit, and the dark night—their own headlights, off—facilitated their mission. The kidnappers were clearly unaware they were being pursued.

"You really think the Russian is in there?"

Gwyneth nodded, smiling.

"What'll we do with him?"

"Oh, just a short conversation, then hand him over to the Brazilians."

"Where do you think they're taking them?"

Gwyneth shrugged his shoulders. "Does it matter?"

"If it's somewhere with lots of people around, our hands'll be tied."

"Then we go back later when things have quieted down."

They continued with this line of conversation, countering the monotony and the strain of a highway full of curves and precipices with their intermittent prattle. The pavement was not the best in the world, and from time to time, without the aid of headlights, the Caravan skidded on the gravel bedding. The smell of jungle drifted in through the open window. The Americans breathed the pure air, their eyes fixed on the twin taillights of the van: two distant, glowing coals in the blackness of night.

General Pessoa, thoroughly exhausted, finally gave up squirming at nearly the same moment the van started to bounce. The Americans tensed up when they saw that the kidnappers had forked off onto a narrow trail in the midst of the forest, some fifteen minutes after entering Itacoatiara, and eventually parked by the side of a placid lake where a seaplane sat in the darkness.

Gwyneth took the same fork and pulled over within sight of a log cabin where the van was parked. A dog began to bark, and from somewhere on the lake a beacon of light blinked three times, to which the abductors responded in kind with the headlights of the van. The two Americans, meanwhile, got out of the Caravan and crept painstakingly toward the shore of the lake, along a jutting promontory that afforded an excellent view of their surroundings even in such darkness.

The abductors finally climbed out of the van, turned on a powerful lantern and commenced to unload their human cargo. The lake began just beyond the slope, and was separated from the shore by a swampy perimeter of low grass and heavy rotten trunks strategically dominated by the point from which the Americans were observing the scene. In order to reach the seaplane, the kidnappers would have to carry the prisoners through this stretch of mud and grass, place them in a boat and row out to the aircraft. There was a canoe already tied up and waiting for them, its prow half grounded in the bog.

Unexpectedly, however, the prisoners were being freed from their sacks and—weapons pointed straight at them—readied to walk on their own two feet. The Americans cautiously descended, cutting through a half-overgrown manioc field, until they reached the most exposed section of the lakefront. Still they remained all but invisible, crawling along the ground, because the bright lantern darkened everything beyond its perimeter, which amounted to the vicinity of the cabin where the kidnappers had unloaded the van.

They watched while one of the men ran down the slope and untied the canoe and two others, armed with machine guns, began to shove the prisoners toward the lake. The Americans realized that they had to act immediately or they might lose their quarry for good.

As the two prisoners stumbled along toward the muddy slope, Carson glanced at his partner and they both placed silencers on their weapons. They crept swiftly along, their anxiety redoubled by the desperate barking of the dog. Gwyneth took a grenade off his belt and gripped it in his sweaty palm. They were now some ten meters from the guards, when Gwyneth pulled the pin out of the grenade with his teeth and hurled the oblong weapon at the van. The missile slammed like a stone against the side of the vehicle, but before it hit the ground a violent explosion illuminated the cabin and tumbled the splintered, flaming van onto its side, instantly killing those standing beside it and the driver who had yet to climb out from behind the wheel. The three men who had been guarding the prisoners ran back toward the explosion, but the two of them who were armed with the machine guns never got more than a couple of steps before they were gunned down by the Americans. The survivor, still holding the line to the canoe, instinctively raised his hands and placed them on his head.

The prisoners, eardrums deafened by the explosion, continued to march marionette-like toward the canoe. From the manioc field there emerged first Gwyneth, the most agile of the two, zigzagging in the direction of the man with his hands up on his head. Close behind, panting hard, a chubby Carson was attempting without much success to keep up with his swifter companion.

The seaplane started its motors and went gliding through the calm surface of the lake, maneuvering deftly among the islands of grass. Carson halted, took out a grenade, pulled the pin and hurled it at the plane. The explosion raised a column of water and smoke, but the craft was already banking safely in the air and soon disappeared into the night.

Gwyneth ran toward the prisoners, expecting to come face-to-face with a Russian from the KGB; but what he discovered was a white-skinned young woman with shapely curves and an expression of panic, as nude as a Greek Venus. Beside the surprising prisoner stood a myopic General Pessoa, straining to assimilate the events around him.

"Who are you?" the general exclaimed.

"Friends!" Gwyneth replied without taking his eyes off the girl.

Carson gave up on the seaplane and trotted up the slope to where Gwyneth was already conversing with the general and the other prisoner.

Pessoa was still suspicious, but relieved.

"Don't worry, General," Gwyneth insisted. "I told you we're friends."

"I hope so," the general answered, lowering his hand to adjust his dirty, wrinkled undershorts.

Gwyneth took off his jacket and handed it to the girl. Vera Martins covered herself and stood staring at the only survivor, who still remained with his hands on his head. The man was staring at her with an arrogance, with a sense of impunity that truly revolted her. Overcome with fury, she went up to the man, took the forty-five out from his holster and jammed it against his temple. A thread of sweat trickled down his close-cropped scalp and dripped from his cheekbone.

"Still feeling so high-and-mighty?"

The man did not reply, but Vera pushed the barrel harder, making his head tilt to one side.

The man let out a moan of submission.

Gwyneth grabbed the weapon from her hand.

"He'll be more useful alive, miss. He has quite a few stories to tell us."

Carson went to take a look at the remains of the van, then checked out the deserted cabin. Pessoa put an arm around Vera's shoulders, drawing her to him in a protective way.

"It seems everything's going to be all right now, child."

"Let's get going," Gwyneth summoned them.

"Where to?" the general asked him.

"Manaus, of course. Isn't that where you want to go?"

The general nodded. In some ways the fact of his being dressed only in his undershorts made the general feel slightly constrained in the presence of the two men and their prisoner—oddly enough, a constraint he had at no time felt while imprisoned with a totally naked girl.

Later, Aboard a Military Plane on Its Way to Brasília

"You should be happy you escaped with your life," Raul insisted, seated beside his father and irritated with the sullenness of the old man.

"I have no desire to go to Brasília, as you well know."

"But, Dad, the thing's in the hands of the authorities now."

"The authorities! How naive can you get, son?"

Raul Pessoa turned away and sat watching the clouds drift above the Amazonian immensity. He had barely arrived in Manaus before

THE ORDER OF THE DAY

he was on his way back, his father beside him safe and sound, though terribly ill-humored, since they had not permitted him to go on with his investigation.

"I only wanted to have five minutes with that fellow the Americans captured. I think he might have given me some excellent leads to follow."

His son shook his head. The old man was not one to give up easily, and Raul began to worry about what might happen next.

"Dad, it was the President himself who asked that you not be involved any further in the matter."

"I *know*," the general roared. "He treats me as if I were already senile."

"That's not true, Dad. The President is very decent to you."

"Yes, yes," muttered the general.

Next to them, Vera Martins was curled up in sleep and Raul was wondering why his father hadn't done the same. The general ought to have been at least as exhausted as the girl. True, the preliminary medical examination at the Military Hospital of Manaus did not indicate anything seriously wrong, but the doctor had recommended a complete rest for the general, in order to recuperate his strength.

An Air Force sergeant approached the seats where father and son continued to bicker.

"There's coffee up front. Would you care for some, gentlemen?"

Raul accepted but decided to go up and get it himself.

"Want some, Dad?"

"No," he replied curtly.

"Good enough," Raul said understandingly, attempting at the same time to step over Vera's knees.

But the girl awakened.

"Sorry," he apologized, despairing that he had awakened her.

"No, it doesn't matter," she replied.

"Would you care for some coffee?"

Vera accepted and sat up in her seat.

"Are you feeling better, child?" the general inquired solicitously, placing a hand on Vera's arm.

"Oh, I'm fine. Just dying to get home, that's all. I'll be taking a night flight to São Paulo and I ought to get there by morning. It's six months I've been away."

"Is your family there?"

"My mother and father, yes, but I live alone. I inherited an apartment in Perdizes from my grandfather."

The general withdrew his hand and grew sullen once again.

"You're still disappointed, aren't you?" Vera consoled him.

On their arrival at GHQ for the Military Command of Amazonia, they had been taken immediately to the hospital. The general had wanted to stay behind, insisting that he was fine and wishing to participate in the prisoner's interrogation. But his presence had seemed superfluous to the men from Second Section.

"They're hiding something . . . they don't trust me."

Raul returned with two cups of coffee and handed one to Vera.

"You sure you don't want one, Dad?"

The general turned abruptly to stare out the window. Night was beginning to fall and the clouds were tinted with yellow and violet, drifting above the parched earth of the central plateau.

Raul returned to his seat and paid no more attention to his sulking father.

"I almost never have coffee anymore," Vera confessed.

The young man looked at her and smiled. He didn't feel very interested in starting up a conversation.

The plane was an AVRO, used for carrying high-ranking officers, the seats arranged in rows as in a normal passenger plane. Toward the middle of the cabin, however, the rows terminated abruptly and the plane assumed a more military ambience, with stacks of cases and olive-green bundles, where some sergeants were congregated around an animated game of poker.

In another half hour they would be landing in Brasília, and the pilot had already established contact with the airport tower to prepare for their descent. The craft winged smoothly through the air, with no turbulence and a clear sky ahead. The monotony of the flight and the persistent hum of the engines caused the general to finally drift off into a light sleep, vanquished with exhaustion. His head hung slightly forward and nodded gently. His son, meanwhile, was attempting to put behind him the anxiety of the past few days. The disappearance of the old man had produced total chaos at home. Although Raul had managed to hide the facts from his mother, he and his friends from the NCPR had feared for the worst.

Vera Martins, taking occasional sips of coffee from her cup, was trying to keep her mind blank. She did not want to think about what had happened, preoccupied that the old fear might return. She seemed to have recovered, to have escaped from the kingdom of shadows— a sensation both difficult to describe and common to those imprisoned without a logical explanation. She had had no news of Paulo. Upon falling into the hands of her captors, she had initially felt her predicament might at least lead her to him. But even that simple possibility had been denied her in that boiling cell.

Farther back in the plane, the sergeants continued laughing, betting on the cards, entertaining themselves until the landing. Vera followed the crescendos of laughter and the rivalries of the game, but eventually noticed that the sergeants had become curiously silent. The animation of the game had abruptly broken off, and she turned her head to look back and discover the motive for their silence. The sergeants were all staring mutely out the windows through which a bluish luminescence seemed to penetrate the cabin and bathe the incredulous faces of their now frozen figures.

Vera, almost instinctively, turned to look through the nearest portal that offered a view in the same direction. There outside, hovering at a constant distance from the plane, a great luminous blinking sphere was projecting darting rays of blue light against the body of the plane. Initially, she allowed herself to be drawn in fascination to simply contemplating the phenomenon—it might have been the twilight appearance of the planet Venus which often played tricks upon the observer. But the persistence of the phenomenon, its steady rotation began to provoke a terrible prickling at the base of her skull. She looked fearfully toward the pilot's cabin, which was open in that craft, and immediately registered the agitation of the crew. The copilot was frantically communicating over the radio to the control tower in Brasília, narrating the phenomenon and asking for an explanation.

"We've picked it up on our screens," the metallic voice of the controller replied from Brasília, "but we have no craft airborne in the vicinity."

"The object does not respond to our calls. We've tried all frequencies."

"Attempt to identify," the voice urged from Brasília.

"It is pursuing at a speed of six hundred kilometers and remains roughly five hundred meters to starboard. It must be roughly thirty meters in breadth, but there's no way to describe its precise contours. It's just a damn ball of light!"

Activity in the cabin grew more and more frantic. Next to Vera, the general continued to doze. His son, however, stared out at the apparition mesmerized.

"We are scrambling to intercept," the tower informed.

Another voice entered into radio communication.

"PP-SPD, VASP jetliner here, over."

"AVRO, FAB here, over," the copilot replied.

"VASP, Flight 201 proceeding to Manaus from Rio de Janeiro, via Brasília. We are observing a luminous oval object, moving at tremendous speed to our left. Can you confirm? Over."

"Positive, VASP; repeat, positive. CINDACTA has it on their screens."

"Okay, FAB. Over and out."

"My God! What can it be?" Vera cried.

The object maneuvered itself in a series of arcs above and below their altitude, then began to draw nearer to the plane. The shortening of the distance could be measured by the increasing size of the light, now an enormous ball of oval fire pulsating in different hues from red to yellow.

"It's coming straight for us!" Raul shouted, snapping out of his trance.

Vera Martins had barely the time to lift her hands and protect her face in an instinctive gesture. The ball advanced against the plane at a fantastic velocity and then suddenly lifted, poising itself directly above the AVRO. The pilot and his copilot were trembling helplessly, for radio communication had been cut off completely.

"Good God!" Vera screamed.

The interior of the AVRO filled with a yellowish glow, like the light from a mercury vapor lamp, and suddenly the cabin began to heat up. It was then that the engines started to sputter, though the instruments in the pilot's cabin still indicated everything was normal.

General Pessoa awoke with the first jolt of the plane. The craft shook several more times, as if drawn upwards by a powerful magnet; and the needles of the altimeter, to the pilot's horror, began spinning crazily.

The sergeants had abandoned the cargo compartment and strapped themselves into their seats, livid and sweating.

Another jolt sucked the plane even higher, and the engines finally cut off totally. The craft continued to rise crazily and at tremendous velocity, while the heat of the cabin began to dwindle into an uncomfortable chill.

"It's trying to knock us out of the air!" one of the sergeants yelled fearfully.

Only General Pessoa kept his professional calm, picking up a camera and waiting. He noted Raul's and Vera's agitation, not to speak of the anxiety among the rest of the passengers and crew. Then unexpectedly the camera was ripped out of his hands and smashed somehow into thin air, vanishing into a vortex of incredible forces.

"It's Sylyon," said the general calmly.

"You mean you think that..." Raul paled as he comprehended the significance of his father's statement.

"He can do what he pleases with this little toy," the general continued a bit too indolently.

Outside, as the plane continued its vertiginous ascent, the stalled propellers were twisted beyond recognition, rendered useless by the force of Sylon.

As she observed what was happening, Vera came to the realization that she was going to die. Soon the plane would be plunging to earth, and all that would survive would be the unrecognizable remains of metal and flesh. Faced with the inescapable, strangely she felt only a deep serenity. She closed her eyes, leaned back in her seat and hugged herself with both arms against the extreme cold.

There was no longer any panic on the plane, only the stoic tranquility of sheer fate.

The pilot was the first to observe another light speeding toward his AVRO, coming out of nowhere in the opposite direction. It must have been traveling at a speed of more than 1000 kph, since in less than a few seconds it had closed the distance between them and begun to maneuver more slowly now into proximity, circling the plane at a radius of about one hundred meters' distance. It was a much smaller light, more bluish and more blindingly intense than the other UFO.

"It's impossible what the damn thing is doing out there!" muttered the pilot with astonishment.

The light further increased its own intensity, and the AVRO immediately trembled, released all of a sudden from the force that had been lifting it steadily higher. The passengers felt the tremendous impact of gravity's reassertion as the craft began its vertiginous plunge. None of the instruments were working, and it was only a matter of minutes before the plane would slam into Earth.

The smaller light that had just made its appearance trailed after the AVRO at a steady distance as they plunged in their downward spiral. The sergeants gripped their seats and Vera had the impression that all of her vital organs were shifting positions and moving toward her throat.

Then the craft halted. It stopped falling, to remain frozen in space. It had been a halt without impact. Swift, but without the laws of inertia. As if the AVRO were secured by a fine nylon safety net.

General Pessoa openly applauded before the inexpressive gazes of the other passengers. He clapped his hands like a baby, laughing delightedly, seized by a happiness as absurd as the totality of all that had just transpired.

"It's Quazgaa," he announced.

The sudden choke of turbines drew everyone's attention and the pilot gradually realized that his instrument panel was again showing signs of life. He glanced outside to find that the blades of the propellers had been restored to their original shape. The AVRO craft moved back on course and regained its former altitude, as if it had been subjected to nothing worse than a slight loss of pressure.

All the passengers were staring out the windows, but saw only the sky now, already dark and starry, and down below the lights of Brasília twinkling on the horizon. Not a sign of lights or UFOs in the vicinity of the aircraft. The radio crackled and the copilot switched it back on.

"Hello! Hello! AVRO? Over? Control tower, here. We lost contact—"

"AVRO here. Instrument failure, the last three minutes. Over."

"Everything okay?"

"Everything okay, back to normal. Request permission to land."

Raul, his hands trembling, reached into the inner pocket of his jacket and took out the box of microfilm the sergeant had entrusted to him at the bus terminal.

"Dad, I'd forgotten to show you. . . . Somebody you know sent you this box of microfilm."

The general reached for the box as if he were already expecting it.

"Sergeant Melo, right?"

"That's right, Pop. In the midst of all this craziness I had forgotten to give it to you."

"It's a crucial document, son. It's what Sylyon was trying to destroy—and nearly succeeded."

Raul Pessoa bit his tongue, recalling Sergeant Melo as he pranced through the bus station in Brasília wearing his pair of spiked heels. As the plane touched down on the runway, he felt Vera's hand gently squeezing his arm. He turned to smile at her and let his thoughts drift back to the girl there beside him, very beautiful, very calm, who had faced impending death with such extraordinary courage. The two had certainly shared an experience that would prove the envy of any adventurer in the absurd.

They were driven to a special wing of the airport by bus, where the sergeants and crew boarded another conveyance. They would be taken to Anapolis and there debriefed by research specialists from the Brazilian Air Force for their archives on UFOs. A small retinue, meanwhile, made up of two regimental guards from the Presidential

Battallion along with their captain, showed up to greet General Pessoa.

"Welcome back, sir," said the captain with a salute.

Without returning the formality, the general proceeded toward the exit from the terminal. But the two guards caught up with him and barred his way.

"What the hell's going on here, Captain!" roared Pessoa. "We need a bath and a good night's sleep in our own homes."

The captain attempted to respond affably.

"Sorry, general, but I have orders to take you at once to the President, at Granja do Torto."

He slipped a folded piece of paper out of a breast pocket and handed it to the general. It was a note in the unmistakable handwriting of the President himself, inviting the general and his companions to proceed directly from the airport to the presidential ranch.

"What does he want, to give us a barbecue?" the general said jokingly.

"I couldn't say, sir," the captain replied. "We have transportation waiting outside. Will you come along, General?"

The general turned to Vera, offering her his hand.

"I think we part company here, my child."

Vera gave the old man a hug, kissing him on the cheeks. She was about to repeat the gesture with his son when the captain intervened.

"I'm afraid her as well, sir."

"Her as well?" the general asked with surprise.

"The order was to bring your entire group. And she seems to be part of it, sir, don't you think?"

Vera Martins dropped her satchel on the floor and stood waiting. The captain was silently pleading with the general not to create further problems.

"Fine, Captain," said Pessoa at last. "Come along, child. At least you'll be able to say you've met the President."

Vera's long sigh was not exactly an indication she was charmed by the notion. For whatever it was worth, however, her adventure was finally leading her to the very core of national power.

At Granja do Torto, on the Outskirts of Brasília

The horse was chestnut-brown. Its nostrils flared in the clear air. He was a high-strung animal and the President knew it. A five-year-old, he was growing into magnificent shape: a handsome Arabian stallion that was the President's pride and joy.

As he did every day after setting aside the affairs of office, the

President had put on his riding breeches and his boots and, before having a bath, had disappeared for several hours into the stables. His passion for horses was public and notorious. Not only because he had risen in the cavalry division, but equally from his long years of experience with those same animals, reaching as far back as adolescence, in exile in Buenos Aires. It was there that he had first taken horseback-riding lessons, during vacations. And now he had a small collection of his own thoroughbreds, costing him a fortune to maintain. He lived his life of horses to such a degree that even his figures of speech were derived from this intimacy, which had cost him untold embarrassment until he had grown wise enough to limit such remarks to the circle of his closest friends.

The President was running a brush over the chestnut hide of his Arabian, restoring its sheen, cleaning out the dust and the excess hair, calming the beast as it turned its head from one side to the other. The stallion whinnied contentedly but still demonstrated a hint of nervousness. The intelligent eyes scrutinizd their master, peering about at the freshly provisioned stall. The President, likewise a bit nervous, had actually passed his emotional state onto this extremely sensitive steed. It was no wonder . . . Upon the President's arrival at home, he had been met by an already established pandemonium. The kitchen had been turned upside down, china smashed on the floor, all the servants talking at once while attempting to explain to the secret service men what had happened.

Now, he heard footsteps suddenly approaching, and he set aside what he was doing in the stall to have a look at who was coming. He had not managed to concentrate, in any case, on the work at hand and his apprehensiveness only served to perturb his stallion. On reaching the gate of the stall, the President saw that it was the head of the SNI, accompanied by General Pessoa and a young couple. He picked up his shirt to put it on, placing the brush on a shelf just outside of the stall.

"Did you have a pleasant flight, General?" the President inquired, swinging a bucket into the locker and raising a hand to greet Pessoa.

"Some minor incidents, excellency."

"So they tell me. I do wish to apologize, Pessoa, for forcing you to come here at such an hour."

The minister from the SNI shook his head disapprovingly.

"The general, here, didn't want me to," the President explained, pointing at the head of the SNI, "but you're the only one who can tell me what in the world's going on here."

General Pessoa smiled. He knew that the President, who had under a previous administration held the same ministerial post as this other general now occupied, had little faith in the appraisals of any secret service. It was part of his impulsive spirit not to take them too seriously.

They left the stable together and headed back to the ranch house, followed discreetly by several secret service men in charge of security.

"I guarantee that we'll soon have the whole thing cleared up," insisted the minister of the SNI, still vexed with the presence of these strangers there. "A geologist from the University of Brasília has suggested that it might have been a small earth tremor caused by the pressure building under the entire plateau."

"What's going on?" Pessoa asked, more curious now.

"The kitchen," replied the minister dryly, "was hit by a tremor. ... Evidently the servants, simple people as they are, attribute a supernatural force to the event."

"The servants, you say?" The President was clearly annoyed. "All I need is for the head of intelligence to start telling me *I'm* only being *superstitious*."

The general from the SNI removed his cap and stretched out his hand to protest.

"Please, sir, try to be reasonable," he implored.

"Reasonable? Reasonable! Plates flying from one side of the kitchen to the other, then smashing to the floor... Stones flying up to the ceiling, then zigzagging back and forth until they strike the servants ... The kitchen table spinning up into the air without anybody's touching it... And you want me to be reasonable?"

"There has to be some logical explanation," the minister retorted angrily.

"Of course there does," the President snarled, jabbing the air with a fist, "and the explanation has nothing to do with any shifting of continental shelves. Earthquakes don't twist forks and spoons!"

"Fascinating," remarked General Pessoa dryly.

"Which is why I had you brought here, Pessoa. You're the only one I know who won't be tempted to put me in a straitjacket for what I have to say."

"When did this phenomenon start?" Pessoa inquired.

"Around six o'clock this evening," the President confided.

Pessoa turned to his son and nodded knowingly.

"Almost the same instant all that business took place up in the air, son," he told him.

"More or less," Raul clarified.

"Your son's already a grown man," the President commented with surprise. "What are you studying, my boy?"

"Medicine, excellency," Raul hastened to answer.

"And the girl? His fiancée?" the President continued to Pessoa, openly intriguing with paternal familiarity.

"A friend," General Passoa corrected. "Who happens to be in *my* company."

"I see," the President observed, backing off a bit. "She seems a good filly, good stock."

Only the minister from the SNI managed a laugh, while the President paused to observe the effect of his words on the girl.

"So much the better that you're not one of those feminists," the President added after a moment.

Vera Martins offered no reply but stared back at the President with haughty reserve, which intensified the charm of her face that was slowly losing its tan.

They were nearly at the steps of the veranda of the house when the wife of the President suddenly emerged from a side door, with a facetious smile on her lips and an incredibly stiff, lacquered, anachronistic-looking hairdo. The First Lady, moreover, even at her most intimate moments took care not to be caught without several layers of makeup.

"Welcome, you lovely people," she said with a flourish. "Will you be sitting out here on the veranda?"

"We're on our way to the Trophy Room," the President replied. "We don't want to be disturbed."

He tossed his riding whip onto a wrought-iron chair and summoned his guests to follow him to the Trophy Room—a favorite refuge.

The Trophy Room had more the air of a veterinarian's office, or a rancher's in the old tradition, than that of the preferred solace of a President of the Republic. The single bookshelf displayed a few volumes on horses and the bound collections of American and European magazines on the same subject. The spacious writing desk was practically bare—it was not the habit of the President to mix politics with the hearth. Near the window, an armoire of metal and glass housed a variety of useful remedies for equine ailments. There was not a trophy in sight.

The President sat down and motioned everyone else to do the same. General Pessoa was the first to accede to the invitation; exhaustion had begun to fatigue his senses. The leather chair was soft, comfortable and soothing. He stared out the window and let his eyes wander across the well-cut, illuminated lawn until they encountered the sight of a security guard armed with a machine gun strolling slowly through the grass. Not far beyond, a high wire fence separated the official compound from the half-desolate landscape of open pastures, stunted trees, and red earth receding into the low-lying hills concealed by darkness.

"Would any of you folks care for coffee, or something else?" the President offered, immediately lapsing into laughter. "Of course, it'll have to be in paper cups—we've lost all the china."

No one wanted anything for the moment, however.

"So you mean to tell me that the china began to fly around the room?" General Pessoa inquired.

"When I arrived here, the place was in a turmoil. The thing had just begun to happen. The servants were refusing to go into the kitchen, and then some idiot from the secret service emptied a machine-gun in there, making even more of a mess."

"Sounds like some sort of poltergeist phenomenon," Pessoa reflected.

"That's exactly what I thought," the President eagerly confirmed. "I immediately recalled that film, you know? I wonder if this ranch was built on some kind of cemetery. . . ."

"We've already checked that possibility," the SNI minister interjected.

The President let out with a cackle, which caused everyone to stare uncomfortably into space.

"I can just imagine what the results were," the President chided, barely able to contain his laughter.

The minister stood up. "If my presence is not needed!"

"Oh, sit down, General. You should run for the Presidency so you develop a sense of humor."

The minister sat down again begrudgingly.

Suddenly the wife of the President came in, looking speechless.

"What's the matter?" the President asked, rising from his chair.

"That business! Now it's in my room!"

Everybody rushed to the First Lady's room and through the doorway could see the bed bucking like a wild bronco and small bottles of cosmetics and perfumes taking flight from the dressing table and smashing to the floor.

"It's unbelievable," her husband commented in astonishment.

"My perfumes . . ." lamented the First Lady.

"I'd like to grab one of these spirits by the balls," the President confessed furiously.

The bed tapped the floor nervously while mattress, sheets and pillows leaped as if they were alive.

"We'll have to locate the epicenter," Pessoa advised them. "Why don't we start right here in the house itself?"

"Good enough," the President assented. "Let's get to it."

The minister from the SNI folded his arms and went to sit in an easy chair in the living room. There he remained gaping at a TV set switched on to a situation comedy, absent from the fevered activity under way in all the rooms of the house.

"It's no accident that the Encyclopedia Britannica classifies military intelligence as slightly below animal intelligence," Vera Martins whispered into Raul's ear.

The young fellow smiled amiably at her and continued noting on his pad everything his father was dictating to him. He carried out this mission with great efficiency and equanimity, never looking around, perfectly adapted to the strangeness of the circumstances.

"And what about the staff?" Pessoa inquired. "Have you any adolescents among the servants?"

"None," the President responded, "everybody's at least over thirty." Then he turned to Vera and Raul to qualify: "That is, at least among the domestic staff. You always have a few soldiers on duty as sentinels by the front gate—some of those are fairly green behind the ears."

The First Lady was trailing close behind, sniveling over the loss of her cosmetics.

"You simply must do something! A *fortune* in perfumes down the drain. And it *would* have to be the ones I bought in Cleveland."

"Look here, woman, don't start breaking my chops," the President roared.

The First Lady, her incredible pompadour still intact above her lavishly dowdy evening gown, turned to her husband. "I think you've been impeached but don't know it."

"Turn off that mouth of yours and stop pestering me," the President retorted with increasing rage.

"I will not turn off anything and you're not the man to make me!" riposted his spouse.

The President turned to General Pessoa, a twinge of lividness coloring his dark complexion.

Pessoa resumed his examination out on the veranda, where he traced his way to the First Lady's bedroom window. The phenomenon still persisted, now in the form of a velvet rug floating past the window sash as if it had come straight out of an Arabian fairy tale.

"I'm sorry, ma'am, but until we discover the epicenter, this thing is bound to continue," Pessoa clarified to the First Lady.

"I just don't want this business to attack my horses," interjected the President worriedly.

"You only think of those smelly animals," his wife complained bitterly.

Before the President was able to explode definitively, two servants rushed out onto the veranda.

"Excellency, the cook!"

"What the devil's happening now?"

"It's Dona Nina, excellency," one of the two commenced to explain, "she's been possessed by a saint in the living room!"

Everybody proceeded to hurry into the living room where they came upon an old black woman, very fat, who had been with the President's family for many many years, and was now swaying rhythmically and emitting outlandish grunts in front of the minister from the SNI, who continued to sit indifferently in his chair.

"Let her be!" warned General Pessoa. "We must all join hands and attempt to enter into contact."

A circle was immediately formed around the old woman, which the head of the SNI boisterously refused to join. Some began praying aloud, and the majordomo—a cousin to the cook and also black—made his rhythmical appearance with a lit cigar, handing it to the old woman as she sighed, moaned and shimmied in the center of the circle.

"Speak, sister!" implored the general.

The old cook blew out puffs of smoke but limited herself to unintelligible gruntings. Vera, holding the President's hand to her left and Raul's to her right, felt an uncontrollable urge to laugh.

Another, separate bit of confusion seemed to be erupting somewhere outside. There were shouts, and several men could be seen running to the back of the garden. General Pessoa noticed the President's complexion was shifting rapidly from livid purple to ashen gray.

"Come," said the old cook in a round basso tone of voice.

They all trailed at the heels of the old woman out to the back of the garden, where the grand lawn ended at the foot of the wire fence. Seated, handcuffed, a young soldier was being detained in the midst of rows of red blooming poppies. Security men in plainclothes were already at work with picks and shovels.

"He's confessed to secretly burying something here," explained one of the secret service men who was lifting a shovel, pointing to one corner of the lush poppy field.

"Who is this man?" the President demanded.

Security handed him a roster of names with one of them underlined in red pencil. The President, moving his glasses back onto his forehead, began to scrutinize the document. The soldier was identified as from Minas Gerais State, and currently a member of the President's honor guard.

"What was it you buried over there, my boy?" the understanding voice of General Pessoa resounded rather absurdly in the midst of the confusion.

The soldier, frightened to death, lowered his eyes without comment.

"I think we may have located the epicenter," the general observed triumphantly. They continued to dig where the young recruit had indicated. The secret service men worked furiously, completely destroying the flower bed.

General Pessoa stooped down to the young handcuffed private and conversed with him in a low voice. The lad at one point slowly shook his head, in the gesture of someone who had lost all hope and was prepared to accept his due. Then he uttered something, imperceptible to the others, in the ear of the general.

"A confession?" the President interrupted.

"Not quite, but something very interesting," Pessoa replied and immediately went over to his son. "Raul, you know that boy has also received a visit from Sylyon."

"A visit from whom?" the President insisted, perturbed by his own complete ignorance of what was going on.

"The lad just told me that yesterday he was approached by a very beautiful-looking woman who called herself Sylvia. The woman behaved very provocatively with him and finally convinced him to bury something here in the garden. He says it was some sort of package."

"You think it was the same woman, Dad?"

"Precisely . . . Sylyon is in the habit of taking the feminine gender whenever he manifests himself. The lad only confessed because the ghost of Dead Preto Velho, received by the cook, made him do so."

"If that was the same woman who made me crack up on my bike that night, then Sylyon sure knows how to pick his females." The recollection of the smiling figure, full of vitality, who nearly drove him to his death, was a difficult one to erase.

A shovel being wielded by one of the security men thudded against something solid.

"I think we've found the thing, excellency."

"Don't touch it!" Pessoa warned.

The old cook, who had kept up her swaying by the edge of the hole amid great puffs of smoke from her cigar, suddenly let out a few more groans and proceeded to lift the object from out of the hole. It was a cigar box, wrapped in ordinary brown paper. Unwrapping it slowly, she removed a slim volume with yellowing pages bound in dark leather. The old woman, after passing the cigar over it several times, handed the volume to the President.

Reluctantly, the President reached out and took hold of it by the binding, then commenced to leaf slowly through its crumbling pages. The ashen pallor of his cheeks intensified, and General Pessoa feared a moment for the President's heart.

"It's a copy of the Helsinki Accords," he announced in a baffled voice. "Human rights and whatnot . . . Look here, signed by everybody—but this is *classified!* How did it get here?"

From back on the veranda, the applause of the domestics echoed through the garden. A servant rushed down the lawn to announce that the house had returned to normal, the phenomenon had ceased.

"Because the epicenter has clearly been pinpointed and neutralized," Pessoa declared triumphantly.

"But why," the President demanded, holding up the agreement. "Why this?" he exclaimed with a waxen expression.

"To topple you from power, excellency," was the dry slap of a reply from the general.

"But who? Who wants to overthrow the government?" he insisted, paging distractedly through the volume, his hands trembling, his voice faltering.

"Those who cling to the past, those who believe themselves to be above the law."

"But a coup would be disastrous! With the economic crisis we have on our hands at the moment . . . you could hardly manage by implementing local repressive measures. Why, you'd have to multiply by a hundred what was done in Chile. A soccer stadium, hell, you'd have to have a thousand soccer stadiums spread all over the country and execute ten percent of the entire population to achieve that kind of power."

The President kept opening and reclosing the little volume as he regained a still livid composure.

"Why, you'd have to seal up this country to a degree that would paralyze the nation, wreck the economy and set back development another twenty years. And the response from this society, whether for or against me—"

"You'd wind up with a continental Iranian blood bath on your hands," General Pessoa completed.

"Exactly! And when we eventually came out of it—if we ever did!—you'd have another country, not Brazil; and quite possibly in an alien political orbit."

Everyone walked in stunned silence, following the President back to the house. The First Lady had forgotten entirely about her cosmetics. And it did little for what was left of her composure to have her husband say, without breaking his stride or concealing his thoughts from their guests: "When I go, you go, and let that be a lesson to you!"

Meanwhile, Out on a Highway Somewhere Near Brasília

Pavel Aksentyevich was having trouble getting used to the damnable stick shift in the old Volkswagen he had managed to steal from the garage at the Valley of the Seven Moons. Nonetheless, if he could just keep going at a reasonable eighty kph and leave it in fourth gear, he might possibly make it to the Plano Piloto and the haven of the embassy.

He had taken flight without premeditation. The idea had occurred to him suddenly when the waiter entered his makeshift cell. He had simply decided to make the attempt and, quite unexpectedly, discovered that his prison was not exactly a work of sophisticated security.

First he rid himself of the waiter with a quick blow to the head. The weapon had been a crystal bowl of Jell-O that he had levitated from the dinner cart at high speed and sent flying against the fellow's skull, without the latter's having the time to even contemplate resistance.

In order not to attract attention, he had donned the waiter's outfit—a bit too tight for a man of his stature—dumped the meal from its dishes onto the floor and set out with the cart through the open door, traversing the corridors without incident. To cap his success, he had penetrated the archives room from which he was able to lift the Betamax videocassette on which were registered the extraordinary phenomena that had been filmed by the dead American agent in the Amazon.

Pavel left the cart in the cantina and proceeded to the garage where the old Volks was parked with keys still in the ignition. From what he could observe, the auto must have belonged to an excessively zealous kitchen employee, since two carrots and a half a cabbage sat rotting in the backseat. No matter, his happiness—though still guarded—was assured by the discovery of the tape. Such a piece of evidence would certainly provoke the highest interest on the part of his superiors, and he was already dreaming of the advantages he would reap with this bit of proof of the great victory he had won over the forces of American Imperialism. He might even receive a promotion—not to mention a large apartment in a more fashionable part of Moscow, *without* the help of his sullen brother-in-law. At the very least, he would be entitled to take his family the coming summer to an exclusive *dacha* on the Baltic, where only the most intimately connected with the centers of power had the right to a vacation, with bottles of French champagne, games of *gorodki* and affable soirees with the Presidium's bigwigs.

With a single roll of tape, slipped into the pocket of the waiter's tight-fitting white jacket, he had won his passport to the rosy world of those touched by the grace of the regime.

Later, at the Residence of General Pessoa

Vera Martins stared at the intriguing oil painting hanging on the living room wall in General Pessoa's apartment, at Superquadra Sul 305. Beside her was Raul Pessoa, busily explaining to her the exotic artifacts mixed in with the otherwise conventional decor of the room.

The painting depicted a large circular spaceship glowing in a sky filled with clouds, above a landscape which appeared to Vera to represent one of the baroque cities of the state of Minas Gerais, perhaps the town Mariana. The ship had a distinct row of illuminated hatchways and, from out of one of them, a face was inquisitively peering at whoever approached the painting.

"It's the space ship of Quazgaa," Raul explained. "An artist friend of father's painted that depiction based on records of the first encounter."

Below the painting, on a small table supporting a lamp and several ashtrays, was the plaster mold of what seemed to be the footprints of a duck, even though this particular duck would have had to have the dimensions of an ostrich. Next to the mold another object—this a dark, shining slab—also attracted Vera's attention.

"That's the footprints of an alien being who landed in the mud of a river basin, somewhere in the interior of Piauí State. The local hicks confused the poor extraterrestrial with the Devil and killed it, burying the corpse in an unmarked grave. Unfortunately, we've never managed to locate the site in order to exhume the remains."

"And what's that wavy slab?"

"This? A cropolyte."

"A what?"

"The vitrified feces of an extraterrestrial, found during the excavations of Três Poderes Plaza, in 1959."

"But how do you know it's actually from an extraterrestrial?"

"Well, whoever passed these wastes ate magnesium in a nearly pure state. No earthly food contains the substance in such absolute dosages. According to our carbon 14 tests, this cropolyte dates back more than ten thousand years."

Vera laughed at the notion of some alien being hastily landing his spaceship, right on the central plateau more than ten millenniums ago, for the prosaic purpose of alleviating his exotic bowels.

Maurício, the young lawyer, came into the room, interrupting their conversation.

"It wasn't easy, but I managed to Xerox the microfilm. The guard at Banco do Brasil remained rather skeptical, but I greased his palm and he permitted me to enter the import-export facilities, where they have a machine with a microfilm viewer and copier. I think we now have a pretty good idea of the identity of our representative of Sylyon and Master to the sect of the Valley of the Seven Moons."

General Pessoa, who had been nodding off in an easy chair while browsing through a newspaper, jumped up and practically tore the binder of Xeroxed pages from out of the lawyer's hands.

"Easy, Dad," Raul tried to calm him, "they're not going to fly away."

The general signaled his son and the others to follow him into his meticulously organized study, where he was working on the reorganization of the mostly destroyed archives of the National Center for Paranormal Research.

"Let me read it aloud," the general announced.

FARENHEIT 451

MUTUAL UFO NETWORK
HUMANOID STUDY GROUP INC.
207 OLDSTONE RD
AUSTIN, TEXAS 78712

File 27

TRIP TO AN ALIEN REALM

Date: July 14, 1968
Hypnosis/Debriefing Session no. 5
Attending Physicians: Drs. Melvyn Hill, Rodger Helmstein and Alan
J. Farber.
(Attached Portuguese translation prepared by Norberto Caldas, from
the Brazilian Consulate in New York at the behest of Brigadier General
Bernardo Fischer.)

The day was still light when we began the scheduled session of
hypnosis in the West Room of the Institute of Parapsychology at
Austin. The patient Fischer was, unbeknownst to all, about to undergo
one of the most painful experiences of his life. And his suffering
profoundly affected those of us who were present. What we were
unwittingly about to record went far beyond anything that our intellects
had thus far ever encountered. Fischer was seated in his chair, in a
state of wakefulness, about to enter his deep trance under the direct
supervision of Dr. Hill.

DR. HILL: Fischer, I want you to go back to the moment where
we ended the last session. You had already entered another
time zone? Continue from that point please.
FISCHER: From the moment I entered the other time zone, or
the point at which I was being transported back from there?

DR. HILL: Begin with the moment you entered the other place.

FISCHER: All right . . . but I feel afraid . . .

DR. HILL: Nothing is going to happen to you, I promise . . . relax.

FISCHER: I am proceeding along a white path . . . but it's very dark around me . . . the whole surroundings. I seem to be numb. And the path trails on indefinitely through the darkness. They realize how afraid I am but they continue to march on ahead.

DR. HILL: They? Who?

FISCHER: The little beings . . . the ones who received me on the other side of the door, once I had entered this universe.

DR. HILL: Go on, we're listening.

FISCHER: Now I can make out a sort of luminousness, where the path suddenly halts. (Incomprehensible groans) It's getting very hot here . . . and the velocity keeps increasing. (Moaning and heavy breathing) My *feet* . . . and . . . we're passing right through the *light*. We've entered another realm!

DR. HILL: What is the place like?

FISCHER: It's hot, very hot. And all red, everything. It must be the only color that exists here. But not in the same way that a red sun would illuminate the Earth. Everything is red—emptiness is red. And the edifices there below are red.

DR. HILL: Edifices?

FISCHER: Minarets and walls. All red. Now the white strip is descending, and it becomes possible to see the edifices more clearly. There are lofty walls, incredibly high. And luminous minarets . . . but . . . it's not possible! . . . My head! . . .

DR. HILL: Take it easy, now. No need to become anxious.

FISCHER: They're . . . they're the towers . . . of the Kremlin . . . The wall is there . . . and the tomb, of that *evil* Lenin! . . . The creatures, minuscule-looking, are all queueing up. The two beings also seem to be frightened. I sense this because of how they are floating more rapidly along the strip. (Choking sounds, as if he were suffocating)

My God, agh-agh! I'm in such *pain* . . . It's getting hotter and hotter. We're nearly running now, but the distance is still enormous.

(He's panting now and crying out in pain)

Jesus, I'm burning! Burning inside myself, where am I really? What place is this? The creatures down below there . . . slaves! Slaves of *Communism* . . .

(More desperate cries)

And now it's no longer the Kremlin . . . No, it's, it's Rio de

Janeiro . . . the creatures are women, half-naked, *red* . . . The *heat,* my body is nearly roasted . . . I'm going to suffocate!

    (He enters into convulsions)

DR. HILL: It's all right, it's all right, you're watching everything from the outside. You're seeing it all as if it were on film. Go on . . .

    (Fischer is calming down, his breathing more nearly normal, lighter)

FISCHER: Finally, we've crossed to the other side, and the heat has passed. Now it's lovely, blue, green . . .

DR. HILL: Blue or green?

FISCHER: Like the bottom of the sea . . . blue . . . and . . . green . . .

DR. HILL: You're at the bottom of the sea?

FISCHER: No, it's here above . . . the air is what's blue . . . green. The same way that the color in that other place was red, here it's all greenish blue or bluish green.

DR. HILL: And the buildings, are there buildings?

FISCHER: The path spirals through space . . . neither cold . . . nor hot, like before . . . it's pleasant. But there are some prismatical-looking things off to the side. Large and sparkling . . . veritable jewels! Sapphires, aquamarines, topazes, emeralds! Like twenty-story *buildings!* It's so beautiful . . .

DR. HILL: You may return now to assuming a participatory role.

FISCHER: I feel a pleasant temperature. It must be a nice day out, twenty degrees celsius or thereabouts. And the shining jewels refract the atmosphere into thousands of verdant bands, like a rainbow made of only a single color. It's so lovely, such a lovely dream . . . and he's there.

DR. HILL: He? Who?

FISCHER: He's big and he's . . . he's . . . a *woman* . . .

DR. HILL: Try to be more specific . . .

FISCHER: Tall, with a bluish skin and wearing clothing that somehow blends into the skin itself . . . I thought she was un-dressed. The body is like a sculpted Venus . . . the breasts seem fashioned by a divine chisel . . . the thighs, *powerful.* Her green-ish hair billows as if blown by a wind I myself don't feel. And there is *peace* in her eyes . . . she loves me, she's been waiting for me . . . I know, because it's written in those crystalline eyes . . . eyes that seem like jewels, the purest emeralds gazing am-orously at me, undressing me, entering my *soul.*

    (He twists in his chair, the cries are renewed)

    No, I don't want to . . . for the love of *God,* mercy! . . .

(Vague gruntings)

I want to get *out* of here, take me *out* of here . . .

DR. HILL: Calm down, now. You're perfectly safe, I told you.

FISCHER: I don't want to, it's too much for me.

It's a *huge* responsibility . . . I don't want to!

DR. HILL: What's happening?

FISCHER: She's telling me . . . right here inside my brain . . . telling me that I will *become her* . . . that I will be the Master. That I will help change the world and save humanity, but I don't want to . . . I just want to get out of here! No! No! No-o-o-o!

DR. HILL: Calm yourself, relax . . . relax, now.

FISCHER: But I no longer have the strength to resist. She's completely dominated me, she's mastered my *will*, she knows my innermost secrets! But I don't want to . . . Now her eyes are *changing* from green to blue . . . and the skintight clothes . . . the clothes have vanished, and she's *naked* . . . with not a hair on her *body* . . . only the bluish skin, like marble . . . all perfection . . . My God, it's not possible! . . . she's drawing me closer, I'm undressed as well! . . . where are my clothes? I'm closer and closer, I smell her perfume, a musky fragrance, I'm afraid . . . What's that? She has something—a *phallus*, she's not really a woman at all! Help me! I'm being lured closer and I can see her huge, erect phallus . . . threatening me! I'm writhing . . . I feel its touch—it's *pure* electricity . . . no, I want to get away . . . I'm *levitating* and . . . and . . . my sphincter muscle . . . relaxing, to receive her . . . no! no! . . .

(Desperate screams, gruntings; Dr. Hill attempts to calm the patient who finally relaxes again, breathing heavily)

FISCHER: (in another voice: mechanical, effeminate) I am the Voyager. I am the Master. I am Sylyon . . . Sylyon . . . Sylyon.

SATURDAY, AUGUST 27

The old jeep driven by Major Nelson pulled into the deserted amphitheater of the Valley of the Seven Moons. Hardly had the major turned the key to the ignition, shutting off the motor, when General

Pessoa had already jumped out followed by Raul, Maurício and Vera. Major Nelson had not even taken the trouble to park the Jeep more safely, since the amphitheater was completely empty and no one would be motivated, in any event, to rob an old useless heap like that.

The five ran directly over to the small temple at the base of Sylyon's statue and rushed into the hall. None of the acolytes appeared, however, and they continued to make their way through the building in the direction of the computer complex that was the heartbeat of the sect. General Pessoa had not the slightest idea of what might happen or how he would confront the enemy; but he felt an energy, a species of force that quite literally impelled him to commit his temerarious act.

All the doors were open, which was as unusual as it was unexpected. The absence of acolytes, the total lack of security in general might indicate one of two things. Either all this was no more than a trap wherein they would be captured and immediately liquidated, or Sylyon—knowing that his secret had been unmasked—had decided to abandon the Valley and flee with his followers.

"We better be careful now," the general warned when they reached the door to the computer room.

Major Nelson touched one of the luminous buttons and the door opened automatically. The room was dimly lit and the only sound to be heard was the hum of the consoles. Vera Martins gaped at the array of instrumentation: the videos, the suites, the panels—and found it all much more alien than her concept of an extraterrestrial. She would never have imagined in her wildest dreams that the basement of some crazy sect in Brasília could have housed such a conglomeration of electronic equipment.

"Jesus Christ," she murmured, stepping cautiously into the air-conditioned environment.

It was then that the lights went out and merely the indistinct, diffuse glow of the screens continued to illumine the space.

"Were you looking for me?" warbled a feminine voice sweetly.

A tall and slender shape emerged from a corner of the room, issuing from some secret passage and raising his right arm.

"You've been unmasked, Sylyon!" General Pessoa shouted.

The figure levitated above the consoles and was settling itself in proximity to the doorway, to impede their flight. The lights returned and the tall, skinny figure of Brigadier General Bernardo Fischer was staring at them without expression—a dull, greenish glow emanating from each pupil. He was wearing the tunic of the Master and, at a sign from him, the door hissed shut.

"Why did you want me kidnapped?" Vera cut in, suddenly holding a screwdriver in hand as if it were a dagger.

The Master did not deign to even look in her direction, but the screwdriver felt suddenly to Vera as if it were charged with electricity, burning her hand; and she dropped it.

"You're a sick man, Fischer," said General Pessoa. "You're possessed by an evil entity."

"Evil is Quazgaa," declared the Master.

The lights intensified their glow and General Pessoa fell to his knees, clutching at his chest as if he were feeling the most violent pains. Raul rushed over to help the old man, saving him from crashing to the floor. Maurício and the major, meanwhile, did not dare move—perhaps waiting for the right moment to launch their assault. But the brigadier general suddenly lowered his gaze to notice some yellowish, dense smoke drifting out from under the hem of his tunic.

He began beating frantically at his garment, attempting to put out the fire—a dark and nearly continuous tongue of flame that was licking the fabric of his socks without singeing them. Seeing how the flame was swiftly spreading, already climbing toward his knees, the Master ran over to a cabinet, opened it and tore off one of the shelves a small fire extinguisher normally used in automobiles. Before he could actually turn it upon the blaze that consumed his lower extremities, Major Nelson slammed into him, making him stagger and drop the extinguisher.

A clout of superhuman strength from the Master put the major promptly out of commission; but the desperate Fischer could no longer support himself from the intolerable pain and crumpled to the floor. Slowly, he began to drag himself toward the extinguisher.

At that moment, Vera Martins walked deliberately over to where the brigadier general lay writhing, engulfed by the flames. Watching her coming, he knew what her intention was and gave her a ferocious glare. Like a nauseating reptile, he inched his way along, spewing yellow smoke, trying to reach the extinguisher before her.

Without allowing herself to be intimidated by her horror, Vera came closer.

"For the love of God," Fischer begged her, coughing smoke.

The smoke was already filling the air and Raul struggled to lead the dizzy General Pessoa out of the room. Maurício was busy dragging a still unconscious Major Nelson toward the far end of the room, less contaminated by gases.

Fischer was nearly within reach of the extinguisher when Vera Martins simply kicked it out of reach. It was a slight gesture, merely sufficient to send the bottle another two meters or so beyond the reach of the brigadier's fingers.

Each time that he got near enough to reach it, she repeated the gesture. The flames had begun to transform him into a black, noxious stump that oozed like mucus over the floor, baring the sooty bones of his legs. A strong burst of flames began to lick the trunk, and the last thing that Vera could see, before rushing out to escape sure suffocation in that pestilential smoke, were the Master's arms, outstretched before him, and his hands contracting in their final vain attempt to clutch the extinguisher.

SUNDAY, AUGUST 28

The Sérgio Silva Show, whose smiling namesake with dark straight hair was rapidly approaching fifty, started every Sunday at ten in the morning and went on until eight o'clock at night in a veritable marathon of prize drawings, sophomoric competitions, musical variety acts, quiz panels and film shorts obtained at the lowest possible prices from North American suppliers. In the last two years, however, he had managed to broadcast nationally, via satellite, to more than thirty stations across the length and breadth of Brazil. His viewers were basically made up of what advertisers classified as a Class Z audience: the lumpenproletariat—the little people who eked out a minimum wage, the eternal tightrope walkers of the broadest, lowest sector of society.

His viewer percentages were virtually total for the afternoon hours, forcing other stations to compete with similar formats on prime time. But none could hold a candle to *The Sérgio Silva Show.*

Silva's empire consisted now of far more than a national chain of radio and TV stations. His interests included numerous appliance and cheap furniture outlets, valued real estate in several state capitals, vast holdings in the financial market, and a farming and cattle-raising project somewhere in Amazonia, where he had reportedly invested over twenty million dollars in infrastructure and deforestation.

The puny youngster who in 1938 at five years of age had arrived on the shores of Brazil—the son of Lebanese parents, Maronite Christians—had already surpassed even the most outlandish expectations of his father (a watchmaker) and his mother (a factory weaver who slowly wasted away at the looms of a São Paulo sweatshop).

From the age of eight he had labored hard to help out with the household expenses: first as a shoeshine; later, more profitably, at selling odd lots from a wagon until he completed primary school—the only education he would ever boast beyond the difficulties of life.

It was on those streets that he had also learned to live with the pathos of daily existence, and this lesson would provide the essential theme of his extraordinarily successful programming.

As a traveling salesman offering nearly useless wares, he gradually perceived to what extent the humble masses seemed to live blindly, unaware of where their misfortunes came from, resigned to the tiniest of life's joys. For such people, nothing was shameful or ridiculous, and melodrama served as a nourishment as fulfilling as the dramas of Shakespeare. Such little people were not ashamed to cry over radio soap operas, as atrocious or mediocre as they may have been.

It was by meditating upon such people, the anonymous inhabitants of the great cities, the brawlers with no fixed rules to the game, that he began to fashion his program—first on radio, in 1959; eventually, in the hour he rented on a local television channel.

The final segment of the show was about to begin, and Sérgio Silva (whose real name was Ambrozio Azancoth) felt drained. During the afternoon, he had changed outfits at least four times, taken two baths, spoken nearly five hours of informally rehearsed lines and taken a single break for only half an hour. Silva not only dominated the entire show, as master of ceremonies and main attraction, in front of a live audience of thirteen- and fourteen-year-old girls contracted at two hundred cruzeiros a show and selected for their physical types. He actually supervised and directed the total production, down to its minutest details, including personal conversations with each contestant and careful perusal of sets and wardrobes before going on the air.

The final segment lasted half an hour. It was the shortest of all and the crowning finale of the entire grotesquery. Girls of eight to ten years of age, picked out of the slums and alleys, presented themselves before a panel of judges. They did not need to do anything before the camera; it was enough to remain seated on the illuminated staircase of the set, which led to a velvet throne, and to answer a few questions of the sort like: "And your name?" or "How old are you?" The rest, the production itself undertook to elaborate by presenting a romanticized, cosmetified "biography" of the contestant—prefilmed and now projected on a large screen to the side of the stage.

Each contestant wore a shabby outfit and generally walked onto

the stage terrified of the bright lights and the noisy audience, not to
mention the supreme trepidation at coming face-to-face with their idol
there in the flesh. Silva never ceased to be amazed at how these girls
turned catatonic in his presence. It was as if he were a deity mater-
ializing before them, which filled him with a pride that more than
matched all the sacrifice.

The panel of judges was responsible for choosing the saddest, most
pathetic case of them all and presenting its findings to the audience
for a final referendum—lending an added illusion of popular participation. The child selected was thereupon led up to the throne by a
boy dressed as a prince. Once seated, she received her crown, hundreds
of presents (the majority of them appliances) and other useless domestic articles.

This particular night, the prizewinner was a young black girl from
a slum in the south end of São Paulo; and the production had gone
perfectly. Her "father," an alcoholic, was out of work and caring for
nine children because his wife had been hospitalized in a welfare
clinic for cancer patients.

The applause from the audience had already signified virtual approval, even before the jury had gotten to announce the girl's name,
so poignant was her tale. Sérgio personally ascended the stairs beside
the girl and helped her onto the throne. Immediately, the cameras
commenced to pan over the presents, with soft music in the back-
ground and the program's credits slowly descending the screen. Hardly
had the commercial begun when the girl was led off the throne and
Sérgio Silva began to make his way toward the wings, eager for
another bath and change of clothes.

The sets were already being removed from the stage and the lights
being cut as Silva left the wings and headed for his dressing room.
He flashed his famous smile at the busy stagehands and technicians
and suddenly—before a gathering of astonished employees—vanished into thin air, swallowed by the void.

Inside a Building on Dzerzhinsky Square, in Moscow

Pavel Aksentyevich stared at the commissar.

"I cannot believe it, comrade."

Commissar Ivchenko scowled and slapped his hand sternly upon
the desktop.

"It's a falsification! Your story is a complete fabrication—as you
are, Comrade Aksentyevich."

"But it was the Americans who sent him there to take the pictures in the first place. And the agent *died* because he had managed to get them."

"Tripe! Sheer tripe," replied the commissar, practically spitting his words.

The laboratories of the KGB had attempted various methods to authenticate the videotapes brought back by Pavel. But the definitive confirmation of a fraud had come with the playing of the tape through a system of previewed-animation-for-next-frame. This system treated the videotape as if it were a succession of film frames, as on normal cinematographic film, and thus offered the computer fixed images which could be checked frame by frame. After several hours of such testing, the doctoring became evident, although it was a piece of outstanding craftsmanship, evidently produced by a special-effects studio—something at which the Americans were admittedly still the masters.

The report was sitting there on the desk of Commissar Ivchenko, Pavel's immediate superior, who had just nearly had his career ruined by crediting the views of this idiot in charge of public relations for the Moscow Circus.

Hence, the commissar's near apoplexy.

"I brought that tape back with honorable intentions." Pavel's voice quavered with a still tenuous thread of hope.

"Honorable *intentions?*" bellowed his superior.

The stainless steel ashtray—representing the satellite Sputnik and serving as a paperweight upon the files of a number of court cases that came under his jurisdiction—began to levitate a few centimeters above the desk.

"And stop your idiotic pranks!" Ivchenko howled, visibly foaming with hatred.

The Sputnik heeled over and dropped with a thud, spilling cigar butts and thick ashes on the pile of juridical proceedings. In an instinctive gesture, Pavel Aksentyevich blew away the ashes which drifted onto the impeccable aquamarine suit of the commissar.

Ivchenko looked down in his lap, then looked up at Pavel with a glacially murderous stare.

"Well, you're about to learn, comrade Aksentyevich, where *honorable intentions* finally get you."

Pavel was wringing his hands, and felt the perspiration running down the back of his neck, although the temperature outside was a mere two degrees above zero.

"Be thankful that this is the tenth year of the Great Wheat Harvest of Adjerbazan."

"Yes, comrade commissar."

"And that we are commemorating the twenty-fifth anniversary of the Great Plan for Rural Electrification."

"Yes, comrade commissar."

"And that this is the fifteenth birthday of the inauguration of the Great Volvograd Tractor Works."

"Yes, comrade commissar."

"And the fifty-fifth anniversary of the publication of the complete works of our eminent philosopher Plekanov."

"Yes, comrade commissar." Pavel began to feel cramps throughout his whole body.

"And inasmuch as we are passing through a period of political thawing, I will see to it that you are only transferred to the post of ticket collector at the State Circus in Anadyr."

"Anadyr, comrade?"

"A lovely port city on the Bering Sea."

The cramps melted into torpidity and an urge to vomit.

"In the good old days," hissed Ivchenko, "you would have been interned in a psychiatric ward with orders to never remove your straitjacket!"

Pavel swallowed dryly and turned his thoughts to his wife. Perhaps she might finally prove to be his salvation. Once she found out that their new apartment would be situated in the desolate Siberian taiga, surely she would plan to make use of him as kindling for the samovar.

"Little Havana," in Miami

Tables and chairs lay broken and strewn about the floor, while four men from Narcotics pointed heavy carbines at the two gentlemen dressed in sober attire—suit and tie—who claimed to be working for the CIA and insisted that the whole thing was nothing more than a lamentable mixup.

The heavyset Major Carson unbuttoned his jacket and one of the FBI agents immediately raised his carbine in a defensive gesture.

"Take it easy," Carson shouted, "I'm not armed but this heat is killing me."

The dark surroundings were barely lit by a neon sign, scintillating in red and blue as it methodically flashed the name of the establishment: *The Winged Boar*. Spread across the polished surface of the inlaid oak bar, which stood parallel to the left side wall, were the goods the Narcotics agents had recovered: five kilos of pure cocaine with an estimated street value of nearly half a million dollars.

When the men from the Narcotics Division had first broken into this flimsy dive and apprehended the two Cubans posing as janitors, they had unexpectedly stumbled across both supposed agents from the CIA, climbing into the sepulchral-looking used car inside of which—in the best tradition of the gangster films of the thirties—the coke was stashed.

What intrigued the sergeant of police in charge of the bust, in collaboration with Federal Narcotics agents, was the order that he had received to hold the two additional characters at gunpoint until someone actually from the CIA should come to identify them. He knew that the CIA stuck its nose into everything, but he also realized that once it became involved in this particular operation, the whole thing would go swiftly down the toilet, because wherever the Agency treaded, politics and immunity for "reasons of state" trailed not very far behind. If the sergeant's additional two suspects turned out to be legit, it would mean the end of eight months of sweat involving three hundred officers with special training and a great deal of suddenly futile sacrifice on the part of several undercover officers.

Two hours later a high-ranking officer of the Agency showed up at the bar with the arrogance peculiar to people from Intelligence.

"MacInnes, thank God," Gwyneth exclaimed.

The officer stared openmouthed at the two handcuffed prisoners and gruffly ordered the sergeant and his men to clear out.

"It's your responsibility," protested the sergeant with a sigh, sauntering out the door and into a small crowd of Latinos looking on curiously.

"I don't understand what's going on," Carson grunted attempting unsuccessfully to stand up. His wrists ached from the handcuffs. "At least get these damn things off us," he demanded.

MacInnes did not reply.

"You're not thinking of . . ." Gwyneth began to laugh nervously, interrupting his own thought as his expression paled.

"How the hell did we get into a spot like this?" Carson insisted.

MacInnes, one of the young stars of the Agency, looked over at the plastic bags full of white powder sitting on the bar, then turned back with contempt to the two middle-aged agents.

"You might as well know that the Cubans have already confessed."

"What?"

"They filled us in on the two tons of light arms you supplied them for shipment to Nicaragua."

Gwyneth felt a slight burning sensation inside his chest and the muscles of his arms began to protest their confinement. Beside him, his companion was starting to melt into a pool of sweat.

"You were to have accompanied Gardner's body back to Washington," MacInnes said dryly.

"Obviously," the two hastened to agree.

"Agent Mike Gardner's body arrived yesterday aboard a Varig flight, but accompanied by two Brazilian officials from the Ministry of Foreign Relations. The Brazilian ambassador informed us he had no idea of your whereabouts."

"It's not possible!" Gwyneth protested, but his interruption lost much of its force to the strange whining sounds issuing from Carson. "The last thing I remember is me and Carson were in some military barracks, down in Manaus, participating in the interrogation of a known terrorist."

"Interrogating a terrorist, eh?" MacInnes repeated blandly.

"I swear!" Gwyneth insisted. "The interrogation was particularly hot because at least one official from Brazilian intelligence kept insisting that the terrorist was already dead."

"The terrorist was already dead," MacInnes repeated, raising his eyebrows.

"Colonel Nunes, from the SNI—he insisted the guy had died in an auto crash, in 1978."

Carson was gasping almost convulsively, struggling in his chair and further perplexing MacInnes's apparently limited faculties for patience.

"Nunes demanded to be put personally in charge of the entire operation, until he was forcibly expelled by the commanding general."

"Expelled . . . yeah," MacInnes repeated as he watched Carson floundering in his chair like a drunken sperm whale.

"The dead terrorist was working for some sect of fanatics and also had a dubious hand in protecting the security of a Japanese installation involved in electronics and petroleum."

MacInnes's eyes began to burn and he blinked repeatedly. There they were, the two of them, handcuffed and mouthing absurdities: the most legendary team of operatives in the service. Although the CIA in the past few years had been compromised by the most varied forms of desertion and scandal, this instance had to be one of the most painful of his entire career. Carson had been his first officer during training and Gwyneth was the uncle of his second wife, not to mention a distant relative of General Patton.

"Once Nunes was driven out of the room, the commanding general seemed to calm down a bit and we supposed that the interrogation was about to proceed normally."

MacInnes had all but lost interest in trying to follow the farfetched explanation offered by Major Gwyneth.

"You're not listening to me, MacInnes."

"Sorry, Gwyneth, go on."

"I felt a needlelike prick in the cheek of my ass and imagined it was another one of those damned tropical mosquitoes."

"A mosquito, yeah."

"Next thing I knew, I woke up with Carson here in a room out back there. We didn't even realize that we were no longer in Manaus, but in Miami. It was Carson who decided we should steal that piece of junk out there and make our getaway."

Carson let out another grunt or two and fell forward.

"It wasn't me, you son of a bitch!" Carson reviled, looking up and coughing asthmatically.

"It *was* you," Gwyneth insisted, eyeing with a look of repulsion the fat torso of his partner as it rolled to the floor like a bag of rotten fruit.

"What in hell were you doing at some interrogation in Manaus? You were supposed to have reclaimed Gardner's body and offered the usual explanations to the Brazilian authorities. Whatever else you were doing—if you *were* doing it at all—was, quite frankly, out of line." MacInnes shook his head silently.

"Nowadays, everything is out of line," Gwyneth protested bitterly. "I still remember when it was up to us to decide, not regulations, and certainly not a bunch of bleeding-heart liberals."

MacInnes stared at the two of them with mild commiseration. They were the last vestiges of another era—more difficult; more romantic, perhaps.

Carson sensed MacInnes's hesitation.

"You better believe it, boy. In those days we actually managed to fathom our neighbors to the south. And things were a lot simpler as a result, I can tell you."

"And Brazil—Brazil was a cinch, right, good buddy?" Gwyneth mused nostalgically.

"I ought to know, I was there in '47. Received by the President himself: General Dutra." Carson began to chuckle to himself in a hoarse fashion—a sea lion regurgitating petroleum dejecta on a rapidly thawing iceberg. "Dutra was a naive soul, transparent as a beer glass. Truman walked into his office one day saying: 'Howdy-do,

Dutra.' And Dutra answered him smiling: 'How Tru-man, how true.' It was quite a beautiful country!"

The two old companions smiled heartily at each other.

"Enough!" shouted MacInnes.

"That bunch of fanatics was preparing a military coup," Gwyneth went on anxiously, dropping the smile. "And they had converted various nuclear reactors for the production of atomic bombs."

"Enough, I said."

"It's true! Two German scientists, old nostalgic Nazis, had been flown in just to—"

"I don't want to hear any more of this!"

"But you've *got* to, MacInnes—that Japanese company, for instance, was also—"

"That Japanese company, as you call it, is the property of four Brazilian generals. If you had taken your mission at all seriously, you would have gotten your hands on this magazine."

MacInnes held up a copy of *Isto É*.

"It went on the stands yesterday—it's all here, gentlemen."

"Everything?" Carson stared incredulously at the open pages.

"Nearly everything," MacInnes sighed. "The only thing it's left out is your involvement in drug trafficking. Drugs and arms, to be precise."

Gwyneth watched MacInnes's face take on a bloody hue with each blink of the neon sign. He thought about his forthcoming retirement and the apartment he had been going to buy—a condominium in California. And before MacInnes finally called the Narcotics squad back in, he had one last moment to remember the wild expression on Colonel Nunes's face as he rushed into the interrogation—followed by another lunatic dressed like a medic—with cries of it's not being every day that one had the chance to get a dead man's confession without swinging him from the "parrot's perch"!

In a Bar, on the Rua da Consolaçaõ, in São Paulo

After his fifth caipirinha, Paulo Veronezzi was wholly imbued with a sense of euphoria. He was seated just across from his editor in the not very busy cafe where the staff from *Isto É* would habitually gather before, during and after the constant trips up to the floor of the magazine, in the adjoining building. The bar was totally insipid and, on Sundays, tended to remain fairly empty. Were it not for some extraordinary reason, no one would even think to show up here on his one day off over the weekend.

Paulo—back from the "jungle," as he called it—was vehemently cursing out the editor's lack of an imagination—the only reason for them to be meeting at such an ungodly place, where all one could do was watch through the window the rarefied fauna that sauntered by on a Sunday afternoon.

Two girls suddenly entered the bar, and one of them—carrying an enormous shoulder bag into which one could probably fit a foldable bed—brought back to his mind the recollection of one of the many manias of his friend Vera Martins: forever dragging around some crazy knapsack or other, while sticking her nose where it didn't belong.

The night before, she had telephoned him from Brasília. The crazy dame was staying at the house of some general-gone-bananas who hunted for flying saucers. Obviously, she had finally found what she'd been looking for all along.

"You nearly missed me at home," he had explained to her, surprised by the voice at the other end.

"Well, at least I remembered to call you . . . Everything okay?" she asked.

"Everything's fine."

"I was scared you might turn up a corpse, who knows?"

"I did want to at least explain what happened."

But Vera Martins no longer had an interest in the reasons for his disappearance from Parintins. She did not even *pretend* to be as furious as Paulo imagined she would be. She had just finished reading a copy of the current issue of *Isto É,* and was wild with excitement, and talked on incessantly, muttering crazy fantasies about impossible events in her effort to "fill in the gaps" of the cover story that had finally spilled the dossier on the dead American.

Obviously, Vera Martins was continuing to smoke too much weed.

"Know what she told me?" he was explaining now to the editor, who listened with an expression of indescribable exhaustion (the old seawolf making an effort to be tolerant toward the young admiral, who had just finished his first Atlantic crossing). "That the cover story hit Granja do Torto like a poltergeist!"

"She certainly has an aptitude for *mots justes.*"

"Yes, the image is rather apt, isn't it."

"Is she still in Brasília?"

"I imagine so."

"Maybe you can interview her, tomorrow?"

"What?"

"Tomorrow, you and the director of the magazine are flying to Brasília. Didn't you know?"

"What on earth am I going to be doing in Brasília?" Paulo asked, defiantly.

"You won, Mr. Veronezzi . . . You played the game and you batted a thousand! You get the right to a *full trial* under the National Security Act. This makes it the third time in a year that my editorial staff will have entered the Hall of Fame!"

"I might have guessed," Paulo confessed, starting on his sixth caipirinha.

"The fellows don't seem to appreciate your perspectives on hydroelectric dams."

Maybe because the sixth caipirinha had gone to his ears, or because his editor's words were simply too difficult to digest, Paulo's head had begun to hum and the other's last remark was all but lost upon him.

"Don't worry, old boy," the other continued. "August may be a wicked month, but like everything else in this crazy country, at least it's drawing to a close. . . ."